DELLA
AND
DARBY

OTHER BOOKS BY SUSANNAH B. LEWIS

FICTION

Bless Your Heart, Rae Sutton

NONFICTION

How May I Offend You Today?
Can't Make This Stuff Up!

DELLA
AND
DARBY

A NOVEL OF SISTERS

SUSANNAH B. LEWIS

THOMAS NELSON
Since 1798

Published in Nashville, Tennessee, by Thomas Nelson. Thomas Nelson is a registered trademark of HarperCollins Christian Publishing, Inc.

Published in association with the literary agency of WTA Media, LLC in Franklin, TN.

Thomas Nelson titles may be purchased in bulk for educational, business, fund-raising, or sales promotional use. For information, please email SpecialMarkets@ThomasNelson.com.

Scripture quotation is taken from the Holy Bible, New International Version®, NIV®. Copyright © 1973, 1978, 1984, 2011 by Biblica, Inc.® Used by permission of Zondervan. All rights reserved worldwide. www.zondervan.com. The "NIV" and "New International Version" are trademarks registered in the United States Patent and Trademark Office by Biblica, Inc.®

Library of Congress Cataloging-in-Publication Data

Names: Lewis, Susannah B., 1981- author.
Title: Della and Darby : a novel of sisters / Susannah B. Lewis.
Description: Nashville, Tennessee : Thomas Nelson, [2023] | Summary:
    "Known for her humor and genuine Southern voice, Susannah B. Lewis
    brings readers the heartwarming story of two sisters learning to love who
    they are and face the world-alongside their charming, wise grandmother"--
    Provided by publisher.
Identifiers: LCCN 2022042765 (print) | LCCN 2022042766 (ebook) | ISBN
    9780785248286 (paperback) | ISBN 9780785248286 (epub) | ISBN
    9780785248309
Classification: LCC PS3612.E9867 D45 2023 (print) | LCC PS3612.E9867
    (ebook) | DDC 892.8--dc23/eng/20220909
LC record available at https://lccn.loc.gov/2022042765
LC ebook record available at https://lccn.loc.gov/2022042766

Printed in the United States
23 24 25 26 27 LSC 10 9 8 7 6 5 4 3 2 1

If I'm going to sing like someone else,
then I don't need to sing at all.

—BILLIE HOLIDAY

1

DELLA REDD

Mrs. Rosie Permenter, a sixty-eight-year-old hypochondriac with self-diagnosed bursitis, bronchitis, and the bubonic plague, was a regular at the clinic. She leaned over my counter while I typed on the keyboard and said, "Della, I've been smelling bread. You know what that means?"

"No, Mrs. Rosie, I don't."

"The internet says it's a sign of an imminent stroke. If I closed my eyes right now, I'd swear I was in a bakery. Don't you smell it? Don't you smell buttery croissants?"

"No, Mrs. Rosie. Can't say that I do." I focused on the computer screen and typed "smells bread" next to the complaint tab.

"It's only a matter of time . . ." Her voice trailed off.

"Have a seat and Melanie will call you back shortly." I adjusted the purple flower tucked behind my ear while she struggled to lift her heavy handbag from the counter and limped to the nearest plaid chair in the waiting room.

Mrs. Rosie was the last patient before lunch. Once Melanie called the frail woman to an exam room, I finished coding a couple of charts and then retreated to the kitchen at the back of the building with my purple floral lunch box in tow. As a born and raised southern lady, I believed there was nothing quite as divine as my grandmother's homemade biscuits or the occasional slice of pecan pie, but I firmly believed moderation was key. Seventy years of good old southern eating had wreaked havoc on my grandmother's body (she would have no qualms about licking a stick of butter like a lollipop), and bingeing in high school wreaked havoc on my waistline. Watching Dr. Faulkner's patients sip their Big Gulps in the waiting room chairs made me roll my eyes. Was it any surprise they were in poor health, ingesting caramel coloring and aspartame in such large quantities?

I always packed a healthy lunch with a glass bottle of filtered water. I removed the plain turkey and cheese on whole grain bread from the small Tupperware and took a bite. Although my grandmother, like most southerners, had mayonnaise in her kitchen at all times, I abhorred the texture and referred to it as "the devil's white sauce." In high school, Maryanne Gleason regularly ate bologna and cheese on white bread smothered in ketchup. I nearly vomited at the sight. Only a twisted individual would douse bologna and bread in ketchup. Maryanne was probably currently incarcerated at the women's prison in Jackson for murdering her family.

I rushed to finish my meal before Melanie and Camilla

entered the kitchen with their cheap cups of ramen or salads drenched in runny ranch dressing. On Mondays and Fridays, they usually spent their lunch break at the diner down the street. I was never invited, and that was okay with me. On those days I relished the peace and quiet of the kitchen. However, today was Thursday, and before I could finish my last few apple slices, they bounded through the door in their matching gray scrubs. They didn't acknowledge me as Melanie grabbed an energy drink (don't get me started on the ill effects of those) from the refrigerator and Camilla popped a plastic container into the microwave. Heat and plastic were a dangerous combination, but I would never tell Camilla. I didn't care what kind of chemicals Camilla ingested. The hotter her plastic container, the better.

As the nurses sat across from me at the round table and ridiculed Mrs. Rosie's latest complaint, one of the fluorescent lights flickered above us, and I made a mental note to call Handyman Humphries to come and fix it. I quickly chewed the ripe apple slice, hoping I wouldn't choke and require the Heimlich maneuver. Melanie and Camilla would let me gasp for air. Probably with smiles on their faces.

"Della," Melanie started in, "that's a *lovely* dress you're wearing today."

She condescendingly enunciated *lovely* the way you call chartreuse curtains or a hairless cat *looovely*.

"The flower behind your ear is *lovely* as well," Camilla added.

Camilla, that new shade of foundation you're wearing is also quite lovely. I barely noticed how much darker it is than your neck, I thought.

"Thank you, ladies," I responded as the juice from the apple threatened to drip down my chin. "You are too kind."

Camilla snorted at my comment before shoveling piping-hot plastic soup into her mouth.

"So what's the latest with Faulkner and Shelly?" Camilla quietly asked Melanie.

They often gossiped around me. They knew their secrets were safe with me because I didn't have anyone to tell, other than my twin sister, and everyone knew she wouldn't repeat anything since she never talked to anyone.

"I'm thrilled he finally went through with it." Melanie's voice was unusually soft so Dr. Faulkner wouldn't hear from Mrs. Rosie's exam room across the hall. "He needs to distance himself from Shelly or she's going to take him and this clinic down with her."

It was no secret Dr. Faulkner's wife, Shelly, was addicted to painkillers. She hurt her knee while running a 5K a few years ago, and since the meniscus surgery, she'd become dependent on pills. Dr. Faulkner confided in the nurses that Shelly had stolen scripts from him on numerous occasions, and he was at his wit's end with her addiction. She refused rehab, and since Dr. Faulkner declined to write prescriptions for her, she started getting her fix from drug dealers. Her white Range Rover was regularly spotted in the roughest parts of town. This morning, as I read the paper between patients, I noticed printed in black and white in the Public Notice section of the *Tallahatchie County Examiner* that Dr. Faulkner had filed for divorce. I knew it would be the subject at the lunch table.

"He should have dropped her that first time she came in

here high as a bird, rummaging through drawers for pills," Camilla commented with a shrug. Her messy brown ponytail hung loosely over her shoulder as she slurped her carcinogenic soup.

Melanie agreed, the disgusting white dressing puddling at the corners of her mouth.

"Who do you think will pounce on Doc first, Mel? Nina Blakely? Every time she comes in for a thyroid checkup, she's wearing a low-cut blouse. I thought she'd end up getting a breast exam last time she was here." Camilla darted her eyes toward the exam room to make sure the door was still shut with Dr. Faulkner inside.

"Nina or Della here." Melanie snickered.

"Excuse me?" I asked.

"Oh, Della, we know you've got the hots for Faulkner. We see the way you look at him all googly-eyed," Melanie said. "You turn to mush every time the man speaks to you."

I glared at Melanie. "I won't deny Dr. Faulkner is a handsome man, but I am not interested in him in that way."

"Wouldn't that be a laugh! Oh, Camilla! Can you imagine Dr. Faulkner and Della as a couple?"

"It would be easier to imagine an alien riding a three-legged unicorn." Adolescent Camilla, only twenty-two years old, covered her mouth to stifle her laughter the way an ill-mannered middle schooler would.

Speaking of aliens, I wonder if Melanie's husband will ever grow into his gigantic head?

My grandmother, Birdie, said hurt people *hurt* people. Melanie appeared to have it all: a career as an RN, a successful (though large-headed) husband, and two blonde-haired, blue-eyed daughters who wore matching outfits. Her goldendoodle was always immaculately groomed and her Instagram photos portrayed perfection in a bright, shiny filter, but Melanie must've been hurt in some way because she found great joy in hurting me. She mocked me at the elementary school lunch table twenty years ago the same way she did now. In high school I once spilled water on my pants and she started the rumor that I was incontinent. Because of her malicious lies, I found adult diapers in my locker for months.

It wasn't just Melanie who bullied me in school. Because our mother was the black sheep of the entire town, my sister, Darby, and I were both ridiculed by many of our classmates. I was sure our peers overheard their parents talking about our mother around the dinner table. I imagined they described our mama, Cindy Redd, as despicable and irresponsible. After all, the consequences of her foolish actions resulted in not only her death but the deaths of innocent people. Fellow students bought into their parents' opinions, and Darby and I were abandoned on the playground, left to eat lunch alone, teased and taunted.

I tried to gain acceptance from the A-list crowd, hoping that would somehow redeem our family name and people would forget what our mother did. That didn't work—not here in judgmental Clay Station, Mississippi, where everyone had long memories and loud opinions. Time and again I aimed to befriend my enemies, but I was repeatedly rejected and intimidated, which fueled my bitterness toward them. My self-esteem was at an all-time low in junior high, and I overate to cope. I successfully fulfilled the role of chubby outcast. It wasn't until I got out of this one-horse town after high school graduation that I finally discovered my worth, got healthy, and became a confident woman.

Melanie should have outgrown her mean-girl persona years ago, and maybe she had, but working with immature Camilla every day revived it. They fed off each other, the same way Melanie fed off her obnoxious friends when we were kids. Although I loathed the nurses and was guilty of silently responding to their criticisms with equally juvenile retaliations (which they deserved for the way they treated me), I was far too mature to stoop to their level and actually speak those comebacks aloud.

"Dr. Faulkner is a looker; I'll tell you that. If I wasn't happily married . . . ," Melanie began as Camilla nodded in agreement.

"Well, I'll be going now." I gathered my trash and tucked it inside my lunch box.

"Is that new, Della?" Camilla pointed to the lilac insulated bag.

"It matches your dress so well. And your flower. Della and her purple." Melanie gulped the caffeinated sugar from the brightly colored can.

"I do favor purple, yes," I said before exiting the kitchen. *And I'd like to give you both a fat purple eye.*

● ● ●

Our house was six miles out of the city limits, surrounded by fertile, red-clay Mississippi corn and cotton fields. It was barely visible from winding Yocona Road—hidden by hundred-year-old oaks and pines at the end of a long gravel drive. Birdie had lived in the small white clapboard house since she and Grandaddy married. She raised her only child, my mother, in the home. And after Mama died, it was where she raised my sister and me.

Thankfully the last patient hadn't run late that day, so I arrived home before five thirty to see Darby's small gray truck in the front yard beneath the pine grove. I parked my purple PT Cruiser at the back of the house where the gravel drive ended next to the flower garden. In it, I grew bell-flowers, balloon flowers, lavender, pansies, and gladiolus— all in gorgeous shades of my favorite hue. Although it was October, it was unseasonably warm and the plants still thrived. Morning glory crawled the ground of the garden and up the white trellis, and that was the flower I'd chosen to tuck behind my ear that morning. The petal had wilted throughout the day, and when I got out of the car, I tossed it back to the soil where it originated.

When I walked through the creaking back door, I was greeted by Perry, my tabby cat. He was a beauty with white stripes, swirls, and spots covering his gray coat. He'd shown up on our doorstep several years before, meowing and mal-nourished, and although I've never been an animal lover, I took him in. I wasn't sure if the cat was male or female, so I named it Periwinkle. After the first vet visit revealed he was male, I shortened the name to something manly. He was a welcome sight after I'd been heckled at work by Tweedledum and Tweedledee. He never sneered at my purple clothing or the flower in my hair.

"Hey, sweet boy." I reached down to rub his back as

his tail stretched tall and he brushed against my leg, leaving stray hairs on my dress.

I draped my wine-colored purse on the hook by the back door and called, "Birdie? Darby? I'm home." When I walked into the kitchen, my grandmother and sister were standing behind the bar. Resting on the mint-colored tile countertop was a large, round Mississippi Mud cake with two candles flickering.

"Happy birthday!" they cheered.

"Well, happy birthday to you too!" I said to my twin.

"Your poor sister has been watching this cake like a lion watches a gazelle," Birdie exclaimed. "Let's slice her up."

"No supper first?" The tan loafers slipped from my feet as I sat on the barstool and Perry hopped into my lap.

"I didn't cook no supper. Birthday cake *is* your supper. Prentice brought a gallon of milk by today. I know you ain't too keen on sugar, Della, but it's your birthday. You're allowed to eat cake all night if you want. You barely eat enough to keep a bird alive as it is." Birdie turned to the refrigerator and pulled out the white gallon jug. "But first I reckon I've got to sing to my two favorite girls."

Birdie's raspy voice, hardened by years of smoking Pall Malls, filled our small home, and then we blew out the white candles. Put off by the smell of smoke (or maybe Birdie's warbling), Perry scampered off my lap and disappeared to my room at the back of the house.

"Twenty-nine years ago, on October 20, 1987, at 8:32 a.m., Della Marie arrived first," Birdie said, beginning the traditional birthday story. "And along came Darby Ann at 8:35. Two identical peach bundles with heads full of dark hair and loud, healthy cries that could wake the dead. I remember it like it was yesterday. I may be a senile old woman, but I'll never forget one of the happiest days of my life."

Darby retrieved the decades-old daisy-covered plates from the oak cupboard and Birdie sliced into the decadent chocolate before saying, "Well, Della, you look finer than frog hair. That sure is a pretty dress."

"Thank you." I glanced to the floor-length purple frock. I could always count on my grandmother to compliment my clothing. "I bought it at Taliaferro's a few months back, but I've put off wearing it until today."

There were only two stools at the small bar in the kitchen, so we took our plates topped with Mississippi Mud to the living room. That was where we ate most of our meals anyway. Birdie sat in her worn brown recliner, and Darby and I took our usual spots on the navy-blue corduroy couch. We pulled metal TV trays close to us and set our full glasses of milk on them while the flat-screen television I bought Birdie last Christmas that was on the stand in the corner played *Murder, She Wrote*. It was Birdie's favorite show. I found every season on DVD at a garage sale a long time back and gave them to her for Christmas. You'd have thought she won the lottery. She played a different disc each night.

"Seems like people would leave town when Jessica Fletcher shows up. She goes to a wedding and the groom is stabbed. Visits a friend at work and someone falls out an office window. That old woman is an omen," I commented while I stuck a fork into my cake. "Cabot Cove, Maine, is the murder capital of the world."

"Fiddlesticks, Della. Jessica is a hero. She's a regular

Sherlock Holmes, she is," our grandmother said between bites. "Did you two have a big day? How was work?"

"Same old," Darby answered.

"Della? What about you? Did your coworkers bring in cupcakes to celebrate?"

"No, ma'am. I didn't tell them it's my birthday."

"That's ridiculous. Birthdays aren't to be taken for granted. You should have told them and let them do something nice for you. You both deserve something special. Especially on your birthday. That's why I want you two to have a fancy little party for your thirtieth next year." She talked a mile a minute. "I already know what I want for mine in May. I want a big bouquet of balloons. Bright colors. Not just purple, Della. Oh, and I want a plate of fried green tomatoes. Darby, you can do that. You've watched me make them a hundred times. That's what I want for my seventy-seventh birthday. I never thought I'd make it this long, so I'm going to celebrate. Lord willing and the creek don't rise."

"So you say Mr. Prentice brought this milk by, yeah?" I held up the glass. "That was awfully nice of him." Darby and I exchanged glances.

"Girls, how many times do I have to tell you? Prentice Mims is a friend. He's my chauffeur since I can't see good no more. That's all." Her cheeks blushed crimson as if she were wearing rouge.

Birdie was once a real looker. She had a movie star face, likened to that of Greta Garbo. An old eight-by-ten wedding photograph of her and our grandaddy, Joe Edward Redd, still hung on the wood-paneled living room wall next to her recliner. I'd often look at it and then down to her sitting there doing cross-stitch or watching Jessica Fletcher snooping around a crime scene. Time and numerous health issues surely had taken their toll on Birdie. Her once thick, bouncy, reddish-blonde hair was now thin and gray and always piled in a bun atop her head. Crow's-feet surrounded her pale-blue eyes, deep wrinkles were embedded in her cheeks, and her skin was spotted with dark bruises from blood thinners. She was still the full-figured woman of her youth, but the damaged and aged skin on her hefty arms sagged beneath the housedresses (all plaid in pastel shades) she wore every day. Her ankles were the size of tree trunks, and more often than not, she was barefoot. She always said feet were meant to breathe.

"I think you and Mr. Prentice make a precious couple," I pressed.

"Della, you're making mountains out of molehills," Birdie replied before finishing her last bite of cake. "Are you ready for your presents?"

"You didn't have to get us anything." Darby pushed her empty plate to the back of the TV tray. "The cake was plenty."

"Nonsense." Birdie moved her metal tray to the side and then struggled to push herself out of the recliner while the arms of the chair creaked. "I've always gotten my girls a gift. Just because I can't drive no more doesn't mean I didn't get you anything." She shuffled, barefoot, across the scraped and scruffy hardwood floor and disappeared to the back of the house.

"Birdie the gift-giver," I said. "We don't even get gifts for each other. Never have. Should we?"

"No." Darby brushed crumbs from her navy work pants and settled into the crook of the couch.

Birdie returned with two small boxes impeccably wrapped in solid white paper. A purple bow was affixed to my gift and a black-and-white-polka-dotted one to Darby's. I quickly unwrapped mine to reveal an amethyst teardrop pendant on a silver chain.

"How beautiful, Birdie! My favorite color, of course." I examined the necklace. "When did you have a chance to get this?"

"Don't worry about that." She slowly fell back into her recliner, breathing heavily from the walk across the house.

"Mr. Prentice took you down to Garrity's Jewelry Store, didn't he? You lovebirds browse a few engagement rings while you were there?" I pestered her.

She stuck her tongue out at me and said, "Come on now, Darby. You're slow as molasses in January."

"I don't want to damage the bow," my sister said as she carefully removed it from the package. From the box she pulled a wooden pen.

"Oh, Birdie," she said in almost a whisper.

"It's made of maple." Birdie seemed pleased with herself. "Russell McKenney made it with his own two hands. That man is quite the woodcarver. Always has been. You ever seen that deer head he carved out of a tree trunk? It's something."

"Oh, it's beautiful." Darby carefully examined the pen as if it were fine crystal.

Birdie nodded. "It's to write down all those poems you've got swimming in your head."

"Thank you, Birdie." She stifled tears. "It's my new favorite thing."

"It'll be perfect to address Birdie and Mr. Prentice's wedding invitations with too," I added.

Birdie rolled her eyes and reclined her chair. "I declare, Della Marie Redd, you're incorrigible."

2

DARBY REDD

Each morning on my way to work, Mrs. Dalton's German shepherd chased the back tires of my truck. When he gave up the chase, the big dummy would lie down in the middle of the road, exhausted and panting. Although we didn't have much traffic out our way, I feared he was going to be hit by one of the combines or cotton trailers that occasionally drove by. I'd carry the guilt for the rest of my life. I worried about that dog most mornings while I cooked breakfast, and today was no exception.

My shift at the plastic factory started at seven, but I was up every morning by five. I always left a plate of eggs and bacon on the stove for Birdie and Della, although it was cold by the time they woke up. They were both late risers. Della had to be at work at eight, but Birdie said sometimes Della didn't roll out of bed until seven fifteen. How she so quickly applied all that makeup and stuck flowers in her hair, I never understood. I didn't care for makeup. Or fixing my hair. I only owned translucent face powder and a tube of mascara, but rarely used either.

Like Della's, my hair was long and dark. Unlike Della's, it was lifeless. It would not hold a curl or even a hair clip. Both slipped out within minutes. It certainly wouldn't hold flower stems like Della's did. I often thought of cutting it all off, but then I wouldn't be able to tuck it behind my ears, and that was my go-to mannerism when I was given unwanted attention. We may have been identical in appearance, but Della and I couldn't have been more different. She rarely avoided attention, she was resentful and discontent, she only wore my least favorite color of purple, and sugar and condiments made her retch. Unbeknownst to her, I enjoyed a blob of ketchup on my scrambled eggs every morning and slathered my toast with sugary grape jelly.

The eggs sizzled in the frying pan as Perry entered the kitchen and stretched from a long night's sleep at Della's side. He knew I'd toss down a crumble of bacon or egg to him, so he waited patiently at my socked feet. Once the eggs were fluffy, I granted his wish and he carefully chewed the small, hot bite.

It was still dark outside as I sat at the kitchen bar with my plate and cup of black coffee. The house was silent except for the hum of the refrigerator and Perry's sandpaper tongue giving himself a bath. I thought about the day ahead and eight lengthy hours of popping white caps onto orange pill bottles. Some nights when I couldn't sleep, I heard the beeping of forklifts in reverse and the roaring of factory machinery. Soaking in the silence and solace of the dark morning hours was the reason I woke up before dawn.

I wished I could have the same quietude during my lunch break at work, but Cliff Waters wouldn't let that happen. He kept an eye on me from his line across the factory and took his lunch break at the same time I took mine. He was relentless. Always chasing, just like Mrs. Dalton's German shepherd. He'd sit across from me at the picnic table beneath the Bradford pear outside the main door with a Coke from the vending machine and something deliciously sweet like a honey bun or candy bar. Maybe Cliff was drawn to me because we shared the same childish diet. I didn't know what other reason there could be. I was plain to look at and painfully shy. I walked with my head down at work in an effort to avoid eye contact and conversation.

I was an introvert, but I didn't view my standoffishness as a negative. I was content that this was just who I was. I'd always thought my shyness made me more observant of the world, which made for good poems. Aside from penning rhymes in the seclusion of my bedroom, my idea of a good time was putting on warm pajamas before dusk and watching "mature lady slash author slash detective" reruns that were older than I was with my seventy-six-year-old grandmother.

I knew Birdie was ready for me to find a nice man and set out on my own, but I wasn't interested in dating. I certainly wasn't attracted to Cliff Waters. He was his own kind of peculiar. He bounced around like an excited puppy dog with a full bladder. His long, lanky arms quickly swung back and forth, and he seemed to spring from his heels (maybe from his sugar highs). His thick glasses were too big for his face and often rested on the tip of his nose. Cliff's dark hair was buzzed too short, and his beard was so wiry and unkempt that he was forced to wear a paper face mask that prohibited scraggly hairs from falling into pill bottles. I often wondered why he didn't just shave to avoid the hassle of a mask.

● ● ●

A cold front had moved through the night before and left the October air crisp and cool. Aside from avoiding conversation with anyone other than Birdie or Della, I also avoided being cold. Birdie said I was born with thin blood. Even as a kid, I opted to stay inside with my grandmother while Della stacked on fifteen layers of clothing to make snow angels in the front yard. Shivering while eating my lunch was not appealing, so I decided to sit in the warm (but crowded) cafeteria instead of beneath the Bradford pear.

Cliff sat down across from me when I was halfway through eating creamy peanut butter sandwiched between salty crackers and potato chips. I quickly glanced up at him and was surprised to see his face clean-shaven. There were two small nicks on his cheeks where he had cut himself. I guessed he was tired of wearing that mask after all.

"How is your day going, Darby?" he asked while unwrapping a chocolate caramel candy bar.

"Fine," I said quietly before taking a small bite of cracker.

"I've got a cramp in my hand from the push and turn vials. What you working on today?" The Coke spewed slightly when he popped the tab on the can.

"Standard snap caps."

We sat in silence for a few moments while he glanced around the cafeteria and pushed the thick glasses up his nose.

"Nice day out there. Why you want to eat inside?"

"I get cold." I tucked a strand of limp hair behind my ear.

"My grandmaw don't like the cold none either. I stop by to check on her on the way to work most days. She had the heat on this morning. You know how it smells when you cut it on for the first time of the season? That's what her whole house smelled like. I can't get it out of my nose."

I remained quiet as employees filled the cafeteria. The group sitting at the table behind us was loud and boisterous. One guy kept punching another in the arm as he told a story that the entire table found humorous.

"Forklift drivers," Cliff said. "I bet they talk so loud because their ears are always ringing. Beep. Beep. Beep. Boy, that gets on my nerves. I can hear it when I close my eyes at night."

I was done eating, so I placed my trash into the paper sack I brought from home and pulled my phone out of my pocket. I was aware it was rude for a person to focus on a device instead of another person sitting less than a foot away, but hiding behind the screen felt safe. Comfortable. Quiet.

"What you playing today?" Cliff leaned forward to glance at my phone screen.

"Solitaire."

"You like cards, then?"

I bobbed my head.

"I play poker with one of my brothers every Friday night

in Maw's garage. Maybe you'd like to come sometime?" He took a swig of Coke. "It ain't too cold in there. We've got a propane heater."

"I only like solitaire."

Someone not as withdrawn as me would provide detailed answers to Cliff's questions—to *anyone's* questions—but I knew detailed answers only led to more questions. Elaboration led to conversation. Which led to stuttering, nervousness, and pulling my hair behind my ears, which stripped it of any liveliness it may have possessed.

I could feel Cliff's magnified eyes peering at me from behind his heavy glasses. When the group behind us erupted in laughter, he finally transferred his gaze from me to them. I continued to swipe my finger across the screen and placed the red three that I had been waiting for atop the black four.

"I guess I'll get on back to the floor. Have a good rest of the day, Darby," he said before tossing the empty Coke can and the candy bar wrapper into the trash next to our table and walking away.

Cliff usually stayed with me until the end of the lunch break and accompanied me back to the warehouse. When I silently sat across from him and fiddled with my phone, he'd pull his out, too, and scroll through social media apps. Sometimes he'd shove the screen in my face and remark on a photo or an article he was reading. The last thing I wanted was a social media account. I cared nothing about reading people's reviews of the Jiffy Lube or seeing videos of their children noisily banging on drum sets.

I could have commented on the absence of Cliff's beard. It was the first time I'd ever seen him without that disheveled mess covering his face, after all, but my remark would have led to his in-depth description of the motivation behind shaving. However, as the cards did a victory shuffle across the phone screen, I realized it was impolite of me not to tell Cliff that he looked much better without his face buried in hair.

● ● ●

When the whistle blew at three, my replacement, Kerry, approached the station where I'd been standing for eight hours. I rarely said anything to her, unless I needed to inform her of something significant that would affect production. Kerry was used to my standoffish demeanor by now and didn't even say hello when she took over the line. Cliff was waiting for me at the time clock, as usual. I was relieved, I guess, to see him standing there. Only because I had worried that my silence regarding the absence of his beard and my quick decline of his invitation to play poker had been mistaken for impoliteness. I wasn't a rude person. I was just quiet. However, I was aware the two could easily be confused.

"Have a good afternoon, Darby?" he asked, right on cue.

"Fine." I slid my time card into the clock.

We filed out of the building with the rest of our shift. At the end of each workday, I was drained and annoyed by the roars of the factory, the chitchat of my fellow employees, and Cliff's inquiries at lunch. I couldn't wait to get home and sit on the couch with a steaming cup of coffee in hand.

"Still cold, yeah?" Cliff asked when I wrapped my arms around myself. "If I had a coat, I'd give it to ya."

"Thank you." I tugged on my hair as we approached our trucks parked side by side in the crowded lot.

"Well, see you tomorrow, then. Have a good night, Darby." He pulled his keys from the pocket of his navy uniform pants before stopping at his driver's side door with a dent below the handle.

"Your beard is gone. You look better," I mumbled as I walked past him.

He didn't hear me. His dusty red truck soon sputtered to life and he pulled away.

3

BIRDENA REDD

TUESDAY, NOVEMBER 1, 2016

Prentice Mims and I both grew up on Route 12 near the scrapyard. He and my baby brother, Harwell, were thick as thieves. They liked to toss that old football around in our dusty front yard and fish off the Tippo Bayou bridge. I never paid Prentice any mind back then. I think the most I ever said to him was in February 1962 when we saw Harwell off to Can Tho, Vietnam. Harwell never came back, and Prentice never came over no more.

When Joe Ed and I were honky-tonkers, we used to run into Prentice and his wife, Gertie, at the tavern out by Lake Louise. Gertie was sweet as pie and Joe Ed was fond of Prentice. They chain-smoked and talked about cars and Sophia Loren. The four of us used to cut in on each other while dancing to George Jones. Prentice had better rhythm than my Joe Ed, but I never said it out loud. Joe Ed and I quit running around bars when I got pregnant with Cindy, and the four of us drifted apart. Sometimes that happens.

Poor Prentice watched his soulmate waste away with cancer for two long years. Della drove me to Gertie's funeral last December, and it was the first time I'd seen Prentice Mims in a month of Sundays. After Gertie was put in the ground, I kept thinking about Prentice being all alone out in that big old farmhouse on Sardis Road, so Della took me and a crock of poppy seed chicken out to him. From then on, we'd been like he and Harwell used to be—thick as thieves. Since my stroke left me blind as a bat in one eye and I couldn't drive anymore, he was kind enough to haul me around and run errands for me. We reminisced about our glory days and I taught him a little about cross-stitching. He'd managed to finish a picture of an eagle with red, white, and blue patriotic wings. I wouldn't hang it up in my house, but I'd seen worse. Marjorie Watkins couldn't even cross-stitch her own initials. Always turned out cattywampus when she tried.

I knew the girls were happy that I had Prentice to keep an eye on me while they were at work. They fretted about me so. Since I had my stroke five years back, Della had been scared as all get-out that I was going to die. I *was* going to die. Death and taxes, wasn't that what they said? Maybe when I did go to my heavenly home, though, Della would finally get out of this town for good and be happy again. I'd begged her time and again to go back to Chattanooga. She thrived when she was there, but she wouldn't listen to me none. Pity to watch her waste the prime of her life away in the same house and same old town she grew up in. I knew I was holding her back; I was a burden. Birdena the Burden.

I didn't feel like a burden to Prentice, though. He enjoyed my company as much as I enjoyed his. We was just two old souls leaning on each other for comfort since the loves of our lives weren't here anymore. I was glad to have his friendship, and I thought he was cute as a button to boot.

As fond as I was of Prentice, he weren't no Joe Edward Redd. I'd never love anybody the way I loved that man. We met at the diner on Highway 8 where I waitressed when I was seventeen and he was twenty-four. Some couples boast about love at first sight, but Joe Ed and I didn't have an instant attraction. For a while, he was just the tall, broad-shouldered handyman from Panola County who ordered sausage gravy and biscuits with a big Coca-Cola a couple times a week. He stood out to me because he never drank orange juice or coffee like the rest of the morning crowd. After a few months of refilling his Cokes, we shared a laugh over Mrs. Borden's beehive because that thing nearly reached the diner ceiling and heaven beyond. Our laughs sounded good together. His was deep and raspy, and mine was a high-pitched cackle. Like bass and soprano. In harmony.

Joe Ed came from poor people like I did. He had a no-good pa and a mother who tried to run every part of his life down to which underwear he wore—even when he made his own living and had a full-grown beard. He also had a lazy brother who broke his ankle in 1953 but claimed he still couldn't work because of it in 1964, for crying out loud. But Joe Ed was nothing like them, thank goodness. The apple not only fell far from the tree but rolled on down a hill.

We were married a few days after my eighteenth birthday and bought the white shotgun house on Yocona Road.

Joe Ed did whatever he had to do to pay the bills. Whether it was painting a church steeple or hanging an awning for the jewelry store or shoveling cow manure out at the Packards' farm, he never turned down any job offered to him. He got up every morning at five o'clock and didn't roll back in the house until sometimes fourteen hours later, worn slap out and covered in dust or paint or whatever else he'd been wallowing in that day. Joe Ed slept good every night. And I slept good next to him.

● ● ●

"How's your sandwich, Birdie?" Prentice nodded to the greasy cheeseburger in my hand.

"Just fine, Prentice. Tastes almost like mine. Nothing like a burger straight out of a skillet. Cast iron has to be seasoned, you know? Ain't nothing good come out of it unless it's seasoned." I took a bite and a sautéed onion fell from the bun and onto the table.

"I hear that." He dipped his crinkled french fries in a blob of ketchup.

I hadn't been to Sit a Spell Diner in a good long time. They'd recently remodeled, and I barely recognized the place. Della didn't ever want to eat junk food, and Darby would rather swing by a drive-through than go inside anywhere and risk having to talk to somebody. It felt good to be out of the house enjoying good food and good company. I looked at Prentice over the top of my burger. When he was young, he had hair the color of strawberries. Now it was white as a sheet, but he still had a head full of it. Same thick mustache he'd always had too. Most men my age were bald as newborns. Even I was envious of Prentice's thick mane.

I looked past Prentice and the speck of mustard in his whiskers and nodded to the lady with the orange-dyed hair placing her order at the red counter. "Well, that's Shirley Mayfield, ain't it?"

Prentice slowly turned in his seat. "Sure is. I'll be. I thought Shirley died a few years back."

I chuckled. "Well, goodness gracious, Prentice. You must be awful shocked to see her standing there, alive and well with hair the color of citrus."

"I could have sworn I went to her funeral." Prentice shrugged and ate another fry.

"You must be thinking of Shirley Childers. Now, she *is* deader than a doornail."

"That sounds about right."

"Shirley!" I raised my hand in the air.

She turned on her pearl-white tennis shoes and saw me. After a long squint through her silver glasses, she produced a faint smile, lightly waved, and turned back around.

"Well," I said. "She's stuck up higher than a light pole."

"She's not coming over here, is she? I don't want to get caught up in a conversation with Shirley Mayfield. What would I say? 'Oh, hey there, Shirley. Thought you were dead.'"

"No, she ain't coming." I scowled. "Just like the rest of 'em."

Until Prentice came around, I mostly stayed in my chair doing cross-stitch and watching the greatest detective of all time, Jessica Fletcher. Darby sometimes took me on drives around the county, and Della and I occasionally had a sit-down meal at the Catfish House in Panola because they had a salad bar she could eat off of. The girls and I went to church, but only on Easter Sunday. Other than that, though, I rarely saw any of my old acquaintances around town. I'd assumed they'd forgotten about Cindy's accident, but Shirley snubbing me right there in the middle of the diner proved they hadn't.

"It doesn't amount to a hill of beans, Birdie." Prentice slurped the rest of his sweet tea through the red straw.

"Twenty-three years it's been, Prentice. Think they'd let it go by now. Shirley and I used to pal around quite a bit before Cindy died. We drove up to Branson to see Mel Tillis one time, for crying out loud. Now she won't even say hello." I gathered a napkin and wiped the grease from my fingertips.

"What's Shirley Mayfield matter anyway? I thought she'd been dead all these years. Didn't miss her none." Prentice chuckled. "I heard if you ain't had use for something in six months—you know, clothes in your closet and such—to get rid of it. Well, that's how you ought to feel about Shirley Mayfield. You ain't had a need for her in a long time. Good riddance."

I laughed. "Prentice, you're a mess."

When we were done eating, Prentice asked if I wanted to go riding for a little while and I happily obliged. We took old Route 12 and passed the site of the red wooden schoolhouse, torn down long ago. We chatted about all the homeplaces we passed and those who lived there. Funny how I couldn't remember to thaw out the pork chops for supper, but I re-collected just fine where Jimmy Rogers grew up and all the goats his daddy had. Mr. Rogers had a billy that was meaner than a snake. That big old thing rammed his head against the fence anytime someone got nearby. Had a long beard, just like Jimmy's daddy. Jimmy's daddy was mean as a snake too. Never saw him ram his head into a fence, but I wouldn't have been a bit surprised if he did.

Tallahatchie County, Mississippi, was home, and I was always tender toward it. It was where I was born and raised and where I met my sweet Joe Ed. Cindy came along after Joe Ed and I sowed all our wild oats—in the spring of 1972, when I was nearly thirty and Joe Ed was thirty-seven. She was the best thing to ever happen to us. I'd heard couples say having a baby brought stress to the marriage, but the opposite was true for us. Cindy Jane didn't wedge us apart. She brought us together. She filled our hearts with so much love that oftentimes we thought we would burst. Her coo harmonized with our laughter.

Cindy was shy from the time she was a toddler. She hid behind my dress anytime we encountered people. I thought she'd grow out of that, but she didn't. Even when she was a teenager and we'd been going to Sand Hill Methodist with the same people her whole life long, she was nervous around them as if they'd just met. She didn't even have much to say to my best friend, Gracie, and she was like family. I didn't understand it. Joe Ed and I often stayed awake after Cindy had gone to sleep, wondering why we had such a skittish child. Both Joe Ed and I had big personalities and never met a stranger, but Cindy just wasn't wired like us.

She didn't have but one friend during her school days, Sandra Turner. They met when they were both snaggle-toothed kids at Eastside Elementary. Sandra was about as nervous as Cindy was, so that was their common bond. They were both reserved and stood away from the crowds—but they stood together. I was real thankful Cindy had Sandra in her life. Joe Ed and I loved hearing the sounds of their laughter when Sandra came over for a sleepover. There wasn't an iota of tenseness when they were together, but Sandra's daddy got a job at the steel mill in Columbus the summer before the girls' first year of high school and Sandra was no longer a part of Cindy's life. Cindy went into a funk. She confided in me and my sister, Willa, one day as we shelled peas on the front porch that she felt more alone than ever. Hearing her say that made my heart heavy as a wet towel.

Wasn't too long after Sandra left that Joe Ed was diagnosed with emphysema after years of chain-smoking. It wasn't more than a month after that when I watched the love of my life strapped to a contraption in Dr. Millhouse's office and flipped upside down to drain his lungs. And then it wasn't but a few weeks after that when Joe Ed died. Unlike my own mother when my father died, I was shattered to lose Joe Ed. I couldn't have loved that man more. I got tossed about in a sea of tears and grief, and I wasn't a very good mama to Cindy at that time. She was mourning the loss of her sweet daddy, but I was so paralyzed by my own pain that I didn't help her through hers. I spent too much time in the bed and left her alone. That was when she started sneaking a shot of whiskey here and there out of Joe Ed's liquor cabinet. She soon realized she liked how it numbed everything. She said it made her "come alive." She wasn't scared of people no more. "Liquid courage," they call it.

Wasn't but a few months after Joe Ed died that I was

pulling my fifteen-year-old baby out of Midway Tavern, drunker than a skunk and unable to stand up straight. Once she sobered up, she swore she wouldn't ever worry me like that again. But the demon had already taken hold of her. She was in its grip just like my own daddy was all those years. She kept sneaking down to that tavern until she got pregnant with Della and Darby. I hated to admit it, but I was embarrassed about the whole situation and took her out of school when I found out she was expecting. I wanted to save us both from the ridicule. She said she'd go back to school after the babies were born, but she didn't. She said she wanted to stay home with them every day from there on out. I agreed to let her drop out, because when the girls were born, I hadn't ever seen my Cindy so happy . . . with the exception of the times she'd been three sheets to the wind.

I was sure those babies would be her saving grace. I had faith they'd be the very thing to keep her from drinking. And they did, but only for a short while. Wasn't long before she was coming home late from her job at the box factory. I stayed home with the babies on my days off from Piggly Wiggly and sent them to Willa's on the days both Cindy and I were at work. Willa loved caring for Della and Darby because she never married or had little ones of her own.

Soon Cindy started picking up the girls from Willa's later and later, with whiskey on her breath because she'd been down at Midway after work. Willa started refusing them to her when she was in a bad way. Cindy never argued with her aunt. She loved her aunt Willa as much as she loved me, I think. She'd agree to stay on at Willa's and have a cup of coffee to sober up, and then when I got off work I'd go pick up my daughter and granddaughters from my sister's house in town. Willa'd follow us all the way back out to the house in Cindy's Chevette, and then I'd have to haul Willa back to her place. It was a big hassle and made me so angry with Cindy for doing the things she done.

When the girls started kindergarten, Cindy was still living all wrong, and Willa picked Della and Darby up from school and kept them late on nights when I was working. I couldn't have made it through without Willa. She was a blessing to me my whole life long. Wasn't but two months before Cindy's accident that Willa died in her sleep. Felt like a dagger through my heart, but I was determined not to do like I did when Joe Ed died—not to hole myself up in my room and neglect my girls. I couldn't do it if I wanted to, anyway. I was too busy keeping up with Cindy and caring for Della and Darby. It was a full-time job because Cindy started drinking even more to deal with Willa's death. I was worried it would be the thing to send her over the edge. And I guess it was.

I had my share of bad memories that took place on Tallahatchie County soil, but it was also the place where Willa and I walked cool dirt roads in bare feet. Ain't no dirt quite as smooth as Mississippi dirt. Fertile, soft red clay begging to be planted. Still, I should have left Clay Station when Cindy died. Truth be told, I didn't have the money or the strength to pick up and start over new with two five-year-olds in tow. But if I had moved off, I wouldn't have had to be reminded that other people recalled the dreadful accident. Like Shirley Mayfield. I'd wager she didn't think to thaw out her supper either, but she sure remembered what my daughter did all them years ago.

4

DELLA REDD

The pasta salad was best made a day early. The fresh parsley and basil were more flavorful after marinating in the extra-virgin, organic, cold-pressed olive oil dressing overnight. Now, olive oil was a condiment that did meet my approval. I liked the bitterness and pepperiness of oil drizzled on chicken and French bread and salads.

Birdie was a fabulous southern cook, and she made our Thanksgiving meal from scratch each year. On holidays I threw clean eating out the window and gorged on the starchy feast: the honey-glazed ham and cornbread dressing, mashed potatoes, green beans sautéed in butter and brown sugar, and sweet potato casserole. I couldn't turn down Birdie's pumpkin pie either.

Darby assisted our grandmother with the main dishes, but the pasta salad was delegated to me. As I sliced the bell pepper at the kitchen counter, Birdie sat at the bar in her familiar plaid housedress and crumbled the cooled cast-iron skillet cornbread into an oversized bowl.

"I know it's eleven months away, but let's talk about your thirtieth birthday celebration," she declared. "No one can hold a candle to my cooking, but I was thinking we might ought to have it catered. Be a little fancier that way."

"We don't need a party, Birdie. We keep telling you that."

The idea for the thirtieth birthday celebration had been conceived while Birdie, Darby, and I rocked on the front porch after supper on a humid night last June. While reminiscing to the serenade of katydids, Birdie mentioned she couldn't believe her granddaughters were nearly thirty years old. And then she exclaimed with a sweating glass of sweet tea in hand, "Heavens to Betsy! I know what I'm gonna do. Next year I will throw you girls a party. That will be my gift to you. I haven't been to a party in ages. What fun it will be!"

Darby and I exchanged glances and quickly dismissed the idea. We assumed Birdie would eventually write it off, but she had yet to do so.

"I know you don't *need* one, but I want to give you one."

Birdie's love language was gift-giving. We grew up poor, but she often dug through the donation pile at Coppedge Creek Baptist Church in search of gently used toys or shoes to present to us in shiny paper and homemade bows. She spent hours cross-stitching small round pictures to gift us and hang on our bedroom walls. She often ordered cheap plastic junk from infomercials that ran in the middle of the night. I had no use for the vibrating neck pillow she purchased at three in the morning or many of the other "doohickeys" she'd given me over the years, but I made a big fuss over them because that was the way she expressed her love.

She continued, "I was looking on the internet and saw Garden of Eatin' has great reviews."

I'd heard Garden of Eatin' had catered a charity fashion show that had been all the talk last year. Darby and I had not been invited, but Erin Drake, the chairwoman of the affair, had raved about the scrumptious bacon-wrapped chicken breasts on Facebook.

"Who in the world do you think is going to come to this shindig? You know Darby and I are loners." I continued to slice vegetables for the salad.

"Fiddlesticks!" she said as the cornbread fell through her wrinkled fingers. "Rachel and some friends from Chattanooga can drive in. You've lived here your whole life. You know everybody."

"I do know everyone in this town, and I wouldn't pee on them if they were on fire." I dropped a helping of onion into the bowl.

"Well, I declare. That's not very Christian talk."

● ● ●

Birdie stayed awake fretting many nights because we were harassed in school. Darby and I both had our friend Rachel, but our grandmother still pushed for us to socialize. She once coerced us into going to a high school dance in hand-me-down dresses that garnered snickers and finger-pointing from the corners of the gymnasium instead of invitations to chat around the punch bowl. Anytime she pushed us to "put ourselves out there," it only intensified the resentment I felt toward so many who lived in this small southern hellhole. And it made introverted Darby put up another wall.

Unfortunately, our grandmother was still on a mission for us to "put ourselves out there," and she was also a technologically advanced seventy-six-year-old. While Darby and I were at work, she spent hours on the laptop I bought her a few years back. Darby often received emails from Birdie with subject lines like: "20 Tips to Spread Your Wings and Fly" or "The Introvert's Guide to Owning Any Social Situation." And I regret the day I ever helped Birdie set up a Facebook account. She tagged me left and right in relationship articles. She once left a comment beneath the photo of a bearded stranger in Des Moines, Iowa, that read, "My granddaughter is single. I think you two would hit it off," and tagged me. I could have been stalked and murdered.

Although Darby and I had every right to scold Birdie for interfering in our lives, we never did. We held our tongues as kids and continued to do so. Oh, Darby and I griped to each other in secret about Birdie. But the poor old soul had been through so much heartache in her lifetime, and the last thing we wanted to do was hurt her feelings. We were all she had. And we knew she meant well. Her intentions were for us to be happy. So we allowed her to meddle. Hence the reason we hadn't adamantly shot down the birthday party idea.

"It's going to be such a lovely party. We could use the community center. And who knows? Maybe one of your Chattanooga friends will bring some eligible bachelors along." She winked at me when I glanced her way.

Not only did Birdie want us to have a slew of gal pals with whom to share coffee and phone conversations, but she wanted us to get married too. Darby couldn't care less about a husband. She was too shy to speak to a man, much less date one. However, I did long for love. I hadn't dated since Kevin and I broke up four years ago. I didn't *need* a husband, but I missed being held. I missed the feel of a strong hand in mine and the sound of a deep voice telling me I was beautiful.

"How are you going to pay for this lovely evening, Birdie? A caterer isn't cheap." I tossed the bell pepper into the glass bowl of pasta. "You can't afford it with your disability income."

"Can't never could, dear girl. Can't never could."

● ● ●

Once the brightly colored pasta salad was chilling in the refrigerator, I left Birdie alone in the kitchen so she could finish making the cornbread dressing. I joined Darby on the shabby—but cozy—corduroy couch. She was clipping her fingernails down to the nubs while the television played quietly in the corner.

"Why do you cut them so short?" I settled into the crook of the couch and folded my legs, which were covered in purple flannel pajama pants. Perry leapt into my lap and purred contently.

"They are a nuisance."

"They are so pretty when they're long, Darby. They'd be even prettier if painted." I examined my own lavender fingernails resting on Perry's back. "You wouldn't have to use purple, you know. You could pick any color you wanted."

"It's easier to pop tops on bottles when they're short," she said without looking at me.

I glanced at the television for the remainder of a local commercial. Erin Drake was on the screen in a lovely kelly-green dress with a thin gold belt accentuating her slender waistline. Her dangling earrings blended in with her long, silky blonde hair as she stood in the foyer of Clay Station Community Bank and promised to make home loans easy. Time had been kind to Erin. She hadn't aged a day since high school. No visible lines or wrinkles, and her smile was as welcoming as it always had been.

"She still looks so young," I commented.

"Botox," Darby responded without even looking at the television.

Erin was the only one in her circle who refrained from taunting Darby and me. She helped me pull Darby out of a mud puddle after she was shoved down in elementary school. When we were older, she looked at me apologetically as her friends dug into me for whatever reason. She secretly gave me a thumbs-up when I reached my limit on that spring day of our senior year and decked Kelly Ragan in the eye.

"You're still enamored with her, aren't you?" Darby asked in her soft, low tone as she continued clipping the white tips from her nails.

"I'm not *enamored*," I answered. "That's a terrible choice of word."

"But you are."

"Erin was nice to the both of us. I just haven't forgotten

that. And I'm not *enamored* with anybody. Except maybe Perry." I stroked the purring cat's ears.

"Birdie still droning on about that birthday party?" Darby set the clippers between us on the corduroy couch and gathered the pile of nails from the lap of her gray pajama pants.

"Yes."

"I'm not going. I'm a grown woman. She can't force me." She reached over to the small wire wastebasket beside Birdie's recliner and tossed the nails inside. "Birdie will have to drag me kicking and screaming down to that community center."

"You haven't kicked or screamed a day in your life. Besides, she just wants to do something nice for us." I reached for my phone on the TV tray beside the couch.

"Throwing me into a crowd of people isn't nice. It's cruel and unusual punishment." Darby pulled the chenille blanket from the back of the couch and covered her long, thin legs.

"What crowd of people? I can count on one hand who would show up. I don't even talk to my old friends in Chattanooga anymore. And Rachel is busy living her own life in Florida. The party will never happen." I shook my head.

"She'll find a way, Della. Don't you remember our sweet sixteen? We only invited Rachel, but Birdie asked everybody at church to show up at the pizza place. We spent the whole afternoon with two thousand years of old people who all insisted on kissing our cheeks. We were stained with lipstick for days. She will find plenty of people to invite. She can because 'can't never could.'"

We sat in silence for a little while, and as Darby got lost in the mystery of the murdered wife on *Dateline*, I opened Facebook and the first picture I saw was of Erin. She was wearing the green dress in the bank lobby and the caption read, "Look for my latest commercial now running on Channel 7!" She had tagged Clay Station Community Bank and her husband, Devon.

I never understood how someone as kind as Erin ended up with Devon Drake. They dated throughout high school—the cliché love affair between the quarterback and the head cheerleader. Homecoming king and queen. Every girl wanted to date handsome Devon and look like Erin. An outwardly beautiful couple, I won't deny, but Devon was so inwardly ugly. What a tough guy he thought he was, cracking jokes about our dead mother.

"I declare, that's going to be some mighty fine dressing," Birdie said as she entered the living room. She was wiping her hands on her wrinkled and stained cream apron with orange piping. Her bare feet slid across the floor until she fell back into her snug chair. "I've seen this one, Darby. It's a rerun. The husband did it." Birdie reclined her thick, tired legs.

"Oh, Birdie," Darby groaned. "You spoiled it."

"Well." Birdie coughed. "The husband is always the guilty one. You know that."

"Another reason not to get married." Darby cut her eyes at our grandmother.

"I just want you to have someone to take care of you after I'm long dead and gone. Husbands could make both of you girls happy."

"I wouldn't be happy if I was murdered, would I, Birdie?"

Darby grinned as Birdie dismissed her with a wave of her palm.

"Listen, now. I talked to Prentice earlier this afternoon and invited him to Thanksgiving dinner tomorrow. This is the first one without his wife, you know?" She reached for the nail file on the brown wicker table beside her chair.

"Birdie!" My exclamation startled the cat. "That sounds like a date to me."

"Fiddlesticks. It just wouldn't be very Christian of me to let the man sit at home alone and eat turkey slices out of a package on Thanksgiving. I know it's only been the three of us for as long as I can remember, so I don't want you to think he's intruding."

I enthusiastically clasped my hands together. "Of course not, Birdie. It's fabulous."

"Darby, are you okay with the idea? You've been around Prentice enough to be comfortable with him, haven't you? You won't be nervous and tugging on that hair all day?"

"I can't make any promises, Birdie," Darby mumbled and continued to stare at the spoiled mystery on the television.

"Would you ever consider getting married again?" I asked.

"I'm seventy-six years old, dear. I'm old as the hills and set in my ways."

"Never too old for love." I winked at her.

● ● ●

When Darby and I graduated high school, Birdie urged us both to run as fast and far as we could to start exciting new

lives anywhere other than Tallahatchie County. Darby had a
hard time making eye contact with people in Piggly Wiggly,
so it was no surprise she didn't dare venture outside the
place we'd always called home. However, not twenty-four
hours after tossing my graduation cap into the air, I sped
off to Chattanooga. I'd had an affinity for the mountains
since watching a documentary on the Appalachian Trail in
school. I waitressed at a busy restaurant downtown, moved
into a cheap apartment on the wrong side of the tracks, and
with the help of financial aid, enrolled in community college
and graduated in two years with an associate's degree. I met
wonderful, nonjudgmental people in class and eventually got
a better-paying job working as a receptionist at Hathaway
Insurance. I moved into a pale-pink vinyl-sided duplex with
a front stoop large enough for a white rocking chair and a
clay pot planted with purple impatiens.

Mr. Hathaway was a sweet old man who often arrived
at the office with a box of donuts for us to share and complimented my Christmas attire. I was right on track to get
all the things I'd ever wanted—to meet and marry the love of
my life, to mother beautiful children with their father's eyes
and my fabulous hair. To be a successful businesswoman
with an attaché case and a corner office in a high-rise. To
live where no one knew I grew up the dirt-poor daughter of
an alcoholic who committed vehicular homicide.

After five years of freedom, discovering who I was,
wearing what I wanted without ridicule, and joining a small
group of friends for trivia night each week, Birdie had a
stroke. I rushed home to help Darby tend to her because
Birdie was in a bad way, losing sight in one eye and struggling

with slurred speech. It was evident Darby couldn't handle it on her own, and we couldn't afford a caregiver, so I stayed on a little bit longer. I still hadn't left. They both needed me. They needed my income. They needed my company.

If they both had men to care for them, though, I wouldn't be as apprehensive to say goodbye to Clay Station, Mississippi, again and leave all of its depressing memories and wretched people behind. I'd head straight for Chattanooga and wouldn't look back. I wouldn't be responsible for anyone's happiness but my own.

5

DARBY REDD

My bed was just a mattress and box spring lying on a worn beige rug. It was draped with white sheets, a comforter, and a gray-and-white-striped throw pillow Della gave me one Christmas. The chest of drawers and nightstand were matching oak with brass handles, purchased used sometime in the nineties. The walls were wood paneling, and the watercolor print of a turquoise vase holding spring flowers had remained in the same spot since I was a child.

I was only five at the time, but I remember Mama hanging the painting on the wall the day she found it at a yard sale. The window was open, and a warm breeze swirled around the small room and whipped the sheer white curtains in a tizzy. Della and I were sitting on the bed playing with dolls, I think, when Mama stepped back to examine the print. She remarked on the colors and how they reminded her of the wildflowers that grew behind the house. She told us she loved to lie in that field as a little girl and fashion crowns out of black-eyed Susan petals and pretend she lived in a castle of poppies and Queen Anne's lace.

Della was always the first one to fall asleep in our bedroom at the back of the house. I stayed awake well into the night, fearful of the dark and the sound of wind rustling through the massive trees outside the window. Storms, lightning, thunder all prompted me to run to Mama's room and cower under her covers. Mama would pull my head onto her chest, stroke my hair, and sing her slow, melodious version of "Ode to Billie Joe." Her voice was soothing. It erased my fears and calmed my nerves and sent me into sweet, deep sleep.

Mama was tall and beautiful with cocoa-colored hair parted in the middle and hanging down to her hips. She always wore a woven leather band on her right wrist. I often sat in her lap and stroked the smooth leather with my small fingertips. Unlike me, Mama wasn't shy but exuberant, with a booming, animated laugh. She often snuck up behind her mama while she fried chicken at the kitchen stove and drops of piping-hot oil flew into the air. She'd suddenly wrap her long, thin arms around Birdie and scare her to death. Then she'd laugh and say, "Love you, Birdie Mae," before planting a kiss on her cheek. Soon she was dancing across the linoleum floor to some song only she heard in her head and scooping one of us girls into her arms to twirl us around the room. We never doubted her love and adoration for us, and she was certainly undeserving of the legacy she left in

Clay Station. What happened on that cold winter's night in February 1993 was an accident. Black ice covered the roads. It could have happened to anyone.

I sat on the bed and stared at my tired face in the full-length mirror leaning against the wood-paneled wall. Della and I both had our mother's hazel eyes, high cheekbones, slim nose, and lips. I would always remember my mother as young, only twenty-two when she died, so it was sometimes startling to see an older version of her in the mirror. This dull, thin hair of mine, though. I must've gotten it from my father, but I'd never seen a photo of him to know for sure.

When I wasn't wearing my drab navy work uniform, I opted for blue jeans and T-shirts or sweatshirts, depending on the season. I didn't own a single dress, and nothing outside the color scheme of black, gray, and dark blue. I was content dressing dully and not standing out, unlike my sister. Della emerged from her room daily in bright-purple skirts, flowy blouses, earrings that dangled to her shoulders, and bold lipstick that made her teeth look yellow. On holidays, though, she took it up another notch with huge hats that I found annoying and borderline obscene. Birdie wasn't nearly as flashy as Della, but she did pull an old church dress from her closet on Thanksgiving and Christmas. She'd put on a smidgen of blush and studs, even though we spent the time quietly at home with food she'd prepared—just like any other day.

I once watched a makeover show on television and wondered how drastically different my appearance would be at the hands of stylists: a chic haircut, heavy eyeshadow, lined lips. In each episode, though, the transformation garnered too much attention for the subject of the makeover. I was nauseated at the very thought of such commotion and preferred being a "before" photo. My factory job was mundane, but being on an assembly line wearing hearing protection was what I was best suited for. The uniform took the guesswork out of attire, and it was too loud and busy on the line to talk to anyone. It was easy to keep to myself while earning a paycheck. After eleven years at Simon Container, I still enjoyed the seclusion. It wasn't until Cliff was hired a few months ago and started chasing me around that I felt burdened to interact with anyone.

Because of my tenure, I'd been presented with a promotion, but the thought of dressing up, putting on lipstick, and participating in conversations with strangers around the watercooler was about as appealing as having my toenails removed with pliers. I didn't tell Birdie or Della about my supervisor's recommendation two years ago because I knew they would scold me like a child for not jumping at the opportunity. The way I saw it, people needed their medicines, and Simon Container produced pill bottles for most pharmacies in the southeastern United States. I popped the tops on the bottles that would be popped off every morning, noon, and night. It was monotonous work, but it was essential.

I didn't want Birdie's plan for my life, and I didn't want Della's either. Both wanted me to be an outgoing socialite on the prowl for a husband. They wanted me to refrain from being shy around strangers, as if it were a switch I could flick on and off. They would have loved nothing more than to see me sing on a stage. Once we walked out of Tallahatchie County High School for the last time eleven years ago, Della kissed Birdie and me goodbye, hopped into her beat-up Cavalier, and drove straight to Chattanooga, as she should have.

When Birdie had the stroke, I told Della she didn't have to come back home. I was capable of tending to our grandmother, but she said I didn't have the social skills to communicate properly with Birdie's physicians. Della often complained to me that Birdie still treated us like children, but she was no different. She thought of both Birdie and me as pitiful and defenseless dependents who couldn't possibly get on without her. I often wished my sister would hightail it out of here again and quit peering over my shoulder. I kept my head down and did my job and retired each evening with a good crime show and warm pajamas and pen in hand, and I wished they'd understand that really was enough for me.

● ● ●

I exited my bedroom in worn, comfortable jeans, a solid gray sweatshirt, and thick wool socks that often snagged the nicks in the hardwood floor. I heard Della conversing with Birdie over the sound of dishes clinking and the sink running. When I entered the kitchen, Della was dressed to the nines in a flowery, silky kimono top and a fuchsia pencil skirt. Her hair was loosely hanging over her shoulders and topped with a floppy felt hat that was even bolder than the color of her skirt. The clash of colors made me squint my eyes. Birdie had chosen to wear the green-and-white-plaid A-line dress that she'd owned as long as I was alive, but it was still in good condition. A wide green belt cinched her waist, although Birdie didn't have a waistline. It looked more uncomfortable than flattering, in my opinion, but my grandmother could wear a sack (which wasn't a stretch since she wore muumuus every day of her life), and I would still think she was a beautiful woman.

Della placed the mismatched set of floral stoneware dinner plates on the houndstooth card table in the middle of the kitchen. With Mr. Prentice joining us for Thanksgiving dinner, we didn't have room at the small bar, and it seemed too formal an occasion for TV trays. It was the first time since Della dated Kevin that anyone would be joining us for a holiday. I never would forget the Christmas Eve when he hit Della, right there on the front porch. Through the storm door, I watched her fall to the faded-blue wooden planks with her hands shielding her face from another blow while Kevin hovered over her with his fist shaking. Birdie and I both rushed to her. I collapsed beside Della on the cold porch floor and held her close while old Birdie mustered up the strength to push scrawny little Kevin right off the stoop. He fell into the overgrown holly bushes that lined the house and remained still, with a look of both disbelief and fear on his face. When he stood up and dusted the dirt and prickly holly leaves from his body, our grandmother said to him through stroke-induced garbled speech, "If you ever come around here again, I'll kill you. Do you understand?" He must have understood because that was the last time we saw Kevin.

Although I preferred our normal routine and the comfortable conversation I shared with my grandmother and sister, I was not nervous about Birdie's friend. Mr. Prentice knew that I wasn't one for much talk, and he didn't press me with trivial questions or try to fill the silence with chitchat like most people. I appreciated that.

"How can I help?" I asked my sister and grandmother as they scurried around the warm kitchen.

"Grab a mitt and pull that dressing from the oven," Birdie instructed while she leaned inside the refrigerator.

I did as she asked and set the piping-hot cornbread dish next to the beautifully glazed ham on the stovetop. Perry was captivated by the smell of the meat and watched my every move in hopes that I would toss down a bite to him.

"He's determined to get his paws on that." Della laughed beneath the bright hat. "He's been prowling around the kitchen all morning, licking his lips."

"Well, if he's a good kitty and doesn't rub fur all over Prentice's ankles when he gets here, maybe we'll grant his wish," Birdie said.

I moved out of the way while they lined the food dishes on the green tile counter and Della swatted a dish towel at a fly that was buzzing around the food.

"Prentice is bringing a pie. Chocolate meringue, Darby. Your favorite," Birdie said.

"I hope it's as good as yours."

"Even if it tastes like cat food, we're going to act like it's the best darn pie we've ever had."

I leaned against the doorframe and looked to the yellowed photo of our teenaged mama on the hallway wall. It was a candid shot of her standing next to the magnolia tree in a corner of the yard. She was wearing acid-washed jeans and a colorfully patterned sweatshirt, her arms crossed and her smile radiant. I was used to her being gone after so many years, but holidays prompted the longing to resurface. I wondered what she would look like now, a woman in her midforties. Would her hair still be long and her face smooth? I often thought of all the what-ifs when it came to Mama. What if she hadn't left the house that icy February night? What if she had gotten sober? What if she was standing beside me right that moment, singing a Bobbie Gentry song? What if she survived the accident, got married, and had more children? Brothers and sisters, maybe nieces and nephews, would be running through the tiny house right now while Birdie yelled for them to get out of her way while she was trying to set the table.

I looked out the storm door to see Mr. Prentice's old Chevrolet truck pulling up our gravel driveway, a cold trail of dust following.

"Mr. Prentice is here," I said.

"Heavens to Betsy! He's early and the sweet potatoes aren't ready." Birdie threw her hands up in exasperation.

"Calm down, Birdie. They've only got a few more minutes." Della patted our panicked grandmother on her back.

"If I had my druthers, everything would be ready and setting out when he got here. I don't like to keep guests waiting. Never have. My mother-in-law taught me that. Lottie Redd was madder than a wet hen if you kept her waiting. She was not a patient woman."

Mr. Prentice parked his truck behind mine and slowly got out. He tossed his chewing gum to the gravel before slicking his thick white hair to the side. As he approached the door with a pie plate covered in tinfoil in one hand, he straightened the collar of his light-blue dress shirt with the other.

"You want me to let him in?"

"I reckon so, Darby. Don't let him stand out there and catch his death of cold," Birdie shouted.

I tucked my hair behind my ears and walked to the door. As I opened it, I looked to the floor and muttered, "Hello, Mr. Prentice."

"Darby." He stepped inside. He smelled of peppermint and stout aftershave. "Happy Thanksgiving."

"Yes, sir. Glad you could join us today," I said faintly.

"Prentice! I'm in the kitchen," Birdie called over the sound of pots and pans being tossed into the sink as he slowly shuffled his hunched frame down the narrow, dim hallway.

"Mr. Prentice," Della exclaimed when he entered the kitchen as I followed. "We are so glad to have you with us today. Let me take that pie off your hands."

I should have taken the pie, I guess.

"Well, you girls are pretty as a picture. Boy howdy, it sure smells good in here. Whoo! That's a fine-lookin' spread, Birdena." He stuffed both hands deep inside the pockets of his wrinkled khaki pants.

"Hold your horses, Prentice. Sweet potatoes ain't even ready."

"I don't mind waiting on potatoes," he answered.

"Go ahead and have a seat right here." Della pointed to one of the folding chairs. "What can we get you to drink? Sweet tea? Water?"

"Tea, and the sweeter the better." He sat down at the metal card table. Perry immediately took to his ankles. "Hey there, cat."

I remained standoffish. The kitchen was loud and crowded. Two of my least favorite things.

"Della, get that fleabag out of here. And, Darby, fix Prentice a glass," Birdie said as she continued to situate the casserole dishes on the counter.

While I placed the amber glass on the table before Mr. Prentice, the timer on the kitchen counter buzzed.

"Well, it's about time. Now we're ready." Birdie retrieved the potatoes topped with melted golden marshmallows from the oven.

● ● ●

There hadn't been a moment of silence during the entire meal. If the kitchen wasn't filled with conversation and laughter between Birdie, Della, and Mr. Prentice, the sound of forks and knives clinking against the plates echoed throughout the tiny room.

"The green beans are delicious, Birdena," Mr. Prentice said between hearty bites.

"Well, they are a cinch to make. Just a little chopped bacon, onion, chicken broth, and butter," she answered. "And brown sugar. That's the secret."

"My Gertie was a wonderful woman, but she wasn't

much of a cook. We always ate green beans straight out of the can. No pepper or nothing."

"I remember a salmonella outbreak after she brought fried chicken to the church potluck back in, oh, '87 or '88." Birdie and Mr. Prentice laughed. "Brother Boone was sick as a dog and on the prayer-request list for weeks."

Mr. Prentice shook his head and wiped his mouth with the paper towel. "God rest her soul."

"She was a good woman, Prentice. I know you miss her. She fought a good long fight."

"That she did."

Della changed the melancholy subject. "Mr. Prentice, we sure do appreciate you taking care of Birdie the way you have."

Since Birdie lost sight in her left eye after the stroke, she was no longer allowed to drive. After Mr. Prentice's wife died last year, he started picking Birdie up every so often to take her to doctor's appointments or ride aimlessly around the country for fresh air and scenery. I loved that he kept her busy while Della and I were at work. It beat her sitting at home on the computer all day, forwarding me emails on how to step out of my comfort zone or add volume to my hair.

"Oh, it's my pleasure. I don't mind a bit. I enjoy her company." He gave Birdie a warm smile and her pale, wrinkled cheeks turned pink. It was obvious there was a connection between them.

"One night your grandaddy, me, Prentice, and Gertie went dancing down at the honky-tonk out by Lake Louise and—"

"Oh, Birdie!" Mr. Prentice's hard laugh turned into a cough. "I know just what you're about to tell."

"You remember, Prentice? That Janie Sue floozy asked Joe Ed to dance, and I let her know quick that dog won't hunt. I dumped a pitcher of beer right on her head. The nerve of her to swing those big old hips in my Joe Ed's face."

His shoulders bounced as he chuckled. "You were a pistol, Birdena. Always were the life of the party."

"Well, I'm older than Methuselah now, Prentice. And just can't muster up that spunk since . . ." Birdie's lips pursed in sadness. "We're not going to talk about Cindy today." She cleared her throat and placed her paper napkin in her wide lap. "More sweet potatoes, Prentice?"

DELLA REDD

December was the only time of the year I strayed from my favorite fashion hue of purple. I had two dresser drawers full of Christmas sweaters, dozens of socks, and a pair of white snowman loafers with charcoal eyes and an orange nose on the top. I had a battery-operated necklace made of twinkling red-and-green lights and twenty-five sets of earrings—bells, elves, Santa hats—to wear each day of the season. Last year I purchased a snow globe brooch that played "Jingle Bells" when pressed.

I haven't always worn purple. My obsession with the color didn't start until after reading the book *Power in Color*. It was on a rolling cart at the library in Chattanooga, waiting to be returned to its proper shelf. I casually flipped through it and was captivated by what I read. I learned color holds power. It can impact our attitude, emotions, and behavior. Purple had always been my favorite, but until I read the book, I didn't realize it was associated with royalty, majesty, and dignity. Darker shades often represent luxury or opulence, while lighter lavender shades are feminine and romantic. After reading the book, I decided to invite luxury and royalty and romance into my life by wearing the color every day. It was an extra bonus that I looked fabulous in purple.

As a teenager, I tried to conform to what others thought was acceptable. Melanie and her friends walked the hallways in baggy, unflattering overalls as if they'd milked cows all morning, and I begged Birdie for a pair. She scrounged up enough money to get some off-brand ones, and right along with the popular crowd, I looked like an extra on the set of *Hee Haw*. I pretended to care about MTV Video Music Awards and the latest NSYNC album, when in secret I listened to Billie Holiday and Louis Armstrong. It was exhausting trying to fit in. And no matter how hard I tried, I still wasn't accepted by the A-listers.

While in Chattanooga, I learned to embrace who I was instead of being ashamed of it. My trivia-night buddies found it fascinating that I chose to dress in purple every day, and my dearest friend from community college, Katie Beth, often picked up something for me in purple when she went shopping. She also bought a bedazzled Santa hat for me. Unfortunately, Melanie and Camilla were nothing like Katie Beth and would pester me for wearing a flashing necklace and embellished red-and-green sweaters all month. But the Christmas clothing put me in a festive spirit, and if my appearance could bring a little joy to the sick ones who encountered me at the front desk, that was even better.

• • •

I arrived at work an hour early that Thursday morning. After unlocking the office, turning on all the lights, and firing up the heat in the frigid building, I headed straight for the storage closet. I pulled two boxes labeled "Christmas" from the cluttered nook and got to work. I placed the small table-top tree on the counter in front of my desk and trimmed it with the miniature ornaments and strands of red and green yarn. I taped tinsel over the doorways in the waiting room and hung the wreath filled with pine, berries, lifelike cedar, poinsettias, and velvet roses on the front door of the clinic. Humming "O Little Town of Bethlehem," I walked over to the small radio in the corner of the waiting room and tuned it to the station that played carols 24–7. The volume was low enough not to disturb the patients (especially those with migraines) but loud enough to lift their spirits. I also placed some fresh cinnamon sticks and cloves in the potpourri jar on my desk to fill the room with the cheerful scent of the holidays.

Once everything was in place, I went back to the kitchen and made coffee. Dr. Faulkner enjoyed having a pot waiting for him when he arrived at precisely 7:55 a.m. More than once he had lifted his mug to me and said, "Good coffee, Della."

In the four years I'd worked at the clinic, Dr. Faulkner and I mostly talked about work and coffee, sometimes the weather. It was true that I found him to be incredibly handsome, with his dark hair peppered with gray at the temples, a strong jawline, and eyes as green as the pines in our front yard on Yocona Road, but I didn't gawk at him or turn to mush when he spoke to me, as Melanie had said. I never thought of him in a romantic sense, but I did welcome his kindheartedness. The nurses made fun of me in his presence once, and I overheard him tell Melanie when I left the kitchen, "That was uncalled for. Della does a great job." And I did. I handled everything in the front office. Not only did I check the patients in and out, but I coded charts (Dr. Faulkner paid for the coding class I took online), handled insurance claims, called Handyman Humphries when a faucet dripped or a light flickered, and made the coffee. And, of course, I decorated for every occasion.

While sorting charts for the day and sipping the steaming black coffee from the reindeer mug I'd brought from home, I heard the back door open and the sounds of Camilla's and Melanie's voices. I rolled my eyes as they loudly grumbled and complained about the cold. They were always discontent. If they weren't griping about the weather or the patients, they were moaning about something else. They walked around with a sense of superiority, noses in the air, as if they were neurosurgeons at Cedars-Sinai. They were good nurses and hadn't killed anyone (that I knew of), but they were so smug.

I heard them settling in the kitchen, shaking out their umbrellas from the icy drizzle and putting their lunches in the refrigerator. And then their voices grew louder as they approached the front office.

"Oh, look, Camilla. Elf is back," Melanie jeered when she saw me.

Elf yourself, Melanie.

"Right on cue, Della. December first."

"'Tis the season." I tipped my coffee mug at them.

I was wearing a red sweatshirt with kittens in Santa hats and black corduroy pants. The fuzzy red-and-green-striped socks were visible from the tops of my black flats, and my hair was pulled back with the reindeer antler headband that Melanie had mocked relentlessly last season.

"It's deer-hunting season, Della. Dangerous for you to be wearing that headband out there in the boondocks where you live." She used the same line she'd used the year before.

I wanted to gore her with my antlers like a bull gores a matador.

● ● ●

I sat alone with a turkey wrap and small container of grapes packed in the Christmas-themed plastic baggies that I bought every December. Melanie and Camilla had gone to Sit a Spell and left me to enjoy the peace and quiet of the office kitchen. I checked emails on my phone and saw Birdie had sent Darby and me an article on how to make a balloon arch for a photo booth. She also sent Garden of Eatin's menu and requested we pick a main entrée for the birthday celebration. I closed out the messages without replying because there was no way Birdie could afford balloon arches, photo booths, a caterer, or the community center rental fee. Not only was it unaffordable, but Darby and I couldn't care less about it. I would have to nip this in the bud before Birdie was thousands of dollars in credit card debt for an overpriced soufflé that only she, Mr. Prentice, Darby, and I would enjoy.

"Good afternoon, Della." Dr. Faulkner startled me when he entered the kitchen and pulled a coffee cup from the cupboard over the stainless sink.

"Hi, Dr. Faulkner. Would you like me to make more coffee? It'll only take a minute," I offered.

"No, this is fine. Finish your lunch. I'll pop it in the microwave."

"Yes, sir."

He poured the remainder of the morning's brew into the cup, placed it in the microwave, and glanced at my outfit. "You're awfully festive today."

I blushed. "I think the reindeer antlers cheered up Mrs. Gaskins. And Mrs. Ogilvie loved the Santa cats." I touched my ornate sweatshirt.

"That's great, Della." He retrieved the hot mug. "Mrs. Gaskins could sure use some joy. She's had a rough year."

"You didn't go out for lunch today. Would you like me to run and get you something to eat?"

"No, thank you. I brought a sandwich from home. Too much to catch up on to go out today. I'll be in my office," he said before leaving me alone at the table.

I finished eating and soon heard Dr. Faulkner in his office next to the kitchen, rummaging through the filing cabinet adjacent to his open door and talking on the phone. I ignored the conversation, the "mm-hmms" and "okays," until he said, "Remi, I know how hard this has been on you, but you have to accept that your mother and I are separated."

My ears perked. Shelly showed up at the clinic a week or so ago and caused quite a ruckus back in his office. She slammed her hands on his desk and yelled at him so loudly that patients could hear in the waiting room. At lunch that day, Melanie and Camilla said Shelly had demanded a script from Dr. Faulkner for hydrocodone.

I grinned, though, because I was the one hearing the conversation between Dr. Faulkner and his daughter, who was a freshman at Ole Miss. Usually Melanie and Camilla were the eavesdroppers, but those nosy Nellies picked the wrong day to gorge on burgers smothered in ketchup and mayonnaise at the diner.

"I know, sweetheart," he consoled his daughter. "Your mother loves you, Remi, but she's confused. She needs professional help. I can't help her, and you can't either. No one can until she's ready to help herself."

I empathized with that statement. It didn't matter what Birdie did for our mother, the pep talks she gave or the tough love she showed, because Mama wasn't ready to help herself. Still, Birdie carried a load of guilt thinking she could have done something to save her only child.

"I'm going to be okay. In fact, I wanted to tell you something. I know it's only been a couple of months since I filed for divorce, but I'm thinking of asking someone to join me for lunch. Not dinner. Dinner comes later. I'm not getting married, Remi. I'm not even giving up on the possibility of your mother getting sober and us being a family again. I'm just looking for companionship. That's all," he said as the filing cabinet closed and I heard him sit in his leather rolling chair.

I wasn't going to tell Melanie and Camilla this! This was going to be my secret. All mine. And when they found out later that Dr. Faulkner was in a relationship, I would say, "Oh, I already knew that. Old news, girls." And they would be green with envy that I knew something before they did. But who was it? The nurses were right. It was no secret that Nina Blakely thought Dr. Faulkner was the bee's knees. No respectable woman wore sequin blouses and a push-up bra just to have her blood drawn.

"Just someone I know through work, Remi. She's sweet. A little younger than me, but mature. I'm quite fond of her. She's a breath of fresh air."

My heart began to palpitate. He could not have been talking about Melanie or Camilla. They were *not* sweet. Besides, Camilla was immature and Melanie was married. Dr. Faulkner wasn't the type of man to break up a marriage.

"It's not important now. Maybe you can come home next weekend and we'll talk all about it then?" He paused. "Okay, sweetheart. I've really got to get back to work. I love you."

There was only one person at work left.

The Christmas elf.

● ● ●

I could barely concentrate for the rest of the day. I misplaced an insurance form, forgot to pull Mr. McElhanney's chart, and barely acknowledged Mrs. Dyson's story, inspired by my sweatshirt, of the time her cat climbed the Christmas tree and sent it toppling over the couch. Or maybe it fell into the fireplace. I thought I remembered her talking about the fire department and an arson investigator, but I wasn't sure.

I kept replaying Dr. Faulkner's conversation with Remi in my mind. He couldn't be fond of me—he barely knew me. We rarely spoke because he was always hidden away in his office or an exam room. On the other hand, Dr. Faulkner had been complimentary of my Christmas outfits and my coffee. He had defended me to the wicked nurses in the past. And he was an eccentric person, like me. Over the years, I'd learned he was a stamp collector and an avid Star Wars fan. He was a nerd, as was I. I wore blinking Christmas sweaters and flowers in my hair. I listened to big band and jazz. I drove a purple PT Cruiser, for goodness' sake. And I had seen the first Star Wars movie. Or was it the fifth? I think they were one and the same. So what if it was true? What if he did find me attractive and wanted to share lunch with me at Sit a Spell? I should probably get him a Christmas gift. Nothing purple. Nothing weird. A shaving kit? The expensive cologne he always wore? Gourmet coffee? A Star Wars mug? A rare stamp? Maybe I could find one on the Christie's auction website.

I took a deep breath. I was getting way ahead of myself, just like I did as a chunky kid with diminished self-esteem. Many of the times when Birdie signed Darby and me up for clubs in which we had no interest or pushed us to attend church lock-ins in an attempt to socialize us, I entered those situations with hyperbolic imaginations of all the good things that would come of it. Instead of leaving with a gaggle of new friends' phone numbers and slumber party invitations, though, I left feeling rejected and less than. I got my hopes up time and again, only to be disappointed. Why did I think this would be different?

And yet.

If Dr. Faulkner and I started dating, Birdie's birthday bash would be a wonderful opportunity to introduce ourselves as a couple. He would look so dashing in his dark tux with purple vest and boutonniere as he twirled me across the floor to Glenn Miller Orchestra's "Moonlight Serenade." I could invite the bullies who ridiculed me my entire life just so they could see me on the arm of the esteemed physician. They'd witness him laughing at my jokes, staring into my hazel eyes, grazing his strong, masculine hand across the freckles on my cheeks. I imagined they would loiter around the cake table and mutter about our love. The stuck-ups would be sorry they hadn't accepted me all these years. I would finally have the upper hand. That *was* my idea of a lovely evening.

Once Dr. Faulkner and I shared lunch at the diner, I would give Birdie and Darby all the beautiful details. I'd tell them the sweet words he spoke through smiling, pearly white teeth. How he reached over my plain garden salad and tucked the red poinsettia behind my ear. The way he refused to douse his french fries in ketchup because of my aversion to the runny tomato syrup. As our lunch date drew to a close, I'd confide in him the nasty ways the nurses treated me and the way the entire town looked down on us Redds. He'd be appalled by their behavior. He'd fire Camilla and Melanie. He would join me on my (and Birdie's) mission to marry off my sister. We'd set Darby up on a date with someone he went to medical school with. Yes, an affluent doctor. Better yet, a therapist! Yes, a therapist who could tear down the walls Darby had put up. A highly trained medical professional who could help her overcome her social anxiety issues. He would marry her and care for her like the wounded bird she was.

This time next year I could be living in Dr. Faulkner's elegant house on Magnolia Trace. I'd place little touches throughout the home—knickknacks in purple and vases of fresh gladiolus and a fabulous painted portrait of Billie Holiday. Brian's daughter and I would become fast friends. Everything I'd ever wanted was finally within reach.

But first, I'd have to get through lunch.

7

DARBY REDD

I had been sitting at the cafeteria table, alone, for at least ten minutes. I figured Cliff went home sick before lunch since I'd seen him on his line that morning and he usually showed up by now. Dozens of Simon Container employees were out with the flu, and Della said Dr. Faulkner had diagnosed a bunch of patients with it. Birdie was also sick last week, and Mr. Prentice stayed with her and fed her soup and changed out her *Murder, She Wrote* DVDs while Della and I were at work. He really was a godsend to us all.

Since Cliff wasn't hounding me with questions while I popped Doritos into my mouth, I thought about Della coming into my room last night while I was writing in my journal. She dramatically collapsed at the end of my bed and rested her head on her elbow while her cat pounced on my comforter, molted 2,200 hairs, and then licked his paws. I'd always loved animals, but I didn't know how much cats shed until Della took Perry in. Not only was it annoying to constantly brush hairs from my clothing, but it was repulsive when I discovered them on my toothbrush or in my Neapolitan ice cream.

Della was beaming as she told me quite the elaborate fairy tale about marrying her boss. Because she'd had a chip on her shoulder since she moved back home, it was refreshing to see my usually aggrieved sister excited and joyful. However, as Della droned on about the eavesdropped conversation between Dr. Faulkner and his daughter, I could sense her overactive imagination was rearing its ugly head. She was getting her hopes up, and when that happened to Della in Tallahatchie County, it never ended well.

When Della moved to Chattanooga, she was restored. Being in a new environment helped heal the hurts our childhood had heaped on her, but coming back to Clay Station undid the progress she'd made. Working with the bane of her existence, Melanie Reid, every day certainly contributed to her indignation. She recalled memories she'd successfully blocked out—the cruel things our peers said and did to us, the spiteful gossip the adults shared about our mother at the country club. Della didn't even realize she was reverting back to her former detrimental mindset of bitterness, the way a dog returns to its vomit.

Della often claimed the Who's Who of Clay Station, Mississippi, were cantankerous wives and mothers who stayed in this one-horse town because they'd never amount to much anywhere else. She said they probably still kept their beauty pageant and athletic trophies on their living room mantels and gazed at them often, pining for their glory days. She called them pathetic and unadmirable, but those were the very people Della wanted to be received by, just like when we were kids. When it came to the two of us, Della had always perceived herself as the leader, the alpha, the emotionally strong twin, but I had been the one strong enough to let go of past upsets, and I didn't even have to move three hundred miles away to do it. I had forgiven those who had hurt us. Not for them but for myself.

I tucked my trash into the paper lunch sack and pulled out my mobile phone. With my shoulders slumped and my face hidden behind my long and limp hair, I catapulted a yellow bird into a stack of bricks. Dozens of coworkers passed by, but no one stopped to say hello or to join me, which didn't trouble me in the least. When our designated lunchtime was over, everyone began to stand and head for the floor. I took the last swig of Dr Pepper from the plastic bottle and tossed it and the paper sack into the garbage can. Head down, I watched my black sneakers shuffle across the cement floor and back into the warehouse.

"Darby!" I recognized Cliff's voice behind me. I ignored it until he called again, "Darby! Hey, Darby Redd!"

I turned to see him working his tall, thin frame through the crowd. He had a red-and-white-striped bag in his hand with green tissue paper and a ribbon cascading from the rope handle.

"Hey!" he panted. "I got held up. Problem on the line. Maintenance had to come, so I'm taking my lunch late. But I wanted to make sure you got this here." He thrust the gift toward me.

"What is it?" I asked as the crowd parted around us.

"It's your Christmas present." He smiled from beneath the short stubble on his chin. "Take it."

"It's not even Christmas yet. There are nine days left." I quickly glanced up at him.

"Better sooner than later, ain't it? I want to see you open it. Go ahead now. Ain't got all day." He laughed and pushed the glasses up his nose that was as slender as he was.

"I can't take this onto the floor." I shook my head and shoved my hands into my pockets.

He looked disappointed. I knew I was coming off as rude and ungrateful, although that hadn't been my intention. I was merely uncomfortable. "Okay then. How about I put it in my locker until the end of the day? You can open it after we clock out?"

I quickly agreed before turning on my heels and marching to my line.

● ● ●

While I placed caps on pill bottles for the next three hours, I thought about the gift. Did Cliff giving me a gift mean I had to give him one? What would I say when I opened it? What if I hated it? What if it was clothing? Something in a bright, bold color that I'd never wear? I would pretend. When Mr. Prentice asked if I liked his chocolate pie on Thanksgiving, I said it was enjoyable, when in reality it was bland. I knew how to be polite. I wouldn't go over the top the way Della did—clapping her hands and skipping around like someone hopped up on speed—but I would tell him thank you. I would smile and be cordial like a normal person. I was an introvert, not a jerk.

I was terribly nervous when the whistle blew at three. I thought about avoiding the time clock altogether. When questioned by my supervisor and HR, I would say I simply forgot to clock out for the first time in eleven years. It would be worth those conversations to avoid the whole gift scenario with Cliff. But when I trooped off the factory floor, Cliff was standing beside the clock with the present in his hands, grinning goofily like the famous Disney dog in the turtleneck and vest. As soon as I slid the paper card into the clock, he shoved the bag into my arms.

"Well, go ahead. I've been waiting all day now, Darby. Open it on up." He skipped alongside me as we exited the glass double doors and were pelted with a blast of wintry December air.

Continuing to walk across the parking lot, I reached into the sea of green tissue paper and pulled out a journal. It was charcoal-colored and my initials were in white cursive lettering on the front. *DAR*. I stopped as he continued bouncing from one foot to the other, and I looked up at him, past the glasses dangling from his nose, and into his shiny blue eyes.

"I called your grandmama a few weeks back. Wasn't hard to get her number since she was the only Redd in the phone book and hardly anybody's got home phones anymore. I asked her what kind of stuff you like. You know, your favorite colors and the like. She told me your middle name is Ann. She said what a good writer you are. Said you can sing like a bird too. I didn't know that, Darby. So this is a journal for you to write in. She said she gave you a pen for your birthday. She's a real sweet lady, your Birdie." His warm breath left puffs of smoke in the frigid gray air.

I was speechless, as usual.

"You like it?" He searched my face for approval, but I remained silent and looked back to the journal in my hands. I rubbed my cold fingers across the dark cover. "You don't like it?"

"Why are you so nice to me?" I finally spoke.

"Because I like you, Darby."

"You don't even know me."

"I'd like to, Darby. I'd like to know you," he said kindly, genuinely.

"I—I do like the journal." I looked back to him. "It was— It is nice of you to get such a gift, such a thoughtful gift."

"Well, I'll be. You *can* talk." He smiled and revealed a small chip in his front tooth that I'd never noticed before.

"I can. I just don't like to."

"That's all right. You'll talk to me a whole lot one day." He continued to grin while turning toward his truck. "Have a good night, Darby. I'll see you tomorrow."

● ● ●

I left Della and Birdie sitting in the living room watching the *Murder, She Wrote* episode where J. B. tracked down a killer on the rodeo circuit and I disappeared into my room. I pulled the journal from my chest of drawers where I'd hidden it after work and sat on the bed. Birdie, of course, knew about the gift since she was the one to suggest it to Cliff, but I didn't tell my sister. I didn't want Della's unsolicited opinion on the matter. She would urge me to buy a present for Cliff, and although I knew that was probably the decent thing to do, I was uncomfortable at the notion. Just because Cliff Waters gave me a Christmas present didn't mean I was going to reciprocate the action. It didn't mean I was going to date him. It didn't mean I was in love.

The stiff spine of the new book resisted, but I successfully opened it and ran my hand across the first bright-white page. There was something beautiful, even magical, about a crisp, blank sheet. The possibilities were thrilling. Oftentimes feelings I didn't even know I possessed came to life on crisp, blank sheets. I pulled the pen Birdie gave me from the bedside-table drawer and started scribbling. The words came to me quickly, effortlessly.

> This rampart has shielded me for so
> > long now,
> Layers upon layers of impenetrable stone.
> You approach with chisel in hand,
> Determined to tear it down all on
> > your own.
> I'm safe behind this brick and mortar.
> I am contented with this wall.
> It's my sense of security and protection,
> But my preference isn't going to deter you
> > at all.

BIRDENA REDD

Looking at Christmas lights had always been good for my weary soul. Those twinkling bulbs took me back to a time before the patina of life had formed, when my future still seemed chock-full of possibilities. I grew up dirt poor with parents who weren't much count, but Willa made sure Harwell and I had fine Christmases to look back on. On Christmas morning, Ma was usually too depressed to get out of the bed and Pa was sleeping off a hangover next to some other woman, but Harwell and I woke up on our floor mattresses in the room we shared with Willa to bacon sizzling in the skillet and some little gift under a baby spruce in the corner of the living room. Mama had more needles in her sewing basket than what was on whatever small tree Willa could cut down and carry back to the house in her teenaged hands, but it was just fine for Harwell and me.

When Cindy was a little one, Joe Ed and I made a point

to ride her around to look at all the lights in the county on a crisp winter night leading up to the holiday. And now the girls and I took a drive to Beverly Woods subdivision in the heart of town to see them. My favorite was the redbrick house at the end of Birdsong Cove. In the side yard, half the grass was blanketed in blue bulbs to resemble the ocean and an inflatable Santa on a surfboard stood right in the middle. You could roll the window down and hear the Beach Boys blaring from a speaker hidden somewhere in the darkness. I got such a kick out of the sight and wondered how long it must have taken the family to put up all those lights.

Joe Ed tacked up a string of multicolored bulbs across the front porch one time, and it was so much work he left them up until well past Easter. And that said a lot about the labor involved because my Joe Ed was a real hard worker and it took a whole lot of aggravation to make him procrastinate on anything.

Della got more excited than a pig in mud about Christmas. She wore the most fun outfits for twenty-five straight days—sweaters decked out in ribbons and yarn, lights, and fluffy Santa beards. I owned a red-and-green Christmas apron with prints of trees and snowflakes on it when she was a kid, and she'd wrap herself in that tattered thing and parade around the house singing carols. I found the most adorable Christmas turtleneck in the donate pile at the Mustard Seed one year. It took batteries and played a little jingle when you squeezed Rudolph's red nose. She was so proud to wear it to school, but those little devils must have said something to her because she only put it on around the house after that.

Della had always been unique in the way she dressed,

and she didn't like the same things other kids liked—pop culture and the like. I could probably take credit for her obsession with Billie Holiday and all things jazz, as that was what I played on the big old record player in the living room while I dusted the place or cooked in the kitchen. And she'd just as well watch episodes of *Columbo* and *The Rockford Files* with me than care what show had topped the Nielsen ratings. That was who she was—at home. But at school she wore clothes she didn't much care for and walked around with fashion magazines she begged me to buy for her in the checkout lane at Piggly Wiggly. It wasn't until she moved off to Chattanooga that she started expressing herself the way she always wanted to. Even though I wasn't too thrilled about her dyeing her hair purple for a little while when she lived up in Tennessee, it was a relief she was no longer scared to be herself or do what she wanted to do.

Since Della had come back, I'd seen her old insecurities creeping in. I'd catch a glimpse now and again of that verbally abused little girl who longed to fit in and hid away in her room to process the school day's mistreatment. One day last year she even asked me, "Do you find it odd that I wear purple so much? Should I quit doing that?" Made me think someone at work might have said something about it. Made me realize again how badly she needed to get away from here. I wouldn't even care if she dyed her hair purple again.

Unlike Della, Darby ain't ever been too worried about what people said and thought of her. Rolled off her like water rolls off a duck's back. I didn't think she was introverted because she was bullied as a kid. That was probably part of it, but I thought that was just who she was—who she'd always been. She was shy like her mama, that was all. Still, I'd always tried to persuade her to step out of her safety net and share her servant's heart and angelic voice with others. When she was knee-high to a grasshopper, she'd go looking for neglected animals in the field around the house just so she could bottle-feed a baby squirrel or put a Band-Aid tightly around a frog's bad leg like a cast. I thought she'd surely go off to be a veterinarian or a nurse someday. But she refused and said the world was too big and noisy for her. Darby seemed content going to work every day at the factory, writing poems in her mama's old bedroom, and tending to me when I was sick. I should've accepted it and thanked God she didn't turn to alcohol like Cindy did because she *was* unhappy being alone. Still, though, something kept telling me if Darby would just get a little taste of friendship and love, she'd be content in that too.

● ● ●

"Well, I'll be. There are lights on that deer head. That may be the most redneck thing I've ever seen," Della said from the driver's seat as we slowly drove down the street with all the brightly colored lights.

"That's Russell McKenney's place. He carved that deer out of a tree stump. Can you believe that? Darby, the man who made your pen lives there. Right there where that deer head is." I tapped on the window.

"That's a pretty impressive deer head," Darby mumbled from the back seat of Della's car.

"Girls, this is just a world of fun. Thank you for bringing

me out to look at the lights every year. Does my heart good." I pulled on the seat belt digging into my chest. "Are you having a good time back there, Darby?"

"Yes, ma'am," she answered over the heat roaring through the car vents.

I'd spent a lot of years worrying if Darby was having a good time. If she was, no one ever knew. She wasn't one to get riled up about much. I thought the happiest day of her life was when she received word that a poem she had anonymously sent in to a writing contest in Tupelo won first place and was going to be printed in the local newspaper there. She was happy as a lark, but no one aside from me and Della ever would have known it. To a stranger, it would have appeared more like her dentist told her she only had one cavity instead of two.

"Oh, *whew*! I'm sweating like a sinner in church," I said as Della turned the red thermometer knob.

"What's your favorite Christmas memory, Birdie? When you were a little girl, I mean," Della asked as we continued to gaze at the bright homes lining the sidewalks.

"Oh, that long ago?" I laughed. "Well, that's easy. More than anything, I wanted a Betsy Wetsy doll. 'Course we couldn't afford one, but Willa bartered with Mr. Williams. He owned the drugstore in town and had some dolls for sale in there. Willa spent two whole Saturdays painting Mr. Williams's fence, and he paid her with that doll. It was wrapped up real nice under the tree on Christmas morning. One year she worked all weekend raking Mr. Williams's leaves to earn a big set of army men for Harwell. Willa sure was one of a kind. She rarely had any time to be a child because she was taking care of us all the time. I guess you girls were too young to remember her before she died."

"I remember a little about her," Della said. "She had a Coca-Cola sign over her kitchen sink. And she made us chocolate milk in those extra-tall glasses with blue stripes on them."

"She sure did." I half turned in my seat. "What about you girls? Darby? Your favorite Christmas?"

"I remember a little about the last Christmas with Mother. I guess that's my favorite." Darby spoke softly from the back of the car.

"What do you remember? You were only five, sweetheart."

"Just bits and pieces. I remember spilling hot chocolate on my foot. I cried in her lap on the couch for a good long while. It was Christmas Eve, I guess, because she told me I could open a present early. It was a mermaid coloring book."

"That's sweet, Darby. I'm glad you have those memories." I felt sorrow right then that Cindy wasn't there. That she'd killed herself and left these girls without a mama or any memories past the age of five. And then that regret seeped into all the empty places like Mississippi River floodwater. Cindy wouldn't have turned to drinking if she could have turned to me when her daddy died.

Darby added, as if she knew recollections of her mother were bittersweet to my ears, "And of course, Birdie, hearing you hum 'Silent Night' in the kitchen while you cooked. Watching *A Charlie Brown Christmas* with Della on the living room floor while we ate chocolate-covered pretzels. That's all good stuff too."

"Yes." I smiled and looked out the window at the white

lights lining the bare branches of a Bradford pear. "Della, what's your favorite memory about Christmas?"

"Same as Darby, I guess. *Charlie Brown*. Forsaking my clean diet for sugary pretzels. And my Christmas attire, of course." She removed her hand from the steering wheel to tap the green-sequined tree on the front of her sweatshirt.

"It's a special time. Everything seems right at Christmas." I nodded.

"I also really enjoyed the time Jenny James forgot her lines during the Christmas pageant. It was one of the best moments of my life watching her frozen in that angel costume in front of the entire assembly. The next year she got bumped down to donkey." Della guffawed.

"That?" Darby asked from behind me. "That's what comes to mind when you think of Christmas?"

"It was pretty good," Della said.

"Are you still twelve, Della? Are we in some kind of Benjamin Button situation here where you are aging backward? Don't forget to add Noxzema pads to your grocery list. Pick up a poster of Freddie Prinze Jr. too," Darby scoffed.

"Girls . . . ," I began. "I don't know about buttons and pads and princes, but let's not—"

Darby leaned forward and huffed loudly. "Don't you think it's pathetic, Birdie? That she's still consumed by things that happened twenty years ago? It's not normal." Darby rarely showed emotion, but this time it was obvious she was ready to spit nails.

"I'm sure your sister was just kidding," I said. "Come on now, Della, you don't really think about that when you think on Christmas, do you?"

Della quietly stared at the road while her lips and eyes did what they always did when she was furious—scrunched tighter than Fort Knox.

"And now the silent treatment. Another twelve-year-old tactic." Darby shifted on the cloth seat behind me. "It's like I'm living in *Romy and Michele's High School Reunion.* She's Romy and there's no Michele in sight."

"Who is Michele?" I glanced at Della, whose face was still shriveled like a prune.

The girls had argued their whole lives, as siblings do. Darby said what was on her mind and then let it go. Della stewed on things and glared darting eyes at her sister for days on end. I did what I could to make them kiss and make up, but I'd learned it was usually best to let them settle it on their own. After Della cooled off in a day or two, she and her sister would be just fine.

I tapped on the passenger side glass. "Oh, look at that nativity scene. That's one of those real-looking babies in the manger. I saw those on an infomercial one night. The eyes blink and everything. Well, I declare."

9

DELLA REDD

SUNDAY, DECEMBER 25, 2016

After we'd eaten our fill of the duplicate Thanksgiving lunch, Birdie napped in the recliner, Mr. Prentice snored upright on the couch next to me, and Darby retreated to her room. The six-foot artificial tree I bought for Birdie when I moved back home glowed in the corner of the den, wrapped in bright lights and ornaments crafted out of Popsicle sticks, glue, glitter, and cotton balls our mother made in the late seventies and Darby and I made in the early nineties. Wads of spent wrapping paper littered the hardwood floor, and dirty dishes cluttered the kitchen sink. Birdie had bought all of us gadgets from late-night television. I received a phone holder to clip on my car AC vent, Darby got a rechargeable LED headlamp for reading and writing in bed, and Mr. Prentice seemed thrilled to open a cooling hat with UV protection for working in the yard. Darby bought me a violet scarf-and-hat set off the internet, and Mr. Prentice gave both Darby and me homemade peanut brittle (that was a tad too brittle and threatened to crack my molars) in a decorative tin can we could later fill with odds and ends such as spare change, paper clips, pens, and pencils.

I continually thought of Dr. Faulkner that morning as we opened presents and ate our fill. I'd waited until Melanie and Camilla left on Friday before giving him his gift stylishly covered in shimmery white wrapping paper with a silver bow. It was a bobblehead in a white doctor's coat. I designed it on a website to resemble him with the same hair and eye color. When he pulled it from the box, he belted out a chuckle and thanked me several times. He immediately swiveled around in his chair and set it on his bookshelf, next to a picture of Remi in her graduation cap and gown with multiple academic awards in her hands. I hoped he'd think of me each time he saw it. I imagined him mentioning me and the gift as he shared a Christmas breakfast of chocolate gravy and biscuits with his daughter at their dining table early that morning.

While wearing the nativity sweater I always saved for the twenty-fifth (although it was biblically inaccurate because the wise men weren't in the stable when Jesus was born; it took them months to make the journey to Bethlehem), I picked at the strands of brown yarn on the camel's tail and scrolled through Facebook. I gazed at a photo of my group of Chattanooga friends posing at the top of Lookout Mountain. They were visiting Rock City, and a couple of them were wearing Santa hats as they stood at Lover's Leap, from where it was said you could see seven states—Tennessee, Kentucky, Virginia, North and South Carolinas,

Georgia, and Alabama. I longed to be there with them, amid the breathtaking views and fresh, clean air. Although we sometimes commented on each other's photos or gave a like here and there, we had grown apart. Some of them had gotten married since I'd left, and my favorite friend among them, Katie Beth, was pregnant. I wished I was throwing a baby shower for her at our favorite café on High Street.

Rachel's photos were next in my newsfeed—candid shots of her husband, Franklin, and their two chocolate Labs squeezed next to the tree in their cozy apartment in Fort Lauderdale. I was thrilled Rachel had gotten out of Tallahatchie County. She was a product of a dysfunctional family as well, dirt poor and teased for the holes in her shoes and the time her father was serving in prison. Rachel was a genius and got an academic scholarship to the University of South Florida. There she met her husband, and now she had a fascinating career as a marine biologist. We checked in with each other via text every so often, but that was the extent of our friendship. Rachel used to get angry with me for trying to insert myself into the popular clique. She took it personally, as if her friendship wasn't enough. It wasn't until I moved to Chattanooga that I realized I had tossed Rachel to the back burner and taken her for granted more times than I would like to admit. One night, after obsessing over it for a while, I sent her a lengthy text to apologize, and she replied simply with "Thanks." I was certain she was still aggrieved by my adolescent behavior, and I wouldn't expect her to fly in for our thirtieth birthday party.

As I continued to scroll, I stopped at the photo of Erin's annual tacky Christmas sweater party.

Melanie and Jenny James were front and center. I despised Jenny, but I admired the festive and fun sweater she had on—Santa squeezing down a chimney that looked like it was rough to the fingers, like a toddler's touch-and-feel book. In fact, I saw nothing tacky about the sweaters. I'd proudly wear any one of them. I glared back at Jenny's cheerful smile and remembered when she'd placed a cupcake on my desk chair at a Christmas party in elementary school. I sat on it, and the entire class laughed when the burgundy icing and green sprinkles covered the back of my jeans. Mrs. Dougherty sent me to the bathroom to wash up and later found me in the stall, in tears, because I couldn't remove the stain. She wet a napkin, scrubbed my rear end, and said, "Don't let them get to you, Della."

Birdie tried to get the stain out of the jeans, but a faded pink spot remained. I had to wear them anyway. Birdie worked long hours as a cashier at Piggly Wiggly to provide for us, but we didn't have the luxury of throwing out pants because of an icing stain. Most of our clothes were baggy, tattered hand-me-downs from Coppedge Creek Baptist Church. Thankfully, I now made a decent wage and could afford all the brand-new "tacky" Christmas sweaters and purple dresses I wanted.

I continued to analyze Erin's Facebook photo and wondered how many of those grown women were raising their own children to be bullies. There was probably some poor little girl at Eastside Elementary who came from a less-than-perfect family and dressed weird—some little girl who was never invited to sleepovers or picked for tag. And Jenny's kid probably found great pleasure in tormenting her.

In elementary school Darby spent recess reading next to her teacher's chair while I walked the playground alone. If I was permitted to join in a game with my classmates, I would overdo it by jumping around in excitement and promising not to disappoint them by getting hit with the dodgeball or being tagged. Then I would immediately get pelted by the dodgeball, be told I was a loser, and spend the rest of the day angry with myself and with the stupid kid who hit me with the ball. I wished I could go back in time and tell that young, insecure version of myself to quit basing her self-worth on what those heartless snobs thought of her.

Although we were judged by the sins of our mother, we didn't follow in her footsteps. We didn't become a statistic or carry on the generational curse. Darby never had a sip of alcohol in her life, and although I occasionally enjoyed a Purple Haze martini—grape schnapps, vodka, lemon-lime soda, grenadine, and sour mix—I wasn't addicted and didn't crave alcohol on a regular basis. I certainly didn't get wasted and then get behind the wheel of my car. I hadn't killed anyone.

I'd never understood how the child of an alcoholic could be attracted to an alcoholic. It never made sense to me how someone could purposefully pursue what they knew from experience would not go well. But that was exactly what I did with my ex, Kevin. His dependence on whiskey was evident on our first date, and yet I fell head over heels in love with him. I met Kevin my fourth year of living in Chattanooga. He was a regular at the bar where Tuesday Night Trivia was held. He staggered over to the pub table where our team, Les Quizérables, was seated and told me I was the most beautiful thing he'd ever seen. He was movie-star handsome—tall with dark hair and beard, and blue eyes comparable to the hue of the Caribbean Sea. Gazing into those eyes took my breath away—a literal physical reaction that was the greatest feeling I'd ever known. It wasn't long before we were inseparable.

Kevin was the first male to show me attention. He said all the right things, and I let down my guard with him. We comfortably confided our broken histories to each other. His father was serving time in South Carolina for a string of offenses, and his mother hadn't been in the picture since he was a teen. He'd been a troublemaker in school, an outcast in his own right. We bonded, and I vowed to help him mend his heart the way I'd mended mine. He admitted he drank to forget the damaging memories and promised time and again to quit. He gave his word he'd stop drinking for me. My mother made the same promise.

But, like my mother, he couldn't do it. He didn't even try. When Kevin drank, he was a different person. No longer the romantic, precious man who stroked my hair as I remembered aloud the night Mama died. He morphed into a spiteful monster with a mean streak a mile long. He said I was stupid because I didn't know the first thing about football. He said I was weird when I listened to Louis Armstrong. He said I was too ignorant to ever make it in the corporate world. He said I was weak if I stumbled and fell when he hit me. But even when the pain was so intense from his blows, I never cried in front of Kevin. Not once.

I confided in Katie Beth that Kevin was verbally and physically abusive, and she begged me time and again to end the relationship before I ended up the subject in one of those murder mysteries Darby found so fascinating. But when Kevin sobered up and begged my forgiveness, I took him back with open arms. There was no way I could refuse his apology while looking into those spectacular eyes in the rare and appealing shade of blue. When he pulled me close, I developed amnesia to the callous ways he'd treated me. Kevin was my person, and I knew if I just stuck it out with him long enough, he'd change. My love would make him better.

When I moved home to care for Birdie, Kevin and I continued a long-distance relationship for several months. However, it wasn't long before he quit his construction job in Chattanooga and moved to Clay Station. He said he couldn't bear to be away from me, so he found work as a janitor at the elementary school and rented a basement apartment in the old fire station in town. He spent many evenings at our house, watching *Murder, She Wrote* with Birdie and helping me and Darby tend to her. Even though sober Kevin was sweet as pie to Birdie, something about him didn't set well with her. She had no idea he was a drinker or that he had abused me, but still, she wasn't a fan of his.

When we ran into people I knew while we dined in public or went grocery shopping together, I held on tightly to him as if he were a trophy. I was so proud to be seen with him; to prove to those who'd tossed me aside my whole life that I was worthy of such a handsome man's affection. After being in Clay Station a short while, he earned a reputation as the drunk from Tennessee who spent his late nights at Pickard's Bar and started fights. He was eventually arrested while breaking into cars in the bar parking lot and spent a few hours in jail before I bailed him out. And I was associated with him. *"Della Redd brought that no-good to town,"* I imagined they said. I was embarrassed and angry with Kevin for shining a negative light on us both. Still, brainwashed by his eyes, the sweet words he whispered into my ear when he was sober, and the way his arms felt around my waist, I forgave him and intended to marry him and move back to the mountains once Birdie was better. I had no doubt I could talk him into getting treatment in Chattanooga. He loved me enough to do it, I thought. Before long, I would have that high-rise job and he'd open his own construction company. As Birdie said, we'd be living in high cotton. Babies. White picket fence. Mountain view. The whole shebang.

However, on Christmas Eve four years ago, he showed up at our house with whiskey on his breath. I told him he couldn't come inside because Birdie wouldn't stand for an inebriated man in the house, not after what our mother went through. We argued for a few minutes before he reared his fist back and hit me. I fell to the porch floor, certain my head had been knocked off my shoulders. The ruckus alerted Birdie and Darby, who ran outside, and feeble old Birdie, still recovering from her stroke, tossed him off the front porch. He didn't beg my forgiveness after that. Instead, he packed up and left Clay Station.

When Kevin was gone, I spiraled into a dark pit that echoed with the familiar lie that I wasn't good enough and never had been. I had allowed myself to be disrespected, much in the same way Melanie and her clan had disrespected me. I was without a relationship, or friendship, and stuck in a town I hated. I had sworn I would never let myself be vulnerable like that again.

And yet now I was willing to try again because the object of my affection this time was a decent man with an esteemed reputation. Brian Faulkner would treat me like a queen. Our relationship was going to be all the good things I had with Kevin—and only the good things. If only he would hurry up and invite me to lunch.

I replayed his conversation with Remi in my mind a million times. I analyzed every word, and it only made sense that I was the sweet, mature woman he referred to. When he gently touched the small of my back while squeezing around me at the filing cabinet last week, I knew I wasn't imagining things. I constantly rationalized why he had yet to ask me out. Maybe his daughter thought it was too soon for him to start dating and talked him out of it, or maybe he was too shy to approach me. Maybe I had to make the first move.

The phone on the table next to the couch rang loudly and startled both Birdie and Mr. Prentice from their tryptophan-induced naps.

"Heavens to Betsy! Who in the world is that calling?" Birdie grumbled as Mr. Prentice crossed his arms and cleared his throat.

I gently removed Perry from my lap and stood to answer the phone. A male voice asked for Darby.

"May I ask who is calling?"

"This is Cliff Waters, ma'am. From Simon Container."

"Hold on just a moment, Cliff." I set the receiver on the end table next to Mr. Prentice's UV hat.

I hurried to Darby's door and pushed it open to see her

lying on her bed and writing in a journal. The bright-pink sweater I'd given her that morning was draped across the foot of the bed, never to be worn, I was sure.

"Darby, Cliff is on the phone!" Like a schoolgirl, I shrieked with excitement.

"Cliff? Why?" She tossed the journal to her side.

"I don't know. I guess he's calling to tell you merry Christmas."

She shook her head. "Just tell him I'm busy or that I'm asleep. Make something up. I don't want to talk on the phone."

I sighed. "Darby, don't be ridiculous. You are an adult. Surely you aren't too scared to talk on the phone." I leaned against the doorway.

"Just because I'm shy doesn't mean I'm scared, Della. I talk to that man at work enough as it is."

"Just be a big girl and pick it up." I pointed to the Garfield telephone on her bedside table.

She looked at the orange cat phone that belonged to our mother and then back to me.

"Okay." She exhaled in annoyance and tucked her hair behind her ears.

I shut her bedroom door and hurried back to the receiver on the end table by the couch. I quietly slid it up to my ear when Birdie said, "Hang up the phone and sit your butt back down on the couch, Della Marie Redd."

10

DARBY REDD

Sleet sputtered from the wintry sky as I slowly navigated the winding road. Mrs. Dalton's German shepherd wasn't deterred by the freezing rain. His big old paws remained steadfast on the slippery asphalt as he vehemently pursued my back tires. I certainly wasn't as energetic as the dog that morning. I hadn't slept well and wanted nothing more than to be back at home in my warm bed, surrounded by the wood-paneled walls and the hum of the oscillating heater. The phone call with Cliff had only lasted a few minutes, but I spent most of the night thinking about the short conversation.

He asked what I'd received for Christmas and then droned on about a ratchet and socket set his maw gave him and how it would make removing the deck on his lawn mower a breeze. He also inquired if I'd used the journal, and I told him yes. He didn't ask me to read anything I'd written in it to him, but I could sense he wanted to. He'd have to pry the journal from my cold, dead hands to know what was scribbled on the pages. My words weren't meant for a stranger's eyes or ears. Some things I'd poured out of my heart and soul had never even been shared with Birdie or Della.

I wrote my first poem on the Eastside Elementary playground while I sat on the itchy green grass next to my fourth-grade teacher, Mrs. Thatcher. The words came to me out of thin air, and I penciled them faintly in the back of the book I had checked out of the library—*Ribsy* by Beverly Cleary. I erased the poem only a few moments after jotting it down, but I never forgot it.

> I sit here day after day,
>> no one asks me to play.
>> That's all right. That's okay.
>> I like sitting here day after day.

Even at nine years old, I was fine with being alone. I was satisfied sitting next to Mrs. Thatcher while she talked with the other teachers about her husband and kids and pet guinea pigs with overgrown teeth. I enjoyed getting lost in a good book about a dog or cat or whatever *Ribsy* was about while Della wasted her time chasing our classmates around the schoolyard and pleading with them to be her friends.

Maybe I should read my first poem (and my first poem only) to Cliff so he'd realize that I'd always been a loner and my standoffishness was nothing he should take personally. Maybe then he'd understand I didn't want my phone ringing off the hook or my lunch break spoiled with chatter.

Who was I kidding? I'd never show my poem to the man with oversized glasses and buzzed hair. So instead of hurting his feelings and telling him to get lost, I'd just do what I'd done in the past—remain aloof and hope he'd eventually take the hint and leave me be.

I did this my sophomore year of high school, when a girl named Constance moved to Clay Station. She came from some cold northern town and spoke with a Yankee accent. Her eyelids and fingernails were both painted the color of charcoal, and she moped around in dark clothes with her shoulders slumped. When she pulled up the sleeves of her black sweatshirts, scars and fresh cuts that were often covered in Band-Aids were visible on her arms. Neither Della nor Rachel was on my lunch block, so I was alone when the mysterious Yankee sat across from me and asked to see what I was writing in my notebook covered in scratch-and-sniff stickers. I quietly told her I didn't let anyone read my words, and I went back to the poem I was writing about Mama. I called it "Black Ice," and it was one of those that I'd never let my grandmother or sister read.

Constance didn't press me further, but she sat with me again the next day. And the next. I never once asked about the cuts on her arms or why she painted her eyes as dark as night. I never asked her anything, as a matter of fact, and I responded to her questions with short, generic answers. It wasn't that I didn't have compassion for the girl with the shadowy, depressing aura. When I was little, I liked to take care of baby birds that had fallen out of their nests. Empathy was in my nature. It was obvious Constance wanted my friendship, maybe even my help, but it seemed too awkward a mission for me to attempt. There was no conversation between the baby bird and me when it was lying vulnerable in the grass. And that was the way I preferred it. Constance finally stopped sitting with me, and she didn't return to Tallahatchie County High School the following year. I have no idea what happened to her. Hopefully she found the friend she needed. It just wasn't me.

Birdie had given me devotionals about friendship and how iron sharpens iron and two are better than one and all that jazz. I didn't disagree. I recognized how good Mr. Prentice was for Birdie, and I understood why Della craved camaraderie. Still, it just wasn't something I was interested in. I felt more inspired without random people's voices and opinions and drama in my head. I was energized by silence. Einstein said, "The monotony and solitude of a quiet life stimulate the creative mind." I was creative—I had dozens of notebooks to prove it. I didn't need outsiders. All I needed was a pen and a blank page.

I made it to work safely on the icy roads and walked through the double glass doors. Surprisingly, Cliff was the first person I saw. He'd never waited on me in the morning before. I wasn't one for discussion any time of the day, but certainly not at 6:54 a.m. I rolled my eyes and sighed in exasperation.

"Morning, Darby." He was annoyingly chipper. "Sleep well?"

"Fine," I lied.

"I really liked talking to you last night." He scampered alongside me to my locker. "Sounds like you had a good Christmas, yeah?"

I ignored him and turned the dial on the combination lock.

"You ain't a morning person, are you? I can tell." He incessantly smacked his fruity-smelling chewing gum. "I've always been a morning person. Always made my brothers real mad. Even Maw. She don't care much for talking this early. My brain starts turning and my gums start flapping soon as my feet hit the floor. Like hamsters on a wheel up there." He tapped his temple and laughed.

Still, I said nothing.

"Hey." He grabbed my arm. I jerked away and looked up at him with wide eyes.

"I'm sorry, Darby. I didn't mean to grab you like that. I just . . . I just wish you would talk to me." He pushed his glasses up the bridge of his nose.

"I don't talk much to anyone." I looked away from him. "I keep telling you that."

"I know, but I just—I want us to be friends. Did I do something wrong?" He folded his bony arms.

"No." I shook my head.

"Why do you ignore me, then?"

"Again," I growled, "I don't talk much. I don't have anything to say."

"You write poems, yeah? You must have something to say. Maybe you—"

"Please leave me alone," I interrupted, shoving my purse inside the empty locker. I refrained from looking at him and seeing disappointment on his face, but I could sense his feelings were hurt.

"Okay, Darby. If that's what you want, I'll leave you be," he said before walking away.

● ● ●

I glanced over at Cliff a few times throughout the morning. I watched him unfold one sheet of corrugated cardboard after the other and send the empty boxes down the conveyor belt to be filled with plastic bottles. He looked as if someone had just shot his dog.

I ate my bologna and cheese (with mustard) sandwich in silence, still expecting him to plop down in front of me at any moment with his plastic sacks of sugar and ask how my day was going. When he didn't, surprisingly I felt bad. I never had a reason to feel guilty when it came to other people. If you don't interact with anyone, you can't make mistakes with them. Maybe that was why I ignored Constance. I had always been immune from saying the wrong thing and hurting feelings because I didn't say much at all.

I was mad at Cliff for invading my space. I was annoyed at his actions that provoked harsh reactions from me. I didn't like the expectations he put on me—the expectations for me to be some cheerful, chatty confidant. It was as if he wanted to change me, just like Birdie and Della did, when I was fine the way I was.

When I clocked out at three, Cliff wasn't waiting on me. I soon spotted him bouncing across the parking lot with those long arms of his swaying back and forth, as if they were about to send him into flight. Even though it seemed

I'd gotten my wish that the lanky man with jumbo glasses was finally going to leave me alone, I pulled my jacket close to my thin body and sprinted toward him. I didn't know what I would say when I reached Cliff, but I knew I had to say something. The guilt of my insensitive words had been weighing on my mind all day.

"Hey!" I called when I caught up with him.

He turned to face me and shoved his large, skinny fingers into the pockets of his navy work coat with his name embroidered on the chest.

"Listen, I, um, I didn't mean to, well . . . ," I began. "I have a hard time t-talking to—"

"Apology accepted, Darby." He grinned and revealed the chip in his tooth. "You don't have to say nothing else."

"All right." I felt my lips turn slightly upward. "I'll see you tomorrow?"

"Bright and early."

● ● ●

When I arrived home from work, I changed into my comfy flannel pajama pants, fixed a tall cup of black Folgers, and helped Birdie prepare supper. She fried Salisbury steaks in her seasoned cast-iron skillet while I whisked the brown gravy in a bowl.

"Are you humming, Darby Ann? You're in mighty fine spirits." She flipped the sizzling patties.

I was humming, and I didn't even realize it. I hadn't hummed in a long time. Certainly not since Cliff started working at the factory months before. His presence and his questions had burdened me all this time, carried over at home where I worried too much what answers he would attempt to pry out of me the next day. My humming must have subconsciously signified that I was no longer troubled by Cliff.

"I didn't know I was." I shrugged.

"Sing me a song, sweetheart. You haven't sung for me in a while now. You know your voice is the most beautiful thing these old ears ever heard. 'Amazing Grace,' yeah? That's my favorite, you know."

I wasn't too sure of myself in social situations, but one thing I was sure of was that I had a nice voice, just like my mama. I sang in the car or in the shower, but not much for Birdie. When I did, she always threw a guilt trip on me for not sharing my talent with the world. She meant it as a compliment, but it was just another reminder that she wanted to change me into an outgoing socialite who not only mingled at cocktail parties and had a slew of friends, but was brazen enough to sing for them. It was another reminder that she was disappointed in my reserved nature. Just to appease Birdie, I began singing for my grandmother in the privacy of our kitchen, and I noticed her close her eyes while the hamburger grease popped in the scorching skillet. I didn't know what she was thinking in that moment—if she was remembering Mama's voice or imagining me on a stage in a sequined gown, microphone in hand. Whatever her thoughts, though, they brought her joy.

When I was done, she said, "What a gift you have, my love. The Good Book instructs us to share our God-given talents with others. Lamps aren't meant to be placed under baskets. I wish you'd listened to me and joined the drama club when you were in high school. You would have been spectacular as the lead in *Oklahoma!* You could still join a church and sing for the choir there. You'd get a solo in a heartbeat. What about that *American Idol* show? What's the age cutoff for that? Oh, you'd win it all. We'd all be livin' in high cotton."

There it was, right on cue.

• • •

Once we'd eaten our supper, and my sister complained that the carbs from the mashed potatoes would likely wreak havoc on her digestive system and her waistline, I retreated to my room to write for a little while. Della soon interrupted me, bounding through my door with her cat in her arms, and fell onto the foot of my bed.

"Don't hate me," she started.

"I make no promises."

"I've been thinking about Birdie's birthday party idea." She propped herself up on her elbows covered in purple sleeves. "Maybe it's not so ridiculous after all."

"Della, are you serious?" I closed the journal and peered at her.

"Think about it, Darby. We could invite our entire graduating class. Most of them still think of us as Cindy Redd's blacklisted daughters with the Kick Me signs on the backs of our ragged coats. The last thing they associate with me is Kevin and his bar brawls. You're still the weirdo who wears black and walks around with her head down. We could show up to that party, looking beautiful with dates on our arms, and really show them."

"Della." I sighed. "I couldn't care less about showing them anything. I am not concerned with what anyone in this town thinks of me. When you moved to Tennessee, you didn't care either. But being back in Clay Station has changed you. You're turning into the old insecure Della. When you were living in Chattanooga, you were confident in yourself; you didn't care about proving anything to anyone anymore."

"I'm still confident," she said as she sat up on the bed. "That's precisely what I want to show them."

"Listen to you. Twenty-nine years old and still trying to befriend Melanie and Erin and their little crew. Don't you remember all the times you followed them around like a puppy dog, praying they would acknowledge you? Praying they would accept you?"

"The purpose of the party isn't to be invited to Erin Drake's for Bunco or on girls' trips with them to Biloxi Beach. You think I'd ever spend a weekend in a condo with Kelly Ragan? I'd end up throwing her over a balcony. I don't care about that anymore, Darby. What's wrong with a little redemption?"

"You want revenge, not redemption. Seeking revenge means what they think of you and what they did to us all those years ago still bothers you. You say your self-esteem is intact, but worrying about their opinions of you is the exact opposite, isn't it?"

She avoided the legitimate question and responded, "I've made up my mind. I'm going to take over the party planning and help Birdie with the cost of it. It is going to be the biggest bash this town has seen. And I'm going to show up with Brian Faulkner. You don't have to be on board with it."

I crossed my thin, chilly arms. "Being back in this town isn't good for you. Working with Melanie Reid is damaging. Stalking Erin Drake on Facebook is drowning you in jealousy and comparisons. Why don't you go on back to Chattanooga? Birdie has me and Mr. Prentice. We will get along fine."

"And wait on the phone call for you to tell me Birdie is dead? While I'm five hours away?"

"That's what you're worried about?" I tapped my socked foot against her leg.

"I worry about everything except Mrs. Dalton's dog. You do enough worrying about him for the both of us."

"I remember visiting you in Tennessee, Della. For the first time in our lives, you were carefree. You made friends. You flourished there. You can't just stay here until Birdie dies. You know what a stubborn old thing she is. She's liable to outlive us all."

"I'm scared, Darby," she admitted while looking to her hands with nails freshly painted the color of grapes.

"Scared of what?"

She shrugged. "I know leaving this dump was the best thing for me. But when Birdie almost died . . . I don't know. The long ride back to Mississippi that night was torture. I regretted not being here. If I did move away, I would spend all my time worrying about her. And you. When she's gone, what will you do? Be known as the old spinster who lives alone on Yocona Road?"

"So you're going to stay here until both Birdie and I are

dead? Do I need to be concerned you're going to put arsenic in the mustard? Make us a *Dateline* episode?"

She smirked.

"What about taking Birdie to Chattanooga with you? Have you thought of that? Find a little two-bedroom apartment and fix her up a cozy room to hang all her cross-stitches. You could put her in a wheelchair and push her in the caves to see Ruby Falls. She'd have the time of her life. You could both start over new," I suggested.

Della shook her head. "I've thought of it. I even mentioned it to Birdie one time. She said this is her home. She was born here and says she's going to die here."

"I will be perfectly happy being known as the old spinster on Yocona Road. Because I'm content with who I am, where I am. Birdie is too. Della, you can have the party, the good doctor, the last word, but without contentment, you will never be happy."

"I know what I heard Brian say. He cares about me. I'll be content when I walk into the party with him and the tables turn."

I rubbed my eyes in frustration. "The tables don't need turning, sister."

"Tables always need turning when you're a Redd." She gathered Perry, stood, and walked out of my room, leaving a puff of cat hair floating in the air.

11

DELLA REDD

The vision for the party came to me before I drifted off to sleep with Perry purring at my side. The large gathering room at the community center would be dim, lit only by the tea candles around the floral arrangements of purple chrysanthemums and lilac-colored daisies that would be centered on round tables covered in dark cloths. Velvety deep-violet drapes would conceal the stark cinder-block walls and serve as a backdrop for the room's main attraction: the ornate, white three-tier cake with cascading pansies. Guests would be serenaded by 1930s and '40s jazz. Duke Ellington, Dizzy Gillespie, Glenn Miller Orchestra, Count Basie, and, of course, Queen Billie. Although finding a band to play that genre of music would be difficult. All of the local bands played country or pop cover songs. My birthday party would be much too sophisticated for melodies such as "Small Town Girl."

It was going to be a magical evening. And despite what Darby assumed, I was still a confident woman. I wasn't throwing this party in an attempt to befriend the group of people I had disliked my whole life. That was something the adolescent Della would do. I only wanted to show them that their attempts to ruin my life had been unsuccessful.

● ● ●

When I arrived at work early that morning, wearing my favorite purple cable-knit sweater, I removed all the Christmas decorations. I carefully placed the trees and tinsel and wreaths into their boxes and stacked them in the storage closet. Brian had not arrived yet, so I peered into his dark office at the end of the hall. When I quickly flicked on the light, I smiled at the bobblehead on his desk. What a relief it hadn't been tossed into the garbage like the Dizzy Gillespie CD I gave Kevin on his birthday.

It was a busy morning. We had several positive flu tests and Mrs. Rosie was back with a throbbing calf. She insisted it was a blood clot. After seeing Dr. Faulkner, she handed me a referral sheet to be seen at the hospital in three days for an ultrasound.

"I hope it doesn't travel to my heart or lungs before then," she fretted aloud.

Mrs. Rosie didn't have great insurance. It was going to cost her an arm and a leg, pun intended, to have the scan and be told she just needed some Aspercreme. But Brian cared about Mrs. Rosie, as he did all his patients, and did the right thing in referring her so her mind could be eased.

While I hid out in the office bathroom for a few minutes, I saw Erin's Facebook pictures of the bustling New Year's Eve party and imagined Brian and I would throw our very own party next year, complete with gold hats and horns. My spinach artichoke dip would be a hit among his friends and colleagues. Melanie would be envious of our social media photos because she, along with her cantankerous crew, would be blacklisted from the exclusive affair. They would be the ones to feel left out when they saw the uploaded pictures of Brian and me with our arms draped around each other. I was giddy for the new year and for my birthday party. And for my relationship with Brian Faulkner to blossom. I left the bathroom and headed toward the kitchen, where I found Camilla and Melanie complaining to each other.

"Jake and I went to his brother's Saturday night. I'm still hungover," Camilla said while rummaging through the refrigerator for her plastic container.

"You and me both," Melanie groaned. "I'm getting too old for it. It's Welch's sparkling grape for me next year."

Camilla pressed buttons on the microwave and the plastic molecules seeped into the minestrone. "Even the microwave is too loud." She rubbed her temples.

I chomped as loudly as I could on my celery sticks, hoping the sound reverberated in their brains. By their annoyed looks, I assumed it worked.

"You have a good New Year's, Della? Get kissed at midnight?" Melanie tossed the wet, white, ranch-covered lettuce with her plastic fork.

I wasn't about to tell them I spent the evening playing

Yahtzee with 150 years of old people and my introverted twin who withdrew to her room well before midnight to write a dismal poem.

"I had a great night," I answered.

"What's your resolution this year? To add more purple to your collection?" Camilla smirked.

To slash your tires, Camilla.

"Actually, I have a busy year ahead."

Melanie munched on the salad like a rabbit and asked, "Oh yeah? Doing what?"

"I'm planning a party."

Camilla feigned enthusiasm. "A party? How fascinating. When is it?"

"In October. For my thirtieth birthday," I said proudly.

"October? Geez, Della. It doesn't take that long to figure out how many pizza rolls you need for you, your grandmother, and your sister," Melanie retorted.

I felt my cheeks flush with rage and my lips tighten into a straight line. "Matter of fact, I'm having the party catered by Garden of Eatin'. Honey-glazed salmon. Most everyone we went to high school with is invited, Melanie. Camilla, you can come, too, I guess, even though you're barely old enough to vote. It's going to be at the community center, and it's going to be fabulous," I downright demanded.

Melanie looked to me, dumbfounded. "Well, my, my, Della. How could we resist? We wouldn't miss it, would we, Camilla?"

"Absolutely not. It sounds like the social event of the year." Camilla chuckled. "I'm allergic to fish, though, Della. I'd prefer prime rib."

Request that Camilla's prime rib be cooked alongside the fish. Watching her blow up like a balloon and gasp for air will be the highlight of the night.

Brian surprised us all when he stepped into the kitchen, looking dashing in his starched white coat. The scent of his aftershave overtook the smell of putrid ranch and I felt faint with delight.

"Oh, Dr. Faulkner. Listen to this. Della is planning a huge party for her thirtieth birthday. When is it again, Della?" Melanie asked.

"October." I placed my empty food containers into my lilac lunch box.

"You ever heard of someone taking nine months to plan a birthday party? It ought to be something else. I planned my wedding in less time," Melanie remarked.

"We're all invited. You'll be there, won't you, Dr. Faulkner?" Camilla playfully tapped Melanie's hand resting on the table.

"Sure, that sounds fun." He pulled a container from the refrigerator and the nurses exchanged a surprised look. "Thirty years old? Della, you don't look a day over twenty-one."

My heart pounded with exhilaration. "I'll be sending out invitations closer to time. I'll have a band and everything. Garden of Eatin' is going to cater. Do you like salmon?" I eagerly asked my boss, who was holding a container filled with brightly colored berries and melons.

He rummaged through the drawer for a fork and said, "Well, my stepsister owns the place. And her salmon is fantastic. Maybe I could get you a discount?"

I clutched my hands together and the five brass rings on

my fingers clinked. "I had no idea. That would be wonderful. Thank you, Dr. Faulkner."

"Sure thing, Della." He winked at me before retiring to his office with his healthy antioxidant-infused lunch. I wished Melanie and Camilla had seen his flirtatious gesture, but they were too busy looking at each other, staggered at Brian's kindheartedness and perhaps disappointed he hadn't joined in on their taunting.

"Well, well." I smirked at the atrocious nurses and stood from the lunch table. "I'd better get enough pizza rolls for four."

● ● ●

I was floating on air the rest of the day, lost in the daydream of Brian and me, hand in hand, as we entered the party fashionably late. Remi would be there too. My future daughter. I would provide a shoulder for Remi to cry on when some college boy in a toga broke her heart. I could help her with calculus. I was a whiz at math.

For our first wedding anniversary, I'd present the bobblehead to Brian in a shadow box to hang on the wall of the elegant living room in our house on Magnolia Trace. It would always remind us of the beginning of our courtship. It would be the most cherished and sentimental object in our house. I'd accompany my sweet, handsome Brian to the country club on weekends and the out-of-town physician conferences. Our faces would grace the society pages of the *Tallahatchie County Examiner*. Kelly Ragan would soon sip her coffee on her back porch and stare at our photo in black-and-white and regret every harsh word she'd uttered and cruel trick she'd played on Darby and me.

We'd build a quaint mother-in-law suite next to the kidney-shaped pool in the sprawling backyard. There, Birdie and Mr. Prentice would be taken care of by round-the-clock nurses, and I'd only be a few steps away if they needed me. Maybe Darby could move in with them too. No, I forgot she would be living happily ever after with Brian's hypothetical therapist friend.

• • •

Birdie's savory meatloaf was cooking in the oven, ready to be served with the leftover black-eyed peas and cabbage. I'd only eaten celery at lunch, so I looked forward to the hearty, although unhealthy, meal. I sat at the kitchen counter with Perry on my lap and searched men's clothing websites on my phone. I'd found the perfect lavender vest for Brian to wear under his dark suit jacket. It would coordinate with the purple floor-length seamed lace dress I had saved in my cart on another site. Royalty. That was what we would represent as we walked through the doors of Clay Station Community Center.

"What you studying on over there?" Birdie called from her recliner in the living room.

I didn't remove my gaze from the phone screen. "Just looking at clothes for the party."

"I am so glad you're finally on board with the idea, Della."

"Me too, Birdie." I stood from the stool, Perry pounced to the floor, and I joined my grandmother.

"What changed your mind?" she asked as Jessica Fletcher skied down a mountain slope in pursuit of a murder suspect.

"I don't know," I lied. "I guess I thought it couldn't happen, but like you say . . ."

"Can't never could." She beamed. "I just wish Darby was keen on the idea. Think you can talk her into it?"

I fell into the sofa. "I've tried. She just doesn't know what's good for her."

"I know she's nervous as a long-tailed cat in a room full of rockers when it comes to social situations, but she's such a beautiful and talented girl with so much love and gentleness to offer the world. Maybe she'll realize that after the birthday party."

"I don't understand her. She says she's content being alone, holed up in that room writing poems about Lord knows what. But I don't believe it. She's human, isn't she? Wired for connection. Why doesn't she long for that the way the rest of us do?"

"I've told you time and again, Della. Darby takes after your mother. Maybe her father. I don't know. Only met that scoundrel once. Useless as a screen door on a submarine, he was." She huffed as the suspect in the ski suit on television confessed to his crimes. "Well, except for helping create you and your sister."

"I remember some things about Mama, Birdie. She wasn't shy. She was loud and had a big personality. Darby isn't anything like her," I argued.

"Why do you think your mother turned to booze? Liquor made her loud and fun. Your mama was shy and skittish until she discovered drinking in her teen years and it made her feel comfortable in her own skin. It changed her. And it's ultimately what killed her." Her face clouded with gloom. "I can't talk about this." Birdie stood from the chair and went to check on the meatloaf that filled every inch of the house with the smell of bell pepper and onion.

Birdie rarely talked about Mama, and the only picture of her displayed in the house was a candid of her standing beside the magnolia in the yard as a teenager. The rest of her photos were kept in albums. Occasionally Birdie pulled those picture books from the cabinet beneath the television and took them back to her bedroom and shut the door. Darby and I knew not to disturb her while she thumbed through the photos of happier days, but we could hear her crying through the door. Mother's death left her brokenhearted.

Birdie didn't talk much about our father either. We only knew he was contracted out of New Orleans to work construction on the very building where Darby now worked—Simon Container. His first name was William; no idea about his last. Mama was fifteen when she ran into him at a local bar. Birdie only met him one time when she went down to the tavern to drag her drunk teenager home. He didn't even help Birdie haul our stumbling mother to the car, and he was the one who'd been filling her with whiskey all night. Mama must have snuck out to see him again, though, since Darby and I came along nine months later. By then he'd already left town and didn't know we even existed.

I wondered if Brian was privy to our family's past. He was older than me—closer to my mother's age than mine—but he had lived in Clay Station his whole life, and everyone here knew the story of Cindy Redd. The tragedy was talked about nonstop for years and still remembered every time someone saw old Hampton Goolsby hobbling around town, all alone in this world. Mama's mistake left scars on multiple hearts that would never heal or be forgotten.

As we held each other close in our king-sized bed on Magnolia Trace, I would tell Brian all about my mother. I wouldn't defend her actions, but I would introduce him to memories of the kind, caring woman who loved her daughters fiercely. He would know who she was before she made the mistake of getting behind the wheel of her Chevette—drunk out of her mind—hitting a patch of black ice, and killing a mother and her three innocent kids.

Marrying Brian would redeem not only my reputation. It would redeem Mama's too.

12

DARBY REDD

I tried to ignore the chills running down my back as I fried bacon at five fifteen that morning, but there was no doubt about it. I was sick. I could only breathe through one nostril and the sinus pressure in my cheeks and ears was so intense I expected my head to blow right off my shoulders. The thermometer revealed I had a low-grade fever, so I called my supervisor to let him know I wouldn't be coming to work. I didn't like feeling bad, but I didn't mind missing work. Especially on this day.

Most people believe Valentine's Day originated from Pope Gelasius I, who made February 14 a day to honor the Christian martyr Saint Valentine. However, few know that ancient Romans first celebrated the feast of Lupercalia from February 13 to 15 by sacrificing goats and dogs and whipping women with the hides of the animals they had just slain. The women lined up before the men, drunk and naked, believing that being beaten with the bloody skins would make them fertile. That certainly wasn't my idea of a good time, and neither was the thought of my coworkers watching Cliff approach me with a box of chocolates he'd picked up at Piggly Wiggly on his way to work.

I wasn't certain about the candy, but I assumed he would give me something because he still pursued me the way Mrs. Dalton's dog chased my back tires. Thankfully, though, he had finally accepted I just didn't have much to say. He didn't aim to fill our time together with mundane small talk, so we actually shared moments of comfortable silence during lunch. I continued to keep my distance emotionally, but I was no longer annoyed that he was always nipping at my heels.

When Birdie discovered me sick and shivering beneath my heavy white comforter, she got to work in the kitchen. I wished I could breathe through my congested nose and stared out the window as pots and pans clanked on the stove. I hated winter. I despised the cold blasts of wind that demanded hats and gloves be worn and the view from my bedroom—the knotty, bare tree branches, the dismal sky, the dead grass, the cold wind whipping gravel dust into a mini tornado. It was during my least favorite season when Birdie told us Mama moved to heaven. I didn't know where heaven was. With the way Birdie cried, I supposed it was far off. I thought it must be on the other side of Jackson, maybe even as far down as Biloxi. A year or so after Mama died, I heard someone come through the front door and I ran into the living room expecting to see her, but it was Mrs. Gracie toting a casserole dish and hot biscuits wrapped in tinfoil. That was when I realized our mother was never coming back.

Della and I started asking a lot of questions about Mama after some kids at school called her a murderer. We didn't know what that meant, but when we brought it up to our grandmother, she was furious. She raked her hand across the kitchen counter and sent several glass dishes smashing to the linoleum floor. She pulled out the stepladder she kept hidden beside the washer and dryer, climbed it, and searched the back of a top cupboard for a pack of Pall Malls that had been there no telling how long. As she choked on the first stale cigarette she'd had in years, she sat us down and told us what happened the night Mama died.

I didn't know how I felt about my mother for a while after that. What she'd done seemed unforgivable. Her choices left a ripple of heartache in their wake, but I clung to the cheery images of the woman I adored. I refused to let that tragic night in February 1993 cloud all the blissful days and nights I had with her.

If any good came from our mother's accident, it was that it instilled a fear of alcohol in both Della and me. Della had a cocktail once in a while, but I completely abstained. I once read an article in some medical magazine at the dentist's office on how socially awkward introverts often turn to drinking and drugging in an effort to feel normal. It wasn't worth the risk of hurting anyone to feel normal. I'd just keep staring at the floor and tucking my dang hair behind my ears.

After Birdie brought me a big white bowl of her steaming, flavorful homemade chicken noodle soup and some green decongestant capsules that were meant for nighttime, I passed clean out. I didn't wake up until it was nearly dark outside and I heard rapping on the front door. On the other side of my wood wall paneling, Birdie squealed with delight and thanked whoever had visited. I recognized the unmistakable sound of balloons bobbling down the hallway, and I propped up on my elbows before she walked through my door, grinning like a Cheshire cat, with the huge bouquet of white, pink, and red balloons in her hand. There was one extra-large Mylar heart with "Happy Valentine's Day" written on it in silver cursive.

"Well, Darby Ann Redd, this ought to make you feel better," she exclaimed. "Who in the Sam Hill are these from?"

I already knew, but I leaned forward and took the small white card from Birdie's pudgy hand. She set the balloons on the chest of drawers, switched on the small brass lamp beside my bed, and sat her heavy body at my feet. I read the chicken scratch on the card. "Hope you feel better soon. Happy Valentime's Day. Cliff." I grimaced at the misspelling.

"That guy from work. Cliff Waters." I placed the card beside me on the bed.

"The same one who called me about a Christmas present for you?" she asked. "The one who calls you sometimes?"

"That's him."

"Did he ever give you a Christmas gift? I don't recall you telling me one way or another."

"I told you, Birdie. That journal." I nodded to it on my bedside table as Birdie cocked her head and grinned.

"Well, I declare. You sure did. I can't remember Bo Diddley these days." She rubbed her chin. "Waters. Is his grandmama the lady with the birthmark on her cheek who cleans all the big houses on the north side of town?"

"I don't know his family tree, Birdie."

"Well, he sure seems like a nice young man, Darby. Awful thoughtful of him." She glanced over at the tall bouquet scraping against the spackled ceiling. "First that stylish journal and now this."

"He's nice." I sniffled and leaned back onto the pillow.

"How do you feel about him, dear?" She tucked the comforter around my cold, skinny legs.

"I don't."

"If you care about this boy at all—"

"This *boy* is thirty-two, Birdie." I felt like a teenager about to be schooled on the facts of life for the first time. Birdie had been saving this conversation for decades.

"Well, *man*, then. If you care about this man at all, don't be afraid to let him in. Don't be afraid of his company. I know you prefer being alone, but you are worthy of all the good things. And it seems this Cliff fella is good."

"Yes, ma'am," I said to appease her.

"Are you hungry? Thirsty?" She stood to her weighty legs and her knees creaked.

"Any soup left?"

"There's plenty, dear girl. Give me a few minutes to warm it up." She disappeared through the bedroom door.

I stared at the balloons bobbing around on the chest and knew what I needed to do. Cliff had always been the one to call me, so I didn't have his number. I reached for the card on the bed and called the flower shop only moments before they closed, and I asked for it. The woman on the other end of the line happily gave it to me, her tone enthusiastic, as if she were responsible for a love connection. It took me a few minutes to work up the nerve to dial, and he answered on the second ring.

"Cliff? It's Darby."

"Hey." I could tell he was stunned that I'd actually phoned him. "You doing okay?"

"Fine."

"Missed seeing you at work today. Your supervisor said you was sick. Anything major?"

"Just a cold, I think."

"That's good. Well, it ain't good you got a cold, but at least you ain't down with something serious."

"I just wanted to call and, well, and thank you for—for the balloons. It was a very nice gesture of you to think—to send them to me."

"You're real welcome, Darby."

That was it. That was all I needed to say. I was prepared to hang up.

"Think you'll be at work tomorrow?"

"I don't know yet. I am—will try. If I feel better."

"Get a whole lot of rest. You need me to bring you anything? Dollar General is right down the road from my house. I can get you some cough drops or something. You need some menthol rub? Maw swears by it. That always helps me when I'm sick. Cuts through congestion like a hot knife through butter."

"No. Thanks—thank you. I'll be fine."

"Glad you got the balloons. I was going to have them delivered to work, but when you wasn't there by lunchtime,

I sent them to your house. I got the address from the phone book. It's helped me out with you a whole lot of times."

What a bullet I had dodged. I could imagine all the conversations my coworkers would initiate if I walked out of the factory with the bouquet of helium. Not to mention keeping the gigantic bundle contained while I stumbled across the windy parking lot and then struggled to shove them in the small cab of my S-10.

"Okay. Thank you again."

"So what are you doing?"

This was why I avoided talking. The conversation should have been over. I said what I needed to say, as did Cliff. Why did he keep droning on? Why fill silence with words that didn't matter?

"I'm on the phone with you," I said, and he chortled.

"Aside from that, silly."

I was at a loss.

"I am sitting on the bed talking on the phone to you. That is what I—that's what I'm doing."

He didn't laugh that time.

"I'm at my maw's house. My brothers are about to come over. My youngest brother, Mitchell, is a pillhead. He only comes over to Maw's to steal out of her medicine cabinet, so I got to keep an eye on him. And my older brother, Gary, and his girlfriend, Tanya, fight all the time. So I work real hard to keep the peace between them. It's a full-time job with them around."

"Yeah," I replied, unsure how to respond.

"Your family is pretty normal, I guess?"

"Hardly," I said before thinking.

"That sweet old granny of yours. She seems real nice. And you got a twin, right? If she's like you, then she must be a pretty good gal."

"She's nothing like me." I twisted the phone cord between my fingers. "I want to go back to bed now."

"Oh. Well, okay then," he said with disappointment.

"Thank you again for the balloons."

"Get some good sleep. Feel better tomorrow. Remember what I said. If you need anything, you got my number now."

I tossed the receiver back onto the orange cat cradle and pulled the covers over my head. I was spent.

13

DELLA REDD

On the way to work, I stopped by Piggly Wiggly to buy myself a small spray of roses. This early in the morning the store was probably still well stocked with flowers lightly misted by the sprinklers in the produce section. All the good stuff wouldn't be picked over until the end of the workday when forgetful men scrambled to the store.

I picked a fresh bunch with red and white petals adorned with baby's breath. On the way to check out, I stopped at a large candy display. I wondered what Brian would like. Chocolate-covered almonds? Nougat? Heart-shaped pretzels? I could easily sneak a box of sweets onto his desk while he was in the exam room with the last patient of the day. As I reached for a square red box filled with an assortment, I thought of Melanie and Camilla. They would surely find out if I bought a Valentine's Day gift for Brian. And the teasing I would endure wasn't worth the pleasure I would get from giving it to him. I shuddered at the very thought of the terrible ridicule and left the candy right where it was.

I intended for Brian to become so jealous at the idea of another man giving me roses that he'd ask me to join him at Sit a Spell for lunch. We'd share the Sweetheart Special—two turkey subs, kettle corn chips, and one chocolate milkshake with two straws. I'd happily slurp down cocoa and sugar with him and not think twice about my expanding waistline. As I gazed into his gorgeous green eyes in the secluded booth at the back of the restaurant, he'd invite me to dinner that evening. I had been eager to try the new steak house in town. Erin raved about their New York strip on Facebook.

While admiring the flowers in my hands, I got in line behind a woman with four large bags of kitty litter in her shopping cart. I wondered how many cats she owned. I had toyed with the notion of adopting a few more kittens because Perry was so precious to me, but I didn't need the term "crazy cat lady" associated with my name. I would wait until Brian and I were married to bring more pets into the house. Then it would be acceptable.

"Well, Della!"

I didn't even turn around to see who the voice belonged to. I already knew. I squeezed my eyes shut, hoping it was a nightmare, hoping my ears had played a terrible trick on me.

I turned to her. "Morning, Melanie."

"Well, what have you got there?" She poked the bouquet in my arms.

"What are you doing here so early?" I situated the heart-shaped pendant hanging from my neck.

"I didn't have any lettuce at home to make my salad for

lunch." She held up the bag of romaine and a small bottle of ranch dressing. "You didn't answer my question. Who are the flowers for?"

"My grandmother," I lied.

"Why not pick them up on your way home?" She raked her long dishwater-blonde bangs out of her eyes. I caught a whiff of her fruity-scented shampoo.

"All the good ones will be gone by the end of the day."

She stifled her laughter. "You know what I think, Della?"

Enlighten me, troll.

"I think you were going to bring those flowers with you to work. And I think you were going to let me and Camilla and Dr. Faulkner believe that some guy sent you those flowers. Am I right?" She playfully punched me in the arm of my purple peacoat.

I chuckled. "You're absurd, Melanie. I don't care what you or Camilla think."

She dramatically gasped like the conniving star of a soap opera. "You didn't think I remembered, did you?"

"Remembered what?"

"That time you sent yourself the big Valentine's bouquet and balloons at school. Oh, Della! That big old cupid balloon. With a diaper on. That was a riot!" She dramatically threw her hands in the air.

I felt my face turn warm. "I did no such thing."

"Of course you did. Devon's mom owned the flower shop back then, remember? She was certain it was you who called and placed the order. You paid over the phone with your grandmother's credit card. Didn't even try to cover your tracks."

"You know what's real pathetic?" I shook the roses at her. "That you were all so concerned with me getting a Valentine's Day gift that you had to call Devon's mom and investigate. You didn't have anything better to do? And here you are, eleven years later, still thinking about it."

"Someone has to call you on your bull, Della." She shrugged. "God doesn't like a liar."

God doesn't like hatefulness either.

"I think there's a vase on top of the kitchen cabinet at the clinic from when my husband sent me flowers on my birthday. I'll get it down for you if you'd like."

"No, don't go to any trouble." I sneered.

"You're up." She pointed to the sleepy-looking cashier impatiently waiting to scan my flowers. "See you at work."

My hands were shaking so badly from rage that I could barely slide my debit card through the reader. When I got into my car, I threw the roses onto the passenger side and several petals fell onto the floor. I banged my hands on the steering wheel and let out a long, loud groan.

Melanie was right. I had sent myself a Valentine's gift in high school. In fact, I had lied to make myself look better many times over the years, but what harm did it do? There was nothing wrong with a little white lie.

I invented a boyfriend once. His name was Houston and he went to Panola High School, right across the county line. I occasionally mentioned Houston in front of others at school—how we enjoyed going to the Panola skating rink on the weekends and when he'd taken me to the theater to see *50 First Dates*. Until one day Jenny James said her cousin went to Panola and verified no one named Houston attended school there. I argued that her cousin was wrong, and several of the snobs asked me to produce a picture of my fake boyfriend. I dug around our photo albums in the cabinet beneath the television and found a picture of a cousin from Wynne, Arkansas. He was nothing like the broad-shouldered, athletic boy I envisioned Houston to be. Cousin Ray was quite unattractive, actually, with a thin, wispy mustache and a face full of zits, but he was the best I could do.

The photo didn't pacify my peers. They insisted I produce a picture of Houston and me together. After weeks of being pestered about it, I told them Houston moved to Virginia Beach and we couldn't make the long-distance relationship work. They didn't believe me, of course, but eventually they found something else to give me a hard time about. Some would see my fabrications as a cry for help, but not the Tallahatchie County High School class of 2005. They only used my lies as ammunition to tease me even more.

● ● ●

It was a terribly busy day. Irritated patients who had been flipping through magazines or staring at soap operas on the television in the corner for over an hour approached my desk to complain. I feigned a smile and tried to placate them as best I could. The nurses and I worked right through lunch, but that was perfectly fine by me. I would much rather sneak drinks of my protein shake while being on hold with Blue Cross Blue Shield than endure Melanie and Camilla's taunting over the Piggly Wiggly roses.

When things finally died down at the end of the day, Camilla stomped into the front office, exhausted and frazzled, her dark hair a mess, and said, "Way to work us to death, Della. I hope you didn't schedule twenty-five patients for us tomorrow." She placed a paper in the copying machine.

"It's not my fault we had so many walk-ins. I couldn't turn away Mr. Bowers. He had appendicitis," I said from my swivel chair. "And Mr. Gallagher was covered in a rash from head to toe. What did you expect me to do?"

"I didn't even eat lunch today. Do you have any idea how hungry I am?" She glared at me as the loud machine spit out copies. "I have the shakes from low blood sugar."

"Mr. Bowers didn't eat either," I mumbled.

"Camilla, that's enough," Brian scolded as he entered the office. "We've all had a rough day. It isn't Della's fault."

She rolled her eyes at him when he wasn't looking, took her papers, and left us alone.

"Thank you, Dr. Faulkner."

"We're all tired. We're all hungry. I'm sure Camilla didn't mean to take it out on you." He rummaged through the file cabinet behind my desk. "You've done a great job handling things today. You kept the office running as smoothly as possible. I'm thankful for you."

I blushed. I wanted to extend an invitation to dinner. Brian and I could forget about this hectic day and feast on an impeccably grilled steak and baked potato (sans sour cream) while being serenaded by the calm sounds of a violin concerto piped through the restaurant's speakers. Over a shared bowl of lemon panna cotta, he'd take my hands into his and profess his love for me.

"See you in the morning," he said before I could pose the offer.

"Good night."

● ● ●

I sat in my frigid car, with the drooping rose bouquet in the passenger seat, while Camilla and Melanie both drove out of the parking lot to spend the evening with significant others. A cold drizzle fell from the foggy sky and my windshield wipers screeched across the glass. I watched Brian emerge from the back door of the clinic, turn to lock the double bolt, and then enter his black Mercedes. I pretended to rummage around the floorboard of my front seat when his lights shone on my car.

Once he'd been gone a few moments, I pulled onto McLemore Avenue. There were a couple of cars between us, but I hadn't lost sight of him. I followed him through our town, past the packed parking lot of Rare Company Steak House, and on to Magnolia Trace. I kept my distance, so as not to be noticed, when he pulled his luxury car into the garage of his stately home and the door closed behind it. The front-room light came on first, which I gathered was the kitchen, and slowly other rooms in the house came to life. Such a big house for one man. It must have been lonely for him after the divorce and with Remi away at college. I wanted to run across the damp, dormant Bermuda grass and pound the gold-plated knocker on the navy door. I wanted to tell him he didn't have to be alone anymore. And I didn't either. We needed each other.

I sat across from his home, with my headlights turned

off and my heater roaring, imagining every room inside the beautiful house. I envisioned our wedding portrait in a crystal picture frame on the built-in bookshelf that was visible through the large front window. I imagined us rocking in the white chairs on the front porch on a warm summer night, sharing laughter and a refreshing glass of reverse-osmosis water. I could envision us lounging by the swimming pool in the backyard while he grilled pork chops.

I sat there in my car for fifteen minutes daydreaming and hoping that he wouldn't leave to meet someone for Valentine's dinner or that no tall, gorgeous blonde was going to pull into his driveway with a bottle of cabernet.

● ● ●

When I walked through the back door that evening, I was bombarded with the welcoming smell of savory chicken noodle soup. I looked down the hallway and saw Birdie sitting in her recliner with the TV tray pulled close to her. The DVD player was fired up and Jessica Fletcher was crouched over a dead man in a hotel room. Perry zipped between my legs and purred with delight as I massaged his gray ears.

"Hey, Birdie." I pulled the purple scarf with red hearts from around my neck and slipped my red loafers off at the back door. I walked to my grandmother and set the pathetic bouquet on the cluttered wicker table next to her. "Happy Valentine's Day."

"How thoughtful, Della. Thank you, dear." She pushed the TV tray away and took the bouquet into her wrinkled hands covered in liver spots.

"They got kind of cold and wilted in the car all day. It's the thought that counts, though, right?"

"Nothing a good vase of sugar water won't cure. That'll perk them right up." She gave them a sniff. "Prentice dropped off a little box of chocolates for me, but don't go getting any ideas. Just a friendly gesture."

"Sure." I smiled. "Where's Darby?"

"In her room. Stayed home sick today. I think she's awake now if you want to pop in and see her. I'll put these roses in water and fix you a bowl of soup?"

"Sure, thanks," I said as she pushed herself out of the chair and I walked to my sister's room.

I lightly rapped on the door before I pushed it open to see Darby sitting up in her bed with the familiar journal in her lap and a wooden pen in hand. I immediately noticed the huge bunch of balloons on her chest of drawers.

"What in the world is that?" I asked, surprised.

"Cliff sent them to me," she said in a nasally tone.

"Oh."

Usually I would be ecstatic that my sister had received a gift from a man—elated at the notion of her finding her happily ever after. Instead, I was overcome with jealousy. My sister was a recluse who barely said two words. She walked around with her head down, hidden behind her stringy hair, in clothes as drab as mud, and yet someone took an interest in her? She didn't even want a relationship.

"You feeling better?" I looked away from the balloons.

"Yeah, I guess," she said. "Just doing some writing."

"You need anything?"

"No, I'm okay. About to get up and shower. That ought to make me feel better."

I nodded and shut her door. I bypassed the kitchen where Birdie was ladling soup into a bowl for me and went to my bedroom at the back of the house. The mauve room was illuminated when I turned on the lamp beside my cherry poster bed. Perry joined me when I fell onto the floral comforter. I buried my face into his loose fur and cried.

14

DARBY REDD

I parked my truck beneath a stately oak tree on the back side of White Rose Cemetery. The small green buds sprouting from the thick, knotted limbs were a welcome sight. Spring was closing in, but it was still too chilly for my liking. I'd worn my heaviest wool coat over my black sweater and dark dress slacks I borrowed from Della.

When Cliff asked me to come to his grandmother's funeral at lunch a few days before, I was dead set against it. I figured sending a peace lily to the service with my name scribbled on the card would suffice, but the sorrow in Cliff's eyes, amplified by his eyeglasses, changed my mind. I still considered him an acquaintance, our rapport simply consisting of brief conversation in the work cafeteria and an occasional short-lived phone call. I still had no interest in the two of us going down to Gulfport for the weekend to shop and charter a fishing boat and take selfies or whatever it was that friends did.

I hadn't attended the funeral at Payne's Bluff Baptist. The long-standing white, wooden church was small, and I couldn't go unnoticed there. I didn't want people gawking at me or asking who I was, and I definitely didn't want to feel obligated to hug anyone. I rarely knew what to say to people on a normal day, so the idea of consoling a grieving stranger was terrifying to say the least. But I figured the least I could do was attend the graveside service. I'd be out in the open instead of sandwiched between the bereaved and four wooden walls with stained glass windows. I could fade into the background much easier outside.

The shiny black hearse, followed by a long trail of cars, entered the expansive cemetery and parked alongside the royal-blue tent over the gravesite that read PRESCOTT FUNERAL PARLOR in white block letters. I remained inside my truck as an assembly dressed in dark colors exited their vehicles and filed around the hole in the ground. Pallbearers, including Cliff, soon slowly toted the mahogany casket and disappeared beneath the tent, and the black masses enclosed them.

I stepped out of my warm truck into the nippy March air and buttoned the gray wool coat. My black flats crunched the dead leaves that peppered the green sprouts of grass while I shoved my hands deep into the lined pockets and glanced over at the far-left corner of the graveyard. That was where my mama was buried. I noticed a hickory limb lying in front of her headstone. I knew I wouldn't leave without paying my respects and cleaning up her gravesite, but I wished I had done it before everyone arrived for Cliff's grandmother's burial. I didn't know how long these people would stand around talking, but I preferred visiting my mother without strangers watching me from across the sea of tombstones. Someone could recognize whose grave I was visiting and bring up the accident. Most everyone knew where my mama was buried because her headstone had been vandalized over the years and the story was plastered on the front page of the *Tallahatchie County Examiner*.

I quietly snuck behind a man at the back of the crowd. He looked rather impatient instead of sad. He sighed loudly and checked his gold watch twice in the few minutes I hid behind him. But there were dozens of people who were crying. Many had wadded tissues in hand, at the ready to smudge their wet mascara, and sniffles echoed through the cool air. Scanning the crowd, I recognized several prestigious families. They stuck out in their fine clothing among Cliff's relatives in cheap, wrinkled suits and some in jeans and baggy dress shirts they had probably borrowed. Cliff came from poor folks like I did.

The pastor was talking so faintly I could barely make out what he was saying. I knew he concluded the service when he approached each family member standing beneath the tent and gave them a consoling handshake. Several people hugged and placed white geraniums on the casket, and then the crowd trickled back to their cars—many of them old beaters on bald tires with Bondo-covered doors. I finally saw Cliff with his spaghetti noodle arms wrapped around a feeble and stooped old man with an unlit cigarette in his hand. Cliff moved about the tent and patted several people on their backs before he spotted me standing to the side. He gave me a little wave with his large white palm and flashed a smile before walking my way. He was wearing a burgundy tie and a dark suit with pants about an inch too short for his lanky legs. I'd never seen him in anything other than his work uniform. He had a fresh buzz cut and shave.

He bounded over to me in his familiar, goofy gait and said, "Thanks for coming, Darby."

"I'm sorry I didn't make it to the church."

"Ain't a problem."

"Your grandmother . . . Was your maw a maid?"

"Yeah. She cleaned houses her whole life long, except for her own." He giggled. "Cleaned Judge Salem's house since I was a baby. The rich folk loved her. Treated her real good."

"Birdie thought she remembered her."

"I'm worried about my dad. He don't know how to get on without Maw. He's been on disability for a long time now. She's been taking care of him same way she did when he was a kid."

"That's your dad?" I nodded toward the weak man with a greasy comb-over and the cigarette now smoldering in his hand. He looked too old to be Cliff's father.

"That's him. All those years of hard living have treated him bad. Looks about ancient, don't he?"

I didn't know how to respond without sounding rude.

"You want to meet my brother? You ain't got to meet my dad because he's half deaf. I know you ain't a yeller."

"Oh. I d-don't," I stuttered. "I don't think so. I just—"

"It's all right, Darby. I promise Gary ain't going to quiz you none."

"Still. I don't think—" A tall, thin guy with the frizziest hair I'd ever seen interrupted me.

"Who is this, Clifton?" He elbowed Cliff as I focused on the spirals on his head blowing in the breeze.

"We was just talking about you, Gary. This is Darby Redd. I work with her. Darby, this is one of my brothers. The better one out of the two." He chuckled.

"Nice to meet you." Gary extended his hand. I removed mine from the warmth of the pocket to shake it. His nails were dirty and his palms were rough like sandpaper.

"Listen, Cliff, you can't let Mitchell go over to Maw's first. Ain't nobody there and you know he's gonna go straight for the medicine cabinet. I gotta take Tanya to pick up her kids, so it's on you."

"Can't Aunt Burnette—"

"Not Aunt Burnette." Gary shook his head and the corkscrew hair strands blew out of control. "You know she'll let him take everything out of Maw's cabinet as long as he shares a little bit with her. Can't none of 'em be trusted. You got to handle it."

"All right," Cliff said.

"Family is grand, ain't it?" Gary glanced to me and tittered, then looked back to Cliff. "Uncle Clyde is taking Dad out for lunch and then back to his house for a while, but don't forget to pick him up and take him to get his script. I got to be at work by seven."

"You talk to Uncle Clyde about taking Dad in full time? You know he can't stay in Maw's house by himself and can't none of us afford a nursing home."

Gary laughed. "Clyde can't have Dad at his place cramping his style. He spends five nights a week down at the honky-tonk trying to pick up widows. Me and Tanya already called dibs on Maw's house. It's got more room for her kids than our place. Looks to me like *you'll* be the one getting a new roommate."

"I don't want to live with Dad, Gary. You know how I feel about him. And there ain't near enough room in my trailer for the two of us." Cliff sighed. "Can't he stay on with you and Tanya?"

"Maw would want *you* to take care of him." Gary patted Cliff on the shoulder. "You were her favorite."

I recognized quickly how manipulative and controlling Gary was. He probably forced Cliff to eat mud when they were kids.

"All right," Cliff said in surrender as Gary walked away. "That's my other brother, Mitchell." He pointed across the now small group of people to another tall, thin man with hair nearly as long and lifeless as mine. He was wearing jeans and a droopy sports coat over a plain white T-shirt. "Not worth a cent, Mitchell. Ain't been out of jail more than six months and already back on the painkillers."

"Sorry to hear that."

"Every family got a no-good, I guess. We got lots of them." The glasses slid down his nose, as usual. "So are you going to visit your mother while you're here?"

I looked up at him, startled. "You know where my mother is buried?"

"I mean—" He went silent.

"Everybody does," I said, finishing his sentence.

"I shouldn't have said nothing, Darby. I'm sorry. Always sticking my foot in my mouth."

"You know what she did, then?"

He shrugged. "I was just a kid back then."

"But you know? You know what happened to her?"

"Well, yeah. I mean, I heard. I'm sorry. I'm an idiot. You don't talk and I don't know when to shut up." He looked to the ground in remorse and kicked at a small pile of leaves.

"No," I said. "Don't apologize. We live in a small town. Everyone knows. Everyone knows about my mama just like everyone knows crazy Mrs. Perkins washes her car in the rain."

"Yeah." He laughed. "Old Perkins *is* crazy, ain't she? Did you know she lets squirrels in her house? Lets 'em right in. Puts doll diapers on 'em and sleeps with 'em, I heard."

"Yeah."

"I'll let you go on and visit your mama, then. Thanks for coming out here today. I know you don't like getting out none. Really means a lot to me."

"You're welcome," I said.

"I can move that big limb off your mama's grave when you're done. They don't take care of this cemetery the way they ought."

Surprisingly, I was relaxed while talking with Cliff, meeting his brother, hearing about his messed-up family, and carrying on like normal people do. I suddenly didn't mind the idea of him walking over to Mama's grave with me. Wasn't this what acquaintances did? Carried on short conversations in the lunchroom and visited graves together?

"You want to go over with me?" I motioned to the far side of the graveyard with my other hand still inside the deep, warm pocket.

His eyes widened. "Really? I thought you'd want to be alone for that."

"I usually do," I said, "but I don't see harm in it. I can help you with the limb."

"All right." He pushed his glasses up and bounded alongside me.

We carried the branch to the side of the cemetery near a line of pine trees and tossed it on top of other yard waste. On the way back to Mama's gravesite, Cliff stopped to pick up some pieces of trash that were strewn about and tucked them into the pocket of his dark suit jacket. A chilly gust whipped through the trees surrounding us as we looked down at the tombstone. To my wonder, the silence wasn't uncomfortable. It wasn't any different from when Della or Birdie stood beside me at that same spot. I didn't worry about Cliff being there as I thought about the good times with Mama—the Bobbie Gentry serenades, riding the mechanical horse that sat outside Piggly Wiggly while she fed it change and called me a cowgirl. I thought about her broad smile and contagious laugh. And then the unpleasant things resurfaced. The slander, the four burial plots for the Goolsbys at the cemetery across town, the newspaper photo of "Murderer" spray-painted on the slate.

"She was a good person," I said, breaking the silence. "She just made a mistake, that's all."

"Everybody makes 'em," Cliff offered.

"Went to the store one night and didn't know there was black ice on Maynard Road and took the curve a little too fast. Marilyn Goolsby and her three kids were coming around the bend after a late night at a gospel singing. Hit them head-on. Police said the youngest Goolsby kid was thrown thirty feet from the car. Everybody loved the

Goolsbys, you know? Hampton Goolsby was the police chief back then. Mama took his family from him and the whole town hated her for it. The whole town hated Birdie and me and Della for it too. Still do. People still think about it every time they see poor Mr. Hampton in the grocery store buying TV dinners for one. I know it isn't right to think this way, but I sometimes wish he'd just die already so he wouldn't be a reminder of it."

It was the most I'd ever said to Cliff in the time I'd known him. No stuttering. No nervousness. No long, awkward pauses. I didn't even tuck my hair behind my ears. I looked over to him, and for the first time, he was the speechless one.

"You don't have to say anything," I said.

He shoved his hands into his coat pockets.

"Well." I bent down to dust some chipped wood from the fallen limb off the stone. "She's in heaven now. No bad reputations in heaven. No judgment up there."

"Nah, there ain't. No maids either. Maw ain't got to clean no rich man's toilets anymore. Ain't nothing needs cleaning up there."

"I'm sorry about your grandmother, Cliff. I don't know if I've even told you that. I've selfishly been worried about coming to her funeral instead of offering my condolences to you." I looked up at his tall frame.

"Darby, you said my name. Ain't never done that before." He smiled and revealed the small chip in his front tooth.

"Guess I'm in rare form today. Didn't know I could say your name or more than three words in a row, did you?" I pulled the coat close to my body.

"I knew you could. I've just been waiting on you to do it."

15

BIRDENA REDD

I grew up in a little old shack covered in flaky red paint out on Route 12, now known as Clayton Sheffield Memorial Highway. Our place sat back off the road a piece beneath a grove of pine trees, and the yard was dirt mostly because the grass couldn't thrive in the shade. It was always freezing inside come winter because there wasn't any insulation, and the flooring was made of plywood lying on a cinder block foundation that sometimes shook when walked on too hard. There were three of us kids in that little place with a mama who cried too much and a daddy who drank every time Mama cried.

Our mother, Melaena, must have had some kind of mental illness because it wasn't regular for someone to cry like that or even to yell like that. Nothing made her happy—not her kids or a warm meal or a good night's sleep. She wasn't even glad when Daddy's liver reached its limit and he died. We thought that might bring her some joy—to be rid of the man who threw her around like a rag doll, but it didn't. Sounds awful cruel to say, but when our mother died, it was a relief for all of us. We didn't have to worry about her feelings or walk on eggshells anymore.

We did all right without any stable parents. Harwell was the baby of the family, and I was right in the middle, two years older than him. Willa was eight when I was born and held me on her hip when she drew water from the well or swept the dirt off the creaking wooden porch steps. She gripped my tiny hand and walked me to the outhouse at night. Coyotes were my biggest fear in the world back then, and they oftentimes came right up to the edge of the yard to hoot and holler like bloodthirsty wolves. I had nightmares about them biting down on my neck while I sat on the toilet and dragging me into the woods. Willa walked me to the outhouse until I was at least fifteen years old. She was a grown woman by then, but still considered me her baby.

It was Willa who took us to Sand Hill Methodist for the first time. There was a boy down there she had her eye on, so she dressed me and Harwell up in our finest clothes, which weren't fine at all. We wore shirts with mismatched buttons, baggy dresses, too-short slacks, and scuffed shoes, but we dug the dirt out from under our nails and brushed the tangles from our hair. Every person in that church turned in their creaking pews to eye us orphans when we showed up for the first time. But Willa didn't let a couple of uppity folks' snickers and whispers deter us from getting the Word of God in our hearts, or her getting a chance to know that tall black-headed boy who worked at the gas station.

After a few visits, the people of Sand Hill Methodist

took to us and started inviting us to lunch after service. We were fed real fine on Sunday afternoons—whether it was fried chicken or glazed ham and all the trimmings. They kept us in nice clothes they didn't have use for anymore and treated us like Jesus taught them to. Nothing ever came of Willa and the tall boy, but Mr. Hill, a deacon, got her on as a secretary at his accounting office, where she worked long after Harwell and I were grown and on our own.

When Joe Ed and Willa died, the church stepped up with consolations and flower bouquets and enough casseroles that I had to put them in the deep freezer. But when Cindy died, something was different. Those same ones who snickered at us the first day we set foot in that church unsuccessfully concealed their judgment when saying, "We're praying for you" after dropping off a fresh cobbler. I suspected they were gabbing over their telephone lines and in the pews while the organ drowned out their judgments, talking about how what Cindy Jane had done was unforgivable. Maybe it was all in my head, but I wanted to avoid overhearing anyone talking about it, so I quit going to church altogether for a while.

I defended my decision to stay home by claiming the good Lord could be worshiped anywhere, including my cozy chair. I could get just as much out of reading His Word on the back porch as I could surrounded by people who looked at me with scorn for what my Cindy did. But then my friend Gracie, God rest her soul, sat at my kitchen table one Sunday afternoon over hot coffee and blackberry cobbler and said church wasn't about me getting anything out of it. It was about what I gave to God—my time and my worship. Gracie wasn't ever wrong about much, so the girls and I went back. I knew they were having a tough time with the death of their mama and the torment at school, and I knew they needed to hear more about the gospel than what I told them. When I had my stroke, though, I got out of the habit of going every Sunday again, but I made sure we were there and dressed in our finest on Easter.

Sand Hill Methodist was a white, wooden church with a white tin roof and tall steeple on Sand Hill Road. Pastures of grazing cows surrounded three sides of the church, and across from it were fields of hay as far as the eye could see. In the summertime it smelled right awful from the sizzling cow patties frying in the hot sun. One time we had to move our homecoming picnic inside and eat in the pews because the horrible stench was carried on the hot, stagnant July air. The youngest church member was well past retirement age. Once we were all dead, the church house would probably become a wedding venue for people who didn't have a church home but liked the idea of being married in a room with pews and crosses.

We walked inside that morning, greeted by Gracie's husband, Napier. He was humped over and shook like a leaf, but he recognized me as if I'd just been at his and Gracie's house playing Rook the night before.

"Thought I'd see you today, Birdie," he said through false teeth. "Was just thinking of you last night, matter of fact. That trip you and Gracie took down to Biloxi that summer? When the tire on her Valiant blew out and you offered to change it?"

"I declare, Napier, you still ain't forgiven me for that?" I hee-hawed.

"You overtightened those nuts something terrible, Birdie. I couldn't get that spare off to save my life. Had to call in help. Took me and both the Steward boys to pry it off."

"Well, you survived, Napier. And if that Valiant had survived that tornado, you'd still be driving that thing, wouldn't you?"

"Wasn't a better car." He dug into his jacket pocket for peppermints and handed one to Della and Darby, as if they were ten years old again.

"Thank you, Mr. Napier," Della said as Darby nodded.

The girls never put up a fuss about church when they were kids and they still didn't. Della jumped at any opportunity to dress to the nines. Darby didn't care nothing about that, but she borrowed a pair of dark slacks from Della and paired them with a sweater and even put a little powder on her face and swiped on some clear lip gloss.

We moseyed to our usual pew—third from the back on the right side. It was the same spot where Joe Ed, Cindy, Willa, and I sat, and after they had all passed, the girls positioned themselves on either side of me. Nancy Delacroix used to sit directly in front of us, but she was long buried beneath a hickory tree down the road at the church cemetery. Wilburn and Sadie Nolen still sat on the pew directly behind us, their hearts ticking barely twenty beats a minute between the two of them. I would have sworn they were either dead or asleep had Wilburn not lifted a shaking palm out to me and muttered, "Birdie Redd. Is it Easter Sunday already?"

"Sure is, Wilburn. Sadie, you're looking finer than frog hair this morning," I shouted so they could hear, but Sadie didn't. She didn't even acknowledge I was standing there. Probably because she was both deaf as a doorknob and blind as a bat.

There wasn't but about fifteen other people in the church that morning, and that was a good crowd, considering it was Easter. I knew each one of them, their backstories, their secrets, their sins. I knew where they were born, which house in Tallahatchie County they were raised in, where they worked when they were young and able and didn't have prescription bottles cluttering their nightstands. As I scanned the room, I realized, as I had many times before, not a one of them had a child who did anything as bad as what mine did.

I didn't know much about Sand Hill's pastor, Reverend Guidry. He'd only been there about three years, a transplant the Methodist Association sent to Clay Station from a church in Louisiana. His accent was as thick as bayou mud and he wore a gold nugget ring on his right hand. I didn't care much for men who wore rings aside from a wedding band. Wasn't sure why. Just a bit too gaudy for my taste.

In his late fifties, he had dark hair, waxy with pomade, and a gold crown visible on one of his bottom teeth when he laughed.

He visited the house one day after he first moved to town. My first impression of him, aside from disliking the ring he wore, was that he talked too much and didn't listen near enough. He droned on about everything under the sun the entire hour he spent guzzling coffee on my couch. He never once asked me about my family but assumed I lived alone because both girls were at work. He sure made a point to invite me back to services. I suspect because the offering plate needed every penny it could get. I could read people well, and I recognized him as the type to take a dollar here or there from the gold plate. If time allowed, I could probably dig up a mugshot of him on the internet.

He slid over to us. "Well, Mrs. Birdie, it's sure fine to see you and these young ladies this morning." He took my hand into his and patted it gently. The gold band on his finger knocked my knuckles.

"Thank you, Reverend. You remember my granddaughters? Della and Darby?"

"Of course I do." He held his gaze on Della a little too long for my liking.

When he was done chatting, he made his way behind the oak pulpit and started preaching from the book of Luke. It was the same Easter message I'd heard all my life, but it didn't mean nothing to me until after I married Joe Ed. I had finally tuned in to Reverend Gatlin one Sunday while Willa sat next to me in the same spot I was sitting now.

Reverend Gatlin was a godly man who shouted about hell and brimstone and stomped his feet and perspired from behind the pulpit like he was hauling rocks up a hill. When I was a kid, I'd count how many times he pulled his handkerchief from his pocket and soaked the sweat from his temples. I'd never forget his personal best was twenty-three. Sometimes Reverend Gatlin would get to jumping around so much his comb-over would flop to the wrong side. I had to cover my mouth to keep from laughing at his hair looking so awkward. Willa pinched my leg more times than I could count as a warning to get my act together.

But on that Sunday after Joe Ed and I were married,

Reverend Gatlin was describing Jesus' beating in graphic and gruesome detail. He said Jesus' skin was cleaved right from the bone. Something about that word, *cleave*, made me sit up at attention. I started crying thinking on all the pain Jesus went through, and if what Reverend Gatlin said was true, He went through it for me and all my wrongdoings so I wouldn't have to go into the eternal hell I deserved. Something in my heart changed right that minute. Willa and Reverend Gatlin said Jesus was going to live in my heart from that moment on, and I was certain it was true.

Even when I skipped out on church after Cindy died, I still believed He was in my heart. I still studied my Bible and watched Billy Graham on television. And believing what Jesus did was for me meant I'd see Joe Ed and Cindy and Willa again one day, because they believed it too.

Cindy Jane was just seven years old when we sat at the kitchen table one hot summer afternoon and read the book of John. She folded her little hands and prayed the sinner's prayer as a pot of peas nearly boiled over on the stove. She asked God's Son to save her, and she was made righteous through Him alone that day. It brought me great comfort to know that nothing could separate her from His love—not even her addiction or the accident.

I didn't know why Cindy and Marilyn and those sweet Goolsby kids were taken from this earth so soon, but I liked to think they now had mansions side by side in paradise. I smiled when I thought on Cindy and Marilyn's babies worshiping our Savior together. They no longer knew the troubles and heartache of this fallen world.

I envied them.

16

DELLA REDD

MONDAY, APRIL 17, 2017

Birds chirped in the pine trees shading my parked car on the corner of Pratt and Blakemore. The driver's side window was rolled down and the warm spring breeze circulated through my PT Cruiser as I purchased the purple lace dress that had been sitting in my online shopping cart for weeks. I wanted to make sure I received it early in case it didn't work out and I needed to return it and find something else for my birthday party.

When the order was placed, I checked the clock to see I only had twenty minutes left before my lunch break was over. I tossed my phone to my side and noticed Shelly's yard was already in need of mowing. Mounds of crabgrass had overtaken the property. I guessed she could no longer afford a gardener since she'd been booted from my future home on Magnolia Trace. Aside from the unkempt yard, her new house was rather nice. It was a traditional two-story redbrick with black shutters and a long front porch. I wondered if alimony checks were covering her mortgage since she was not employed. I would put a stop to that once Brian and I were married. Shelly was not going to depend on my husband to pay her bills. She could stand on a street corner and beg for change before I let that happen.

My thoughts were interrupted when her dusty white Range Rover pulled into the driveway that had grass sprouting from cracks in the cement. A thin man with long, greasy hair exited the passenger side first. He was wearing brown work overalls splattered with paint and dirty white tennis shoes. He reached back inside the car to retrieve a McDonald's sack and a large drink. I assumed the rumors were true and he was the pillhead Shelly had been accused of palling around with. It sickened me that he was about to sit on the couch and eat food Brian had surely paid for.

Shelly's car door finally opened and she stood and dusted crumbs from the front of her dark jeans. She said something to make the stringy-haired man laugh, and then they both walked toward the front porch. I knew I had to catch her before she disappeared inside the house, so I hopped out of my car and sprinted toward them. The wind nearly whipped the bellflower from behind my ear.

"Shelly?" I called as they both looked to me and then glanced around to see where I'd come from.

"Yes?" she asked. The drugs had taken a toll on her and she was no longer the doctor's attractive wife. She looked pale and tired, with dark circles surrounding her eyes. In the words of Birdie, she looked rode hard and put up wet.

"May I have a word with you?" I said when I was standing

right before them. I grimaced at the scent of the unknown man's BO hanging in the wind.

"Who are you?" I recognized the look on her face as she scanned me from head to toe. She thought my lavender carpenter jeans and purple floral kimono was a bizarre outfit.

"My name is Della Redd. I'm Dr. Faulkner's friend."

She let out a long, disgruntled sigh and rolled her dark eyes. "Mitchell, take the food inside."

"You sure?" He looked at me curiously.

"Yeah, go on." She waved him away. When the thin man went inside, she placed her hands on her slender hips and asked, "He sent you here?"

"No, he doesn't know I'm here."

"Well, what do you want, then?" The wind tossed her long, reddish-blonde hair into a frenzy. Dark roots proved she was in need of a coloring. At least she hadn't used her alimony check for that.

"I saw you slap him Saturday afternoon."

"What?" She scowled.

"I saw you slap him. Saturday afternoon in his driveway. You can't do that."

She laughed. "Who are you again?"

"Della Redd."

She searched her mind and then said, "The girl at the front desk? You're the receptionist? You're the weird one, always dressed in purple." She sneered at my ensemble. "Yes, I recognize you now. You're Cindy Redd's daughter, aren't you?"

"I am."

"What does any of this have to do with you? Were you at Brian's on Saturday?"

"I was driving by his house on my way to visit a friend and just happened to see what you did."

That wasn't true. I wasn't visiting a friend. I made it a habit to cut through his neighborhood on Saturday afternoons when I ran errands. Someone had to keep an eye on him, after all.

"And how is this any of your business?" She crossed her bony arms defensively.

"I'm here to tell you to back off," I said sternly. "Quit treating him this way. Just leave him and Remi alone."

She laughed again. "Woman, I will slap you into next week."

"I know you're fond of slapping, but I'm not here to have a physical altercation with you. I'm just asking you to quit giving him a hard time." I paused and reached out to gently touch her arm, but she jerked away. "Shelly, you have to accept that he's left you. He's moving on with his life. You have to move on too. Get the help you need. Don't bring him down with you. Don't—"

Her open hand struck my cheek before I could finish. I had felt that sting before when I dated Kevin. I looked down to the bellflower that had fallen from my hair and landed next to my purple and white sneakers on the cracked driveway and touched my tingling face.

She turned to walk in the house and over her shoulder said, "Get off my property."

"Leave him alone, Shelly!" I called as she climbed the porch steps. "And start sending out résumés now. He's not going to pay your bills forever!" The door slammed behind her and I added, "And mow your yard."

I stood silently in the driveway for a few moments and rubbed my warm, burning cheek before speeding back to the clinic.

● ● ●

When I returned to the office, Melanie and Camilla were loitering around the file cabinet and Melanie was harping on about a new teacher at the elementary school. Apparently Melanie didn't like the way the school system presented Common Core math to her little angel. As I sat down at my desk, she went on about how much more simply math was taught back in our day.

"Bella was up until ten last night crying over her workbook. I have to do something about this. I'm bringing it up at the next PTO meeting," Melanie grumbled.

I'd always been good with numbers and knew I could tutor Melanie's daughter, but I would never volunteer to help. Instead, I hoped her kid failed and had to repeat first grade.

I checked the compact mirror in my desk drawer and was relieved to see the redness left by Shelly's hand had faded. I put the mirror away when I heard the back door of the clinic slam closed. Soon Dr. Faulkner appeared next to Camilla and Melanie.

"Della," he said, "may I have a word with you in my office?"

The nurses both looked to me with wide eyes and confusion on their faces.

"Sure." I stood from my desk and followed him.

When we reached his office, he pointed to the brown leather chair in front of his sizable L-shaped desk cluttered with paperwork. "Have a seat," he said while shutting the door behind him.

"Is anything wrong?" I asked as he fell into his rolling desk chair.

This was it. Shelly told him about our confrontation, and he was going to thank me for sticking up for him. He was going to extend the long-awaited invitation to lunch where he would confide in me all the ways Shelly had tried to destroy him. And I would promise to make it better. Our future began now. He folded his hands on the desk and searched for the right romantic words. He looked so handsome in his pale-pink button-down. I took in the dreamy scent of his aftershave.

"Did you visit Shelly on your lunch break?"

I proudly nodded. "Yes, I did."

I was surprised when he didn't look pleased.

"Della." He sighed. "Why would you do that?"

"I-I was driving by your house on Saturday afternoon. Mr. Pete and Mrs. Marion Mahoney are acquaintances of my grandmother. I was returning a dish to them," I lied. "That's when I saw her hit you, Dr. Faulkner. I hated seeing that. You're such a kind man. You don't deserve that." I looked to my hands in my lap.

He paused. "I appreciate your concern, but, Della, it's *not* your concern. My wife—"

"Ex-wife," I interrupted and he paused again. Our eyes locked.

"Shelly is not in a good place, Della." I loved the sound of my name rolling off his lips. "She is, um, she's going through a hard time. I'm working very hard to make our separation a peaceful one, so I don't want anyone causing drama or friction. Adding fuel to any fires, you see?"

"I understand."

"She thinks I sent you to her house to start trouble. She even has this, um, this crazy notion that you and I are having an affair. I mean, it just doesn't look good, Della. You understand?"

I knew the disappointment on my face was evident. I didn't like him saying the idea of us as a couple was crazy.

"I understand, Dr. Faulkner." I looked down to my hands again and picked at a purple thread on the seam of my jeans. I decided to fish for sympathy, play the damsel in distress. "She slapped me today. She slapped me really hard."

"Oh, Della." He leaned forward in his chair. "I'm so sorry about that. Are you okay?"

My heart rate increased thinking he was about to graze my assaulted cheek. "I'm okay," I said pitiably.

He breathed and rubbed his temples. "I do appreciate you taking up for me. That was sweet of you, but it's just—it just isn't necessary, okay? She is not playing with a full deck right now. We're trying to get her help and get her on the right path, but she's got some issues. Just—I need you to just stay away from her."

"I'm sorry," I said like a child who had been caught drawing on the living room wall.

"Thank you," he replied, and we shared a long, uncomfortable pause.

"If that's all, Dr. Faulkner, I need to get back to work. Lots of coding to be done." I stood from the chair, deflated.

"Listen," he said. "I don't want you to think I don't appreciate what you did. I know your intentions were good, and I'm not angry with you. I'm not only trying to keep this separation amiable, but I'm looking out for you as well. I don't want you mixed up in all of this because I care about you, Della, and I don't want Shelly coming after you in some way. Who knows what she might do in her frazzled state."

I was on air again. "I understand. I'm sorry for overstepping."

"You were just being a good friend. I would do the same for you." And then he added as he nodded toward my blouse, "Purple really is your color. I see why you wear it so much."

I blushed. He winked. And I walked out the door.

●　●　●

Although I'd intended to be heroic, I hadn't thought through my actions. I hadn't considered we were dealing with an unstable woman—an addict looking for her next Lortab. It was no surprise Shelly spun the meeting in her driveway and tried to use it to her advantage. She was unwell, and anything I said or did to defend my sweetheart would be used as ammo against him. I vowed not to speak to her again. Not until Brian and I were officially a couple and I'd earned my place to take up for him. Then it would be appreciated by him. It would be the admirable and virtuous thing to do. It would be my obligation as his girlfriend, as his wife.

Still, I wondered why he had yet to ask me to lunch.

Maybe he was waiting on me to make the first move. I thought confronting Shelly would be considered a sign, but it was a bad decision on my part. He needed to know how I felt about him, outright. I had to find the courage to confess my love for him. Then he would understand why seeing Shelly slap him had upset me so. He'd understand why I couldn't stand idly by.

17

BIRDENA REDD

SUNDAY, MAY 7, 2017

Saint Paul talked in Philippians 3 about forgetting the past and straining toward what was ahead; to keep pressing on until the ultimate goal of heaven. Lord knows I've prayed for that—prayed for amnesia. I declare, I wish there was some kind of medicine to take and erase the hard things from both the heart and the head, but I remembered the day of Cindy's accident so clearly. How cold and gloomy it was outside. The trees in the yard void of any life—just bare branches that danced in the frigid wind.

I remembered Cindy drank all that day. I didn't permit her to bring alcohol into the house, but she hid bottles of bourbon in her room and mixed it with Coca-Cola. I knew by the sound of the melting ice cubes clinking in her glass as she aimlessly walked from room to room. And how she grew louder and more comfortable in her own skin by the minute. She walked through the house, singing to herself or playfully poking me in my side while I cooked in the kitchen. She swung the girls around and tickled their feet. All that because alcohol was running through her veins, but I'd admit I enjoyed the sound of her and the girls cackling. I didn't see no harm in her drinking as long as she was doing it in the safety of our little old house.

Once Della and Darby were put to bed that February night, Cindy grabbed the brown rabbit-foot key chain off the coffee table and planted a big kiss on my cheek while I worked on my latest cross-stitch. It was a golden-brown owl perched on a limb with four sparse leaves protruding from it. Cindy said she'd be right back, and I begged her not to go. If I didn't have to wake the babies and load them up in the cold car, I would have taken her down to the store for cigarettes. I wouldn't have let her get behind the wheel. I've never regretted anything more. Waking two five-year-olds from sound sleep would have been worth avoiding what happened that night.

When she hadn't come home within an hour, I assumed she'd stopped off at Midway. Disappointed in her, I went on to bed. I even remember the green-and-yellow-striped flannel nightgown I was wearing. It was too long for me and often got caught up in my legs when I turned over in the night. I promised I'd throw it out every time I woke up feeling like I was tangled in a spider's web, but I never did. Couldn't afford to throw out nightgowns just because they were annoying. I woke up a few hours later to pounding on the front door, and I assumed Cindy was too drunk to unlock the dead bolt. When I saw a deputy in uniform on the other side of the glass storm door, my worst fear was confirmed. I knew what had happened before I even let the young man with the downcast eyes inside the house.

My wailing woke the twins. Bless their hearts. They were so confused and scared, and they stayed that way for years to come. It was a long time before they understood what had happened to their mama and that she wasn't coming back home. And even longer before they learned what happened to Mrs. Goolsby and her young'uns. Losing Cindy would have been enough heartache to last me two lifetimes, but what she did to the Goolsby family only intensified the sorrow. It was my daughter's fault that another family—a kind, decent, good family—had been ripped apart. Marilyn Goolsby had a servant's heart. When my Joe Ed died, she brought us the most delectable cherry pie made from scratch. I ain't ever seen such a perfectly pinched piecrust. She also dropped off hand-me-downs for Della and Darby a time or two. My newborn granddaughters had a baby blanket that belonged to the very kids Cindy killed. Heavens to Betsy, it was too much for me to bear.

Still, I knew I couldn't hide away in my room and grieve the way I did when Joe Ed died. I couldn't let the despair devour me. I couldn't be so consumed by sorrow that I neglected Della and Darby. I accepted that it was my fault Cindy turned out the way she did. Because of my absence after Joe Ed died, she went wild and reached to alcohol for comfort. I wasn't there for her to lean on, and I wouldn't dare make the same mistake with my grandbabies. So I stuffed it all down best I could. I cried in private—in the break room at Piggly Wiggly or in my car on the way to work or on my days off while the girls were at school. I mourned after they were fast asleep, and I made sure I was done in time to fix them breakfast and send them off to school with a smile on my face.

When I thought, *I can't go on*, I remembered can't never could. I worked real hard to make life good for my grand-babies, and it made me madder than a wet hen when class-mates excluded them because they overheard their parents talking about their mother. Those kids treated Della and Darby like black sheep instead of realizing those poor little things were without a mama and needed love and prayers too.

God had granted me seventy-seven trips around the sun, some years better than others. Willa and Harwell were on the other side of heaven, and it was true I often longed for the good old days when we ran barefoot in the silty dirt down Hammermill Road or when we caught bugs in a Mason jar. All those hot summer afternoons when we swung from a cypress limb and dropped into the cool, flowing water of Tippo Bayou. The times when we weren't worrying about our mama or daddy. I also thought on dancing in the kitchen with Joe Ed while chicken turned crispy in the cast-iron skil-let. I thought of the nights we sat on the front porch swing of our little shotgun house, the air dense with humidity and the sky like a watercolor painting. I could still see our barefoot Cindy Jane walking for the first time in the front yard while wearing a blue pinafore Willa made. I'd never forget my daughter holding her twin baby girls in swaddling clothes and covering their peach cheeks in kisses. I adored watching her watching them.

I thought on those good things, the pure and lovely things, during my birthday party. I soaked in the sight of

Della in her fancy purple hat and Prentice smiling at me with adoration and the sound of Darby sweetly singing "Happy Birthday." As the colorful balloons the girls had presented me danced on the kitchen counter and the plate of Darby's perfectly crunchy fried green tomatoes sat next to the rich chocolate cake that promised to spike my blood sugar, I knew that through it all, I was blessed.

I'd see my Joe Ed, Willa, and Cindy again one day, sooner rather than later. I'd give Mrs. Marilyn Goolsby a big hug too. I knew it was true because that was what Saint Paul was talking about in Philippians 3.

18

DELLA REDD

I was not surprised to see Kelly Ragan limping through the door of the clinic since I'd made the appointment for her less than an hour earlier. Her husband had informed me on the phone that she'd hurt her ankle while working in her yard, but I could not picture prim and proper Kelly with sweat on her brow, dirt under her fingernails, and grass stains on her expensive running shorts. She'd always thought herself too important for such lowly, common chores. Maybe she'd realized she wasn't too good to plant a rosebush instead of hiring a day laborer to do it. Maybe she had changed. Maybe she had matured.

Her husband, Rob, gripped her under her arm and helped her wobble toward my desk. I faked a smile.

"Hi, Kelly."

"Eleven o'clock appointment," she replied. No pleasantries. No "Well, hello, Della. Haven't seen you in a while.

How are things? Your grandmother doing well? What about Darby? Is she okay? I sure am sorry for that terrible thing I did to her our senior year. Get her on the phone for me, will you? I'd like to talk with her and make amends." No, Kelly Ragan hadn't changed a bit. She was a thirty-year-old snob.

"Just have a seat and Melanie will call you back soon." I motioned toward the empty chairs in the waiting room as her husband thanked me and helped her to the closest seat.

I placed her chart on the cart for Melanie and eyed Kelly sitting there, rubbing her foot, obviously in pain. Her pale eyes squinted and she took slow, deep breaths. I was delighted to see her feeling discomfort, without makeup and her hair in a messy ponytail. Her lime-green tank top and black shorts were still dusty from her fall.

Melanie soon grabbed the chart and called her name. "Oh, poor Kel! What on earth did you do?"

"Working in that dang flower bed. Man's work, but Rob was too busy out playing golf," she scoffed, rolling her eyes at the man helping her limp down the hallway to the exam room.

When they disappeared from sight, I thought of senior English with Kelly. It was one of the few high school classes Darby and I had together. Our old spinster teacher, Ms. Purdue, seated us in alphabetical order and Kelly sat right in front of Darby. She repeatedly slung her long brown hair back so that it draped over Darby's desk. It annoyed my sister to no end, but she never complained. However, I wasn't afraid to frequently tell Kelly that it was rude. She ignored me while I had visions of chopping it off at the neck.

In the spring of our senior year, goldenrod was in full

bloom and Darby had terrible allergies. She couldn't help but sneeze every few minutes, so she kept a little package of Kleenex on her desk all season and made sure to cover her nose. Still, Kelly made such a ruckus about it.

"Ms. Purdue, Darby Redd is blowing her disgusting snot all over my hair," she'd yell out while the entire class snickered. When Darby's eyes watered from the hay fever, Kelly would ask in such a hateful tone, "Oh, did I make you cry, Darby?" while my sister looked down at her desk, deflated.

Ms. Purdue reached her limit with Kelly and told her to stop exaggerating. Still, Kelly was relentless and Darby was soon terrified to sneeze, bless her heart, because she knew Kelly would either have an outburst or turn around and glare at her, both of which caused the classroom to erupt in giggles.

One April afternoon Darby reached for her menthol-scented pack of tissues to wipe her runny nose and watery eyes, and it wasn't a few seconds before huge tears streamed down her cheeks. She turned to me with a fire-red rash covering her nose and swollen eyelids and whispered, "Della, my face is burning. I'm blind!"

All eyes were on us when I interrupted our teacher's lecture on *Macbeth* and asked to see the nurse. By the time we reached her office, Darby was groaning in pain. Her face was blistered and swollen like a birthday balloon. Nurse Palmer flushed her eyes with water and gave her a Benadryl, and then we waited for the puffiness and redness to subside.

"Some kind of irritant," Nurse Palmer guessed as she examined Darby's bloodshot eyes. She excused her for the rest of the day, and I took her home in my Cavalier, put her to bed, and covered her face with an ice pack. By the time Birdie came home from work, she was much better. We couldn't for the life of us figure out what had caused Darby's allergic reaction.

The next day in English class, it happened again. The burning, tingling, and irritation returned, even worse than the day before. Ms. Purdue excused us to see Nurse Palmer, and I noticed Kelly repressing laughter as I helped my poor, blinded sister out of her desk.

"What did you do to her?" I demanded.

"It's her allergies," Kelly said, her legs crossed and her foot kicking casually while she malevolently smirked.

I glanced down at Darby's tissues, sitting open right there on her desk while class came to a halt and Ms. Purdue was comforting my wailing sister. I reached for the Kleenex and gave them a sniff. My eyes began to water. That was not menthol I smelled.

I furiously waved the small package at Kelly Ragan. "What did you do?"

"Nothing, Della." She swatted at the bitter-smelling Kleenex.

I quickly reached for Kelly's colorful woven purse hanging from the back of her desk and rummaged through it while Kelly yelled at me and grabbed for it.

Poor Ms. Purdue was flabbergasted and said, "Della, what's gotten into you? Give Kelly her belongings!"

I ignored my homely teacher and pulled a small bottle of capsaicin spray from the woven bag. Kelly had sprayed Darby's tissues with the potent medicine used for muscle aches. She might as well have rubbed a jalapeño in my sister's eyes. I explained to Ms. Purdue what Kelly had done, all the while Darby continued to frantically paw at her face, and whispers and snickers floated throughout the classroom adorned with posters of Poe and Faulkner. Kelly's smug grin made me rear back and strike her cheek with my fist. Gasps echoed throughout the school room.

Soon we were all three in the office. Darby was with Nurse Palmer, and Kelly and I were behind Principal Mayer's closed door. Kelly refused to admit what she'd done, but Mr. Mayer was no fool. Kelly was sentenced to in-school suspension for three days; not nearly long enough for such a heartless joke. I was punished too. During my three days of in-school suspension, I delighted in seeing Kelly's swollen cheek change from black to blue to green. I'd never been prouder of myself.

The night of our altercation, Kelly's mother called Birdie, not to apologize for the agonizing and dangerous joke her daughter had played on my sister but to complain about me rummaging through Kelly's purse and hitting her. Birdie didn't hold back as she pulled out the stepstool again and reached for the stale nicotine hidden in the cupboard. Mrs. Ragan was surely terrified of Birdie after that phone call. When Kelly came back to class the next week, Ms. Purdue moved her to the other side of the room and she never looked our way again.

None of Kelly's friends approached Darby to apologize on Kelly's behalf. My sister could have been blinded, but no one cared. Instead, they talked about my "assault" as if I were the heinous one. They probably thought the prank was funny. Everyone except Erin. I saw her casually and quickly give me a thumbs-up before we left class that day and went to the office. I also noticed she didn't sit next to Kelly at the lunch table after that. I appreciated the small gesture when no one else seemed to care what Kelly had done to Darby.

Some of them probably still talked about it at their ugly Christmas sweater parties and long weekends at Biloxi Beach. I could just imagine their nasally, nasty voices saying, "Kelly, do you remember that time you put capsaicin spray on Darby Redd's tissues? Nearly blinded that weirdo. That was a riot!"

Darby was more skittish after that ordeal. She even shied away from Rachel and continually looked over her shoulder for the next debilitating prank—would it be a bucket of pig's blood suspended over the door? My hatred for Kelly and her clique reached an all-time high, and I couldn't wait to leave Clay Station for good.

After Kelly was sent home in a boot with a prescription for Percocet, Melanie and Camilla went out to lunch and left me alone in the kitchen to enjoy my meal in peace. I was reading the menu on the Garden of Eatin' website, although I had nearly memorized it by now. I was unwavering on the salmon, but I enjoyed looking at photos of it on the menu—pink and glazed on a shiny white plate with garnish. I had already reserved a jazz band, Dizzy Davis. I was paying extra for them to make the trip from Memphis, but they promised the best horn section in the South.

I was startled when Dr. Faulkner entered the kitchen. I thought he had left, too, as the office had been so quiet. Since I'd confronted Shelly two months earlier, things had returned to normal between us. He told me I made good coffee and remarked that the sombrero and poncho I wore on Cinco de Mayo were festive. One day his hand lingered as I dropped paper clips into his palm, and he intentionally grazed my fingers with his. Still, he had not invited me to lunch, and I'd not worked up the nerve to invite him.

"Oh, Dr. Faulkner," I said. "I'm glad you're here. Did you have a chance to talk to your stepsister about a discount for my birthday party in October?"

"No, I'm sorry. I completely forgot, Della. I'll send her a text right now." He pulled his phone from the pocket of his white coat and tapped on the keys. "When is it again?"

"October 20 at 6 p.m. at the community center. I'm expecting about a hundred guests."

"Big party," he exclaimed, still typing on the phone. "She's given the family discount to a couple of my friends before. I'm sure she won't mind a bit. Twenty percent is usually what she offers."

Friend. Friend turned lover. That would be our story.

"Wow, that would be a huge help. Thank you so much for asking her."

"Sure thing. I'll let you know what she says." He dropped the phone into his pocket and poured a cup of that morning's coffee. Then he stuck it in the microwave.

Now was my chance. We were alone. The party was approaching, and we needed our first date out of the way. He ought to clear his calendar and have his tux cleaned. He had to find the perfect gift for me. We had to fall in love. I didn't want him to accompany me as merely my friend or my boss but as the man who was completely and totally infatuated with me. My heart pounded as I mentally prepared to steady my voice when making my request. No slurring. No stuttering. I was beautiful. I was worthy of his love. I was royalty.

"I've been wanting to ask you something," I blurted while he retrieved the steamy mug from the microwave.

"Shoot." He turned to the cutlery drawer to pull out a spoon.

"You are planning to come to the party, I hope?"

He eagerly nodded. "I sure am. Sounds fun."

"Would you consider coming as my date?" I asked confidently. My smile was wide, optimistic, and I was positive he would say yes.

Instead, silence. He paused stirring the creamer in the yellow cup. But then, uneasy at the stillness, I assume, he started stirring again. Quickly. Loudly.

"Della." He turned and glanced at me, then looked back down to his coffee cup. "That's not a good idea."

"Why?" I continued to smile.

"Work relationships aren't a good thing." He shook his head topped with beautiful, thick hair that I had often imagined running my fingers through.

"Oh, Dr. Faulkner. That's a bit old-fashioned, isn't it? Work relationships aren't frowned upon anymore," I insisted.

"Della, I do appreciate the invitation, but—"

"Dr. Faulkner, I heard you on the phone," I stated. "I heard what you said about me."

"What's that?"

"A few months back. I was in here and heard you on the phone in your office. You told your daughter you were interested in someone at work. It can't be Melanie. She's married, and she's one of the most deplorable human beings on the planet. Camilla is merely a child. So you were talking about me, weren't you?" I tipped my head to the side, my smile beginning to fade. "Weren't you, Dr. Faulkner?"

"Oh." He looked to his shiny leather loafers with tassels and then joined me at the table. It was obvious he was avoiding eye contact with me. "Sue Simpson."

"The medical rep?" I asked, surprised.

"Yes," he said in a consoling manner as if I were a child who just found out Santa wasn't real.

Of course. The blonde bombshell who dropped off Pfizer samples. The voluptuous one with dangling earrings and tight dress pants and two-inch heels and nails always freshly painted and monthly Botox appointments.

"We went to lunch a couple of times, but it didn't work out."

"Oh." I sighed. "Well, silly me. I'm so embarrassed." I nervously chuckled and buried my face in my hands so he wouldn't see the fire I felt in my cheeks.

"Della, don't be embarrassed. I'm flattered, really." He reached out and touched my forearm. "That must be why you approached Shelly. You were hopeful for something between . . . between us?"

I nodded and hesitantly removed my hands from my face. "Yes. Oh, Dr. Faulkner, I feel so ridiculous." I refrained from crying. I was going to be tough and not dare let him know how wrecked and heartbroken I was.

"I really am sorry. I think you're a beautiful woman, Della. I really do." He stirred the coffee again.

"What about that right there, Dr. Faulkner? The compliments? The winks? Touching my hand, my back? You were flirting with me, weren't you? Or did I imagine it all? I'm so stupid. I have such an overactive imagination."

"No, Della, you didn't imagine things. I can see how you'd mistake my gestures for . . . I can see how I led you on. But with the divorce and Shelly's condition, I'm not ready to jump into another relationship. I realized that when I took Sue to lunch. The timing just isn't right. It's not you, I promise. You're pretty and kind and fun." He nodded in a consoling manner. "You're an asset to this office, and I do consider you a friend. I would still be honored to come to your birthday party. As that. As a friend."

"Sure." I faked a smile. "I've, um, I've got a lot to catch up on before your one o'clock. I'd better get back up front." I quickly gathered my trash and darted out of the small room, feeling humiliated. As I scurried toward the front office, I wiped my eyes.

I didn't cry when Kevin hit me and sent me barreling to the floor. But when my sister received balloons from her co-worker and Brian Faulkner rejected me, I did.

I ignored Brian's flattering words about my appearance and personality and focused instead on how utterly stupid it was of me to think someone like Brian Faulkner would be caught dead with me. He'd never be seen in public with the weird woman in purple who had a murderer for a mother and a painfully awkward twin. I was a stalker too.

I thought back to my actions over the past months. Brian wasn't on social media, but I had watched his daughter's public accounts like a hawk. I learned, through Remi's post of her grinning father with a dab of chocolate pudding on his nose, that he loved the sweet treat. One night I had asked

Birdie to whip up her homemade pudding and I took it to work the next day. When he proclaimed it was his favorite snack, I said my grandmother made too much and insisted I bring what was left to work. He gave me another flirtatious wink before fixing himself a bowl and alluded to it being the best pudding he'd ever had. He had tenderly squeezed my shoulders in gratitude.

One Saturday it was early evening when I cut through his neighborhood, and I took it so far as to park down the street and dart across his lawn, like a SWAT team member, to peep inside his house. His back was to me as he stood at his stove with freshly washed hair in a gray T-shirt and plaid pajama pants. As he lingered there in bare feet with the faint sound of the Eagles playing on the radio inside, I begged God to allow me to one day stand beside him in that kitchen to stir sauce while he chopped carrots for the salad.

I'd been a fool, consumed by the overactive imagination and senseless fantasies of my youth. It was reminiscent of the obsessive way I had watched Josh Tucker from the bleachers as he ran the football down the field during practice. I wasted entire afternoons gawking at him and imagining walking into senior prom on his athletic arm. I trailed him to the arcade on the weekends and peered at him from the dark corner beside the pinball machine. I sometimes drove by his house, hoping to catch a glimpse of him washing his truck in his driveway or tossing the football on the lawn with his little brother. I left love notes in his locker and chose his mother's teller line when Birdie asked me to deposit her paycheck at Tallahatchie First Bank. I incessantly and insanely chased that boy until he demanded, in the crowded cafeteria, that I leave him alone or he'd have his police-officer father file a restraining order.

I had reached out for love, companionship, and friendship to countless people in Clay Station, Mississippi, only to be reminded that no one here wanted me for the same things. When Birdie was dead, Darby was liable to marry Cliff Waters and leave *me* alone in the clapboard house.

Della Redd, the weird old spinster on Yocona Road.

19

DARBY REDD

Cliff Waters was my friend—the friend I didn't know I wanted. Or needed.

Slowly, over the last several months, he'd hammered away at the walls that had enclosed me my whole life. He started by removing little specks of clay and spackle. Then whole bricks began to crumble. He kept working on those walls until conversation flowed freely from my lips. Until the shyness I possessed around him faded. And now I laughed with him. I playfully punched his bony arm when he told a bad joke. I casually and without apprehension pushed the bulky glasses up his nose. We talked on the phone into the wee hours of the night. We shared lunch without much silence. We sat in his truck in the parking lot after work and listened to the nineties rock (at low decibels, as I'd never be a fan of noise) he favored. He'd coaxed me into singing along with Alanis Morissette. We met for burgers at

Sit a Spell Diner once in a while. He'd sat on the corduroy couch across from Birdie and watched J. B. Fletcher infiltrate a drug ring while I pulled white-chocolate macadamia cookies from the oven. He'd talked with Mr. Prentice about tree trimming and deer blinds and the coyote invasion. He'd mowed our yard while singing loudly to the Nirvana songs blasting through his headphones. He'd complimented the purple pansy behind Della's ear.

I'd learned to raise my voice so Cliff's father could hear me after the mean old man demanded Cliff or I bring him medicine or a grilled cheese sandwich. I'd even played poker with him and Gary in his grandmother's garage, which was now filled with Gary and Tanya's things. I won four dollars.

I woke up in the morning eager to see him and hear his voice.

This was what I'd been missing all my life. An arm to pull me close when I recollected memories of my mother's death. An ear to hear me vent when I was so angry with Della I could spit nails. A warm presence to share comfortable silence. Inspiration when I had writer's block. This was why people met for coffee. This was why Della begged to be let in on a dodgeball game. People need people. I needed Cliff.

Cliff needed me too. He wasn't reserved in letting me know that he desired me to be his girlfriend. He said he was attracted to me because of my meekness, gentleness, humbleness. He saw beauty where I'd always seen homeliness and limp hair. He recognized my strength in forgiving those who'd browbeaten me. He recognized my contentment, and he appreciated it. Maybe I'd desire him romantically someday, but not yet. Maybe never. Either way, he was patient. He was kind. And he kept chipping at the walls.

For as long as I could remember, Della wanted me to have friendship and possibly love. And now that I'd obtained it, she seemed angry with me. As Cliff and I laughed at the kitchen bar, I saw her glare at us from the stove. She was probably fantasizing about hitting me in the head with the skillet. Jealousy, that was what it was. This was supposed to be happening to her, not me. The painfully awkward, shy one who had long tucked her hair behind her ears and looked to the floor had what she wanted. She'd chased this dream I was living and she had nothing to show for it but a tear-soaked pillow and a shedding cat. I felt for my sister. I wanted this for her. I wanted Della to have male companionship. I wanted her to find happiness. And I wanted her to be happy for me as well.

• • •

The hot, humid Mississippi air gave my hair some life and warmed my thin blood. I'd never complained about the heat, although Birdie certainly did. She sat in the webbed lawn chair in the shade of the oak tree canopy with beads of sweat on her gray hairline and flapped a paper fan with a Popsicle-stick handle. It read "Bob Neville for Mayor. 1986." Birdie told us time and again Bob Neville was crooked as a dog's hind leg and never got her vote, but he sure made a good fan. When Birdie was long dead and gone, I'd still recall her waving it in the summertime humidity.

Mr. Prentice and Cliff manned the grill, both with red

Solo cups of sweet tea in their left hands. For the first summer in a dozen years, I'd opted to wear shorts. Cliff said my legs were too long and pretty to hide beneath heavy denim. The shorts were dark gray because I still wasn't a fan of bright, flashy shades, but at least my legs were seeing the light of day. My skin even had color from a day trip to Tippo Bayou. Cliff and I didn't catch a single fish, but we had fun trying. He chased me down the bank of the slow-moving stream with a bullfrog in his hands, and I yelled like a banshee. "Glowing," Birdie said. I was glowing. From the sun. From friendship. From Cliff.

Della sat across from me, next to Birdie, in a purple sundress and a straw hat with an American flag bow affixed to it. She sucked down her bottle of water with the usual scornful look on her face. Her eyes shifted from Cliff to me and back to Cliff, and each time I interjected my thoughts into his conversations with Birdie and Mr. Prentice, she looked astounded. She must have wondered who this woman was in shorts sitting beneath the shade of the sprawling tree and conversing freely in more than a whisper. She scarfed down her plain burger, without a bun, and disappeared inside the house before even half my potato salad was missing from the paper plate.

Birdie, Mr. Prentice, Cliff, and I remained at the picnic table covered in a red-and-white-checkerboard cloth while the deviled eggs sweated from the heat, promising salmonella to us all. We didn't care. We kept on talking. Birdie and Mr. Prentice shared memories of Clay Station in the sixties. We discussed the fireworks Cliff purchased from the tent in the Piggly Wiggly parking lot. We argued over the proper amount of sugar in a pitcher of sweet tea. Birdie swore by two cups and Cliff by three.

Birdie and Mr. Prentice eventually joined Della inside the house to cool off and left Cliff and me in the metal chairs my grandparents sat in before I was even born. They were both red with patina on the white arms. Cliff and I rocked beneath the tree in the front yard, waiting on night to fall, as the air cooled by only a few degrees. The temperature would remain in the nineties until well after midnight. Crickets, cicadas, and bullfrogs came to life as the sky dimmed, and the hot breeze rustled the large emerald leaves and flesh-pink mimosa petals above our heads and grazed my neck. My hair was pulled into a high ponytail, inaccessible for me to tug behind my ears.

"Still haven't heard from your mother?" I interrupted the insects' serenade.

Cliff had been worried about her since she didn't call on his birthday several weeks ago. She was an addict last known to be living in a homeless camp in Asheville, North Carolina. Cliff hadn't seen her since he was twelve, when he and his brothers lived with her in Panola County. She took off in the middle of the night with some man who made big promises, leaving her boys home alone to eat generic spaghetti rings and imitation meatballs out of the can for three days. When they realized she wasn't coming back, Gary phoned Maw and she barreled over to Panola to get her grandsons and bring them to live with her. He hadn't seen his mother in twenty years, but she managed to call on her sons' birthdays and Christmas. Cliff said she'd been married two times, been in jail three times, and lived dozens of places.

"Not since Christmas. I ain't too worried about it, I guess." He took off his glasses and rubbed the lenses with the hem of his plain white T-shirt.

The transformation was amazing when Cliff removed the bulky frames from his face. His eyes were no longer magnified like a bug's and his strong jawline was visible. It was as if he'd removed a veil.

"Maybe you'll hear from her soon."

"Truth be told, she should have died a long time ago. I don't know how she's lived this long, what with the drugs and sleeping on the streets and Lord knows what else. Her life ain't been good. Might be for the best if she don't call." He rested the temples of his glasses back on his ears while I reached over and patted his tanned arm.

"Cliff!" Birdie called from the open door on the front porch. "I'm putting the leftovers away. You want me to make your dad a plate?"

"That'd be awful nice, Ms. Birdie. Thank you," he answered before Birdie disappeared back inside the house. "He won't appreciate it none. Probably throw the burger against the wall. Dump the baked beans on the floor. Ornery, he is. Always has been. I don't know how much longer I can have him at my place, Darby. Mean as a dadgum rattlesnake."

"It makes me so angry Gary won't step up to help you with him."

"Gary ain't worried about nobody but Gary. Always been that way. He thinks the sun comes up just to hear him crow."

I snickered.

"But I can't blame Gary for not helping out. Dad ain't

ever been good to any of us, but Gary always caught the worst of it. I've watched the old man slam his head against a wall and break his fingers. Dad ain't ever do any of that to me. Just yelled at me a whole lot. I guess I'm the favorite." He grinned. "I'll keep him on at my place and deal with it. I'm surprised he's still kicking around. Probably won't be living much longer anyway." He paused. "That's awful of me to say, ain't it? Wishing my parents dead because it would be easier on me? I'm a terrible person."

"That's not true. You're sweet and gentle and selfless. I wished the same thing for Mr. Goolsby and he didn't even do anything bad to me. You're just . . . you're tired, Cliff. You're tired of the burden both your parents have put on you your whole life. They haven't made things easy on you. You're tired of worrying. That sounds pretty normal to me."

"I guess." He shrugged and reached for the condensation-covered plastic cup of tea sitting on the grass beside his chair. "I just don't have much love for any of them—my parents or my brothers. Maw, though." He smiled at the very thought of her. "Maw was the best. She was nothing like the rest of them."

"Sounds like you take after Maw."

He took a swig from the glass and looked to me. "Thank the good Lord for grandmothers, yeah?"

"Yeah," I agreed.

"Speaking of family, I've been putting off telling you something."

"About my family?" I wondered.

He set the cup back on the soft grass. "My brother,

Mitchell, called last night. Higher than a kite in the March wind and running his mouth. Telling all his secrets. Let it slip that he's been dating an older rich woman, Shelly Faulkner."

"Dr. Faulkner's ex-wife?" I leaned forward and my legs stuck to the metal chair.

"That's the one. Said Dr. Faulkner gives Shelly pain pills. Passes them out like candy. That's what keeps them both high."

"That can't be right, Cliff. Dr. Faulkner would never do such an immoral thing. Della swears he hung the moon."

"I don't trust my brother none, but I don't think he's lying about it. He said he's nervous the police are watching all three of them. Mitchell said they've got taps on the phones at the clinic. Real movie-like stuff, ain't it?" Cliff shrugged. "If Mitchell gets busted with pills, he won't ever get out of jail. I've lost count how many times he's been in trouble with the law. Got a rap sheet a mile long, I suspect. If he does get thrown back in a cell, I don't think I'll be too sad about it either."

"Oh my." I nervously chewed the inside of my jaw. "Della will be heartbroken to hear about this. She respects Dr. Faulkner. She trusts him. I think she's still infatuated with him. Why would he give pills to his wife and her boyfriend? It doesn't make sense. From what Della says, he's trying to get help for her."

"That I don't know." Cliff bobbed his bony shoulders.

"On the bright side, maybe this will help her move on. Motivate her to get out of that clinic. Go back to Tennessee," I hoped aloud.

"You don't think Della is in on it, do you?" He rested

his elbows on his scrawny knees hidden beneath holey jeans and rubbed his calloused hands together.

"Of course not!" I defended my twin. "She would never be a part of something so dishonest."

But I wasn't so sure. Could she be so brainwashed by love that she turned a blind eye to Faulkner's wrongdoing?

"I didn't think so, Darby, but I had to ask. Don't be mad."

"I'm not," I said. "I have to tell her. You'll back me up?"

"Sure I will. Your sister is too good a person to be left in the dark about this. I'll tell her everything Mitchell told me."

"Okay." I exhaled. "Let's get it out of the way. The sooner she knows, the better."

"I hate to ruin her Fourth of July," Cliff said as we both stood from the rockers.

"Her Fourth of July was ruined the moment I put on shorts."

2 0

DELLA REDD

I had been jealous my whole life. I was jealous of the tight-knit friendships among my classmates, jealous of the name-brand clothing they wore. I was jealous when their mothers dropped them off at school or brought cupcakes to the class parties. I envied people with cars that didn't overheat on the side of the highway and the large homes on the north side of town with impeccable landscaping and two-story columns. I'd been jealous of nearly everyone in Clay Station, except my sister.

I spent most of my life defending Darby to the bullies and pranksters. But I also pitied her. I pitied her because although we were on the same losing team, I was the captain. I carried more rank. I was the leader of our party of two. We were both considered outcasts, but I was destined to receive all the good things first. And that was exactly the way it worked out when I relocated to Chattanooga. I obtained the friends, the boyfriend, the college education. I was first, just like our order of birth, but I lost it all first as well.

Like the race between the tortoise and the hare, my slow and steady sister had passed me. She was sitting outside in the fifty-year-old metal rocking chair, a man gazing at her, and she was laughing; and not a muffled, quiet laugh but one that echoed throughout the countryside and startled birds resting on branches. She was no longer the reserved recluse who stared at the floor and pulled on her hair. She was different. She loudly sang over the water splattering against the mint tiles in the shower. Even on the errands we ran for Birdie—to the grocery or the pharmacy—she wasn't wary of the strangers we passed in the aisle. She no longer held her breath and prayed no one would speak to her when we took Birdie to the Catfish House for supper. Cliff was to her what alcohol was to our mama. He supplied her with some kind of courage and confidence and personality I never knew she possessed. And I was eaten up with jealousy.

Did I mention she was wearing shorts? I hadn't seen her legs since we were kids wearing hand-me-down dresses to Sand Hill Methodist on Sundays. Showing skin was a testament of the person she had become. She'd spent her life hidden, in the background, but now she and her kneecaps were on display for God and everyone else to see.

I silently stared at them through the storm door and wondered if she and Cliff had kissed. I was certain that not once in twenty-nine years had she ever felt a man's lips atop hers. I imagined how awkward a kiss between Darby and Cliff would be and retched at the thought of her stringy hair getting caught in their mouths, his glasses wedging between their faces, the whole debacle looking like cows chewing cud.

At least my only boyfriend had been handsome with twinkling Caribbean-blue eyes and a chiseled jawline. Cliff was no looker. His dark hair was buzzed down to his bright-white scalp, and his face was hidden by the thick spectacles that were two times too big for him. He pranced behind my sister like a basset hound, his ears nearly flopping and his tongue hanging out. No other woman would be envious of Darby on Cliff's lanky arm. Cliff! Cliff in blue jeans that drooped from his thin, gangly frame because his belt couldn't hold on to mere bone. He'd probably never had a girlfriend either. Who in the world would want him?

In the beginning, I urged Darby to reciprocate Cliff's feelings; to talk to him on the phone and buy him a present for Christmas. I thought having someone to care for her would be a little push to get me out of this town, but now I was so resentful of her I could barely see straight. I turned away from the door, from the sight of Darby and Cliff sharing intimate thoughts, and I passed the kitchen.

"Della, where you going? Be time for fireworks soon," Birdie called as she wiped down the counters and Mr. Prentice sat at the bar reading yesterday's newspaper. The Tupperware of food for Cliff's dad, another deadbeat, was sitting next to the sink.

"Just going to the bathroom," I answered before entering the miniature room at the end of the hallway.

I flipped on the light, and it reflected off the sea of baby-blue tile that extended up half the wall. I sat on top of the

DELLA AND DARBY

chipped toilet lid and reached over to turn on the waterspout before tossing my straw hat to the floor and burying my head in my hands. Perry swerved between my bare ankles and my long, purple linen dress got caught on his tail. I thought of Brian. Although he had declined my invitation to be a couple, he continued to rave over my coffee and my purple attire. He made an effort to ensure there was no awkward tension between us. A couple of times he tapped my elbow and said, "We're okay, aren't we, Della?" I guaranteed him we were.

I wished he'd downright slighted me since I made a fool of myself by asking him to be my date. It would be easier to get over him if he snubbed me and called my coffee vile swill before smashing the pot to the kitchen floor. But because he continued to treat me with kindheartedness and respect, my mind was guilty of wandering to a senseless and embarrassing place. When he came to the front office to ask for sticky notes or paper clips, I imagined he'd only come to the office to see me. I dreamed he would tell me he was a fool for rejecting me, and I could visualize him dropping to one knee, while I gripped the yellow sticky notes he had requested, and begging me to be his one and only.

But then I'd claw my way back to reality—the reality that he probably just needed paper clips or sticky notes. Nothing more. Nothing less.

I thought of quitting my job at Faulkner Family Medicine. Even though his generous words proved otherwise, I suspected Brian secretly pitied me and thought I was a lonesome, desperate soul who would forever pine for him. I was also at my wit's end with Melanie and Camilla. Darby was right about one thing: working with Melanie Reid was the unhealthiest thing for me. Her constant insults were catapulting me back into the dark, depressing place of my youth. I didn't know how much more I could take before I scalded Camilla's face with her carcinogenic soup or whacked Melanie upside her blonde head with her energy drink can.

I knew the logical thing for me to do was run as fast as I could away from Tallahatchie County, Mississippi, but it would be selfish of me to do so. I felt responsible for Birdie. Not so much Darby anymore since Cliff entered the picture, but I couldn't bear to leave my grandmother. She sacrificed for us her whole life and I would have to sacrifice my happiness to be here for her.

Without Brian to accompany me, I dreaded the birthday party. Thinking of walking into the community center alone on October 20 made my stomach drop. However, I couldn't call it off because Birdie had charged a nonrefundable deposit for the community center to her credit card, Dr. Faulkner's stepsister agreed to cater and offered a 20 percent discount, and I'd scheduled the band and bought my dress. Canceling would let so many people down and Birdie would lose her money. And most importantly, I didn't want Brian Faulkner to think his rejection had devastated me to the point that I didn't care about celebrating my thirtieth birthday.

I wondered if I could employ a man from some far-off city to attend the party with me. I'd swear him to secrecy. I would carefully plan it out, much better than I did when I invented Houston from Panola County or bought myself roses or sent myself balloons. It just might work, and it would prove to Brian that I was over him. Even better, it would make him so jealous he would whisk me away from the hired escort and we'd spend the rest of our lives together.

As my mind raced with ideas on where to find my make-believe beau, the name and hobbies and background I would create for him to tell the partygoers, I was interrupted by a knock on the bathroom door.

"Who is it?" I asked over the running water.

"It's Darby. Are you okay in there?"

"Yes." I cleared my throat. "Yes, I'm fine."

"We're about to start the fireworks. I was hoping I could talk to you before, though."

"Yes." I stood from the closed toilet lid and examined my dejected face in the medicine cabinet mirror. "Just give me a minute."

● ● ●

Birdie and Mr. Prentice sat in the living room, both eating slices of warm pecan pie topped with scoops of vanilla bean ice cream. Birdie said, "Your sister is looking for you. She's outside. Tell them we're ready for the light show. Be dark soon."

The heavy iron storm door slammed behind me and I saw Cliff and Darby about a hundred yards from the house. Cliff was setting out the fireworks that he'd brought. I couldn't bear to look at them standing so close together, so I focused on the summer sky. The sunset left it beautiful shades of orange, pink, and even purple.

"You wanted to see me?" I asked when I approached them.

"Della, we need to tell you something." Darby looked to Cliff while he situated a cannon on the gravel driveway and then nodded to her.

"Heavens to Betsy," I said, mimicking Birdie. "You're getting married?"

"What? No!" Darby shook her head and the long pony-tail draped over her left shoulder.

"You're pregnant?" I guessed again, much quieter.

Cliff laughed and dusted his hands on his tattered jeans. "You've gone crazy as a betsey bug, Della."

I impatiently crossed my arms. "Well, what is it, then? You want to get to the point?"

"I'll tell her," Cliff said to Darby. "Della, do you know my brother Mitchell?"

"No." I shook my head. "And I'm glad I don't."

"Della, why are you being so hateful?" Darby growled. As Birdie would say, she was fit to be tied. "Why are you so angry with me and Cliff? It's obvious you can't stand the sight of us together. You're jealous, and I don't understand why. This is what you've wanted for me my whole life. To have a friend. And I'll admit, you were right. Birdie was right. Being vulnerable to friendship, knowing Cliff, has been a blessing. Can't you at least be happy in knowing you were right? Can't you be content with anything?"

I looked down to my nails, ashamed, but I was too hard-headed to apologize. Everything Darby said was true. I had behaved contemptibly toward them. For no valid reason. I hated myself in that moment. Still looking down, I asked, "What about your brother, Cliff?"

"Mitchell's into narcotics. He's never been any count.

When he was only seven, he was spray-painting cuss words on parked trains down at the depot. One time he got caught red-handed with a can—"

"Get back on track, Cliff." Darby gently nudged his arm.

"Sorry," he apologized. "My brother gets his pills from Shelly Faulkner."

I looked up from my hands to Cliff's eyes enlarged behind the thick lenses.

"And Shelly gets her pills from Brian," he added.

I immediately shook my head. "That isn't true. She's come to the clinic asking Brian for prescriptions on several occasions. She always leaves empty-handed. Dr. Faulkner would never—"

Darby interrupted. "I know this is hard to believe, but Cliff doesn't think his brother is lying about this."

I searched my mind. Was Mitchell the guy in Shelly's driveway the day she slapped me? The thin man in paint-covered clothes, dingy tennis shoes, and a McDonald's sack in his hand?

"What does he look like? Your brother."

"He's skinny as a rail. Scragglier than me, even, if you can believe it. He works with a painting crew. Not much of a looker," Cliff answered. "He has this front tooth that juts out . . ."

Cliff continued, but I blocked him out. Without a doubt, Dr. Faulkner's strung-out ex-wife was dating my twin sister's boyfriend's strung-out brother. I'd only ever heard such a mouthful on *Jerry Springer*.

"Just because they're together doesn't mean they're getting pills from Dr. Faulkner. He divorced Shelly because he could no longer live with her drug use. It makes no sense that he would supply her with pain pills. He wouldn't do that. You don't know him, Darby," I pleaded with her. "He's a good man."

"I know this is hard to hear, Della," she consoled me. "Mitchell told Cliff the police are watching the three of them. They may even be tapping the clinic phones. It's possible Dr. Faulkner could get in trouble for this. I don't want you involved—"

"I'm telling you this is not true!" I adamantly declared. "You are believing Cliff's brother over me? You don't even know the man. And he's a criminal on pain pills. How can you trust anything he says?"

She shrugged her shoulders and looked at me with sympathy. The ponytail fell to the side, and that did it for me. I was overcome with acrimony, envy, resentment. Before I knew what I was saying, I blurted, "You think you're so high and mighty, don't you? With your rosy cheeks and ponytail and knees hanging out for everyone to see. I know who you really are, Darby Redd. Beneath that giggly little facade is the same bashful weirdo you've always been. I got out of this town. I made friends. I'm back, not because I want to be but because I feel obligated to take care of Birdie, and you love it, don't you? You love that I was forced to come crawling back and undo all the improvements I made in Chattanooga. Now that you have this loser to show you a little attention, you feel like you have the upper hand for once and want to ruin my good job and relationship with Brian by making up these lies."

Darby remained silent as Cliff gently took her hand. She

stood tall, unmovable, with her shoulders back, while she brazenly stared into my eyes. I waited for her to yell that I was wrong. To point out how bitter I'd become these last five years. I thought maybe she would pull Cliff by the hand to his truck parked next to hers on the grass and they would speed away, leaving Birdie, Mr. Prentice, and me to stare at unlit cannons on the gravel drive. But she did nothing, said nothing.

"That's—that's all I have to say," I muttered, interrupting the awkward silence. Then I walked back to the house.

Birdie and Mr. Prentice stepped onto the porch, a satisfied look on their faces from the dessert they'd consumed, and Birdie said, "Where are you going now, girl? It's time for the light show!"

21

DARBY REDD

I stared out the window of Della's car to the passing field on Chickasaw Road. Miserable-looking cows were grazing in the scorching, heavy heat. It was the first time I'd been alone with my sister since the Fourth of July. Birdie didn't know the conversation that took place on the lawn that day, but she knew something was wrong by the glares Della and I shot at each other from opposite ends of the couch for the last ten days. This morning our grandmother made us sit down and make up like she did when we were kids. We apologized to each other, but neither of us meant it.

"You didn't have to come." Della interrupted my thoughts and the sound of the AC furiously blowing our faces. I was freezing, but I wouldn't dare complain to Her Majesty.

"Birdie said I had to," I answered.

"You don't have to do what your grandmother tells you to do. You're an adult."

I remained silent and continued watching the fields and parched livestock as we drove by. I dreaded spending an hour with Della in Piggly Wiggly while she strutted up and down the aisles in the stupid purple fedora that only should have been worn by Prince on the Purple Rain Tour. She was delusional if she truly believed the vitriol she spewed a week and a half ago. I was not pleased she was back in Mississippi, scorned and dejected. I had always pushed for her to go back to Tennessee and be happy. She'd really hurt my feelings. My own sister wanted to destroy my newfound joy, and it angered me that she'd belittled Cliff. Thanks to his reassurance and some cathartic (oftentimes wrathful) poems, though, her harsh words didn't set me back to a place of timidity and seclusion.

In purple, cruel and vile,
She detests when I smile.
Envious, vicious, bitter,
How's that for a sister?

As I sat on the front porch that morning, enjoying the warm breeze, I overheard her talking with Birdie in the living room. She said she thought she'd found a date for the party but didn't want to disclose any details until it was official. Knowing Della, she'd probably hired someone to escort her. Anything to look good for the crowd. Birdie asked her if I was on board with coming, and she replied, "Not yet."

Yet! She was a fool to think I would attend her ridiculous shindig with "loser" Cliff. I didn't care if she stood in the community center alone all night next to the gigantic uneaten cake that she'd have to bring home in seventy-five doggie bags. She could go down with that sinking ship by herself. It would be what she deserved for the way she'd treated me our whole lives. For continuously thinking she was superior to me. For believing her lot in life was to defend her embarrassingly shy sister. For depending on me to depend on her. She wanted to be accepted by the in-crowd, but she never accepted her own sister as she was. Della was only concerned with how *I* made *her* look to others. And now she resented me because I made her look like the pitiful one. She still wrestled with anger concerning the past, while I'd let it go. Dr. Faulkner had rejected her, while I had a wonderful friend (and possibly a future romance) in Cliff.

● ● ●

When we entered the grocery store, she grabbed the cart with her list in hand. She'd forever been the one in charge, expecting me to follow behind her with my head down and my heart palpitating, overcome with social anxiety. Thanks to Cliff gently easing me out of my shell, I wasn't that person anymore, so I stepped in front of her and the cart, and she brought it to a halt before ramming into the back of my bare ankles. Yes, my exposed ankles, not covered with denim or thick socks and sneakers in the dead heat of summer.

I glanced back at her and read her face—*Who in the world does she think she is for stepping out of line? For trying to take the lead?* I knew the day's grocery list by heart. Chuck roast for Sunday supper, along with red potatoes, carrots, celery, flour for the biscuits, and sugar for the tea. Cantaloupe and strawberries. Sandwich stuff and chips for my lunch all week, and wheatgrass and seaweed or whatever stupid bland thing Della ate at work. I decided I would throw a bottle of Duke's mayo into the cart just to watch her squirm.

By her grumbles and sighs, I knew she found fault with every red potato I picked from the display in the center of the aisle. This was *her* job, after all. She was the keeper of *all* things—even the vegetables and fruits we purchased since Birdie was no longer able to tend to a summer garden.

"That one isn't ripe." She could no longer hold her tongue.

"Looks fine to me." I examined the cantaloupe.

"The rind isn't beige. Don't you see that green?" she mocked.

I tossed the non-beige melon on top of the flawed potatoes.

"You didn't even smell it," she said before retrieving it from the cart and giving it a good sniff. "This one is no good."

I rolled my eyes so far back in my head, I could see behind me. "Don't know what I'd do without you, Della."

We went about the store, arguing over the ripeness of fruits, the brown spot on a celery stalk, and the acceptable thickness of deli ham. I was so frustrated with her nitpicking that I wanted to walk away and let her finish the shopping. But that was what the old Darby would do—back down and fade away. I was going to establish a new hierarchy, the same way a beaten-down omega dog fought its way to the top. I would pin her to the floor of Piggly Wiggly and snarl my teeth if I had to.

As we disagreed on the perfect chuck roast, Della's idol suddenly appeared beside us. In all her glory, with cascading long blonde hair and in her Sunday best, Erin Drake was scouring packages of hamburger meat. I could immediately sense my sister was both ecstatic and a nervous wreck.

"Erin! Hi," she practically shouted over the pork loin display.

"Oh." Erin looked to her, startled. "Hi, Della. Darby."

"I am so—I'm just so glad that I—that we ran into one another. It's been such a long time," Della bumbled from beneath her ridiculous hat. She sounded ten years old again.

"Yes, it has." Erin glanced back to the meat.

"I'm, well, Darby and I are having a big party in two months—well, three, October 20, actually. At the community center. It's for our thirtieth birthday. I'll be sending out invitations on Facebook, but I want to personally, right now, extend an invitation to you and Devon. October 20."

I had secondhand embarrassment for her, just as I did when she invited herself to Morgan Doyle's slumber party in the sixth grade.

"That sounds nice." Erin looked over to her. "I'm not sure what I've got on my calendar. I'll be sure to check, though."

"But you will come, won't you? I mean, if you aren't—if you don't have a previous engagement, I mean? October 20. At the community center," she repeated while I hid my eyes behind my hand.

"Sure, Della," Erin said. "We're friends on Facebook, aren't we?"

"Yes, we are."

"Send me the invitation. I'll be there if I can."

"Garden of Eatin' is catering. Dr. Faulkner is my boss, but he, well, he's my friend and his stepsister owns the place and she's doing all the food. I p-picked the salmon," she stuttered.

"That's right. I forgot you work for Brian." Erin placed a package of meat in her shopping cart.

"Oh yes. I started working for him when I moved back from Chattanooga a few years ago. We're good friends." Della grinned like a Cheshire cat.

Erin looked around and then asked in almost a whisper, "Are the rumors true, Della?"

"What do you mean? What rumors?" Della whispered back.

"The rumor that Brian is going to be arrested for forging prescriptions for Shelly." Erin raised her perfectly plucked eyebrows. "I heard he's been supplying her and her less-than-reputable friends."

"What?" Della shrieked. "Well, no! Who—why would you think that? Who said that?"

"That's just the rumor." She shrugged. "Clay Station is a small town, you know."

"Erin, he—Brian is a good man. Some bad people are trying to bring him down. There's no truth to it. I've been with him for years. I've never known him to do anything dishonest. He's a good man."

"I'm glad to hear that. Brian has always seemed like

such a nice guy. I was hoping it wasn't true." She smiled. "Well, I'll be seeing you. Bye, Darby."

"Bye, Erin," I said.

"Don't forget the party. Be looking for the invitation," Della called as Erin walked away.

"Well, that was something." I looked back to the roast options.

"You see that?" Della looked to me, her face beet red and sweat forming beneath the brim of her hat. "You see all the trouble you and that boyfriend of yours are causing Dr. Faulkner?"

"What?"

"Cliff and his brother are telling people Brian has done something wrong. Erin is talking about it. You're ruining his reputation, and I'm the one who has to defend him," she protested through gritted teeth.

"No, you don't have to defend him, Della."

"I do. I just hate you, Darby!" she shrieked, loud enough to capture the attention of passing customers.

I took my usual place behind the cart and let her lead the rest of the shopping trip.

22

DELLA REDD

I was so livid I ground my teeth the entire drive home from Piggly Wiggly and could taste specks of my metallic filling in the back of my mouth. Darby and I didn't speak a word as I hurriedly navigated the country roads and she sat stiffly in the passenger seat with crossed arms. When we got to the house, I quickly unloaded the groceries while Darby put them away, and Birdie began to brown the roast on the stove. I told Birdie I had another errand to run and scowled long and hard at Darby before driving to Magnolia Trace. I had to speak with Dr. Faulkner and apologize for my idiot sister and her meddling boyfriend and his no-good brother for spreading malicious lies that could cost him his medical license. I had to help him get ahead of this and clear his name.

I sped past my familiar parking spot on the street and pulled into the paved driveway for the first time. The scorching summer sun pelted me as I hurried to Brian's front porch and banged the gold-plated door knocker. The navy-blue door opened and I welcomed the gush of cool, refreshing air on my flustered face. Brian was standing before me, so handsome, in khaki shorts and a lavender beach shop T-shirt. Lavender. I almost fell into his arms.

"Della, what are you doing here?"

"I'm sorry, Dr. Faulkner. I had to come talk to you. May I please come in? I won't take but a few minutes of your time." My heart pounded.

"Of course you can." He opened the door wider and I stepped over the threshold. "It's nice to see you."

His home smelled magnificent. No specific odor—just the smell of him. The same smell attached to his white coat. Clean. Manly. Enticing.

I followed him through the attractively decorated two-story foyer and thought a painting of Billie Holiday would look exquisite on the large wall to the left. We soon entered the modern kitchen that I'd only seen through window-panes and he asked, "Is everything okay?"

"May I sit down?" I motioned to the rectangular table with a linen cloth.

He pulled out a chair for me and sat in the one beside it. I removed the hat from my sweaty hair and placed it on the table next to shiny salt and pepper shakers. I wanted to pause and take in everything—every photo on the wall, every rug on the floor. But I didn't have the time. We had to solve this problem. Together. He'd be so grateful I had come to him that he'd pull me close and tell me—

"Well?" he asked curiously. "What brings you by? Were you visiting the Mahoneys again?"

"No. I'm sorry. I'm a little frazzled." I pulled sticky hair from my forehead. "My sister. My stupid, stupid sister."

He looked puzzled. "What do you mean? Does Darby need some medical advice? I'd be glad to help."

"No, Dr. Faulkner. Thank you, though. You're always so kind. So considerate," I said. "Which is why none of this makes sense."

"I'm not a mind reader, Della. You want to fill me in here?" He folded his hands on the table.

"My sister is dating Mitchell Waters's brother. Do you know Mitchell?"

He squinted his eyes. "No, I don't think so."

"Mitchell is the guy Shelly has been seen with all over town. He was at her house the day I went by and confronted her back in April." I mumbled, "How embarrassing that was."

He flinched, uneasy, in the ladder-back chair. "Oh, I see. I guess I do recall her mentioning his name. Tried to block that out, you can understand."

"Of course," I said. "Mitchell told his brother Cliff, who is my twin sister's boyfriend—"

"Do I need to write this down?" he teased.

"I know it's confusing." I grinned. "Mitchell told Cliff that you have been writing prescriptions for Shelly. That you are the one supplying their pills."

He shook his head. "I can't believe that."

"May I have a drink of water, Dr. Faulkner?" I asked. "I'm sweating bullets here."

"Sure," he answered as he walked to the Sub-Zero refrigerator and pulled out a bottle. "So Mitchell is saying that I give Shelly pain pills? Why would I do that?"

I took the bottle from him and said, "I know it's absurd," before guzzling the water.

He sat back down at the table. "I have worked tirelessly to get Shelly into a treatment facility. I have loved her for twenty years, and her drug use ruined all our lives. There is no way I would give her the poison that has torn our family apart."

"Well, of course, Dr. Faulkner. It's such a ridiculous claim. You've got to do something about this. Word must be getting around because I saw Erin Drake today at the grocery store and she asked me if it was true."

He sat back in the chair. "Erin Drake? Devon's wife?"

I nodded.

"That Devon Drake is quite the Chatty Charlie. I'm sure he's told everyone at the club. No wonder I got some odd looks while I was playing golf this morning."

"Mitchell probably doesn't even remember telling his brother all this. He was high when he did, but he also said the police are watching the three of you. They may even be tapping the clinic phones."

"Well, this is all very interesting, Della." He rubbed his chin and looked out the kitchen window. "Sounds a lot like something you'd see on television, doesn't it?"

"I just had to tell you so you would be prepared if anything does come of this."

"I appreciate you telling me." He tapped his fingers on the table. "I will speak with my lawyer about this. It's libel. That guy can't get away with spreading these false accusations."

"Oh good, Dr. Faulkner." I sighed in relief. "I just don't

want to see you get mixed up in this. I don't know why they would make up such a cruel thing."

"Shelly probably told him she gets her pills from me. She will do or say anything to hurt me. She's so angry Remi stays with me when she comes back home because she doesn't want anything to do with her mother. Addiction is a terrible thing. It has a domino effect and impacts everyone in its path." He winced.

"Isn't that the truth?" I nodded. "I'm sure you know who my mother was, don't you?"

"I do." He looked at me sympathetically.

"Her alcohol addiction is what killed Mrs. Goolsby and her three kids. My sister and I have been punished for her mistakes our whole lives. Melanie still ridicules me, the same way she did when we were children. It's something we've never been able to live down. Even my grandmother has been ostracized because of it."

"I had no idea." He reached across the table and took my hand. I soaked in the incredible, natural feel of our skin touching. "I was in middle school when your mother's accident happened. My father and Hampton Goolsby were dear friends. A tragedy for them, yes, but I did think of your mom. So young and beautiful. It was a terrible mistake that could happen to anyone. I know it has been devastating for your family as well."

As he still held my right hand, I quickly used my left to wipe the tear before it streamed down my cheek. "Thank you for that, Dr. Faulkner."

"Would you like me to say something to Melanie? She's an adult now and shouldn't be acting like that. I didn't know the extent of her mocking, Della, or I would have addressed it already. I don't want that kind of adolescent and cruel behavior going on in my place of business."

"That's okay." I smiled. "I'm an adult too. I can handle it."

He patted my knuckles before letting go and said, "Listen, I'll get this all figured out. You didn't have to tell me this, so I sincerely appreciate it."

"I—I would be remiss not to."

"You're a good woman." We both stood from our chairs and I placed the fedora back on my sweaty hair. "I like that hat. Always been a fan of the fedora. Wish it was still standard for men to wear them. I think I'd pull off the look just fine."

"You would." I felt my face turn warm as I followed him to the front door.

"Really, Della, you're a loyal employee. Friend," he said as I crossed over the threshold and into the quiet heat. He unexpectedly leaned toward me and wrapped his arms around my waist. I closed my eyes, rested my head on his shoulder, and slowly inhaled the smell of his neck. I felt faint in his strong arms.

"Of course," I whispered.

"Don't worry about this another minute." He pulled away. "I'll get it all squared away before I see you at work on Monday morning, okay?"

I could no longer speak, so I silently nodded before he shut the door.

23

DARBY REDD

I yawned while the thick cuts of bacon popped in the cast-iron skillet. A line of storms rolled through after midnight, and it was impossible to sleep over the booming thunder rattling my bedroom window and the heavy pine limbs scraping the roof. I texted Cliff to see if he was awake, too, and he was. We messaged each other until there was a long pause between seeing the lightning and hearing the thunder. Although I'd downed two cups of dark coffee from Della's purple-striped mug that morning, I was still exhausted and wanted only to curl up in the bed for another hour or two. Perry was alert, though, sitting at my socked feet and waiting for a crumble to fall to the linoleum floor.

When the bacon was crisp, I sat at the bar and sleepily dipped it in the maple syrup that puddled around the mound of pancakes on my plate. I thought about the conversation with Cliff only a few hours earlier. Cliff revealed he was anxiously awaiting autumn because he favored the chilly night air and campfires. He was already twisting my arm about camping on Tippo Bayou when the leaves started changing from lively green to burnt colors. I had no desire to dress in fleece and freeze in a tent all night or eat Beanee Weenees from a can along with Cliff's catch from the creek, but I would probably agree if he insisted enough. He influenced me to try new things and be more outgoing. If it wasn't for him, I'd still have a crick in my neck from staring at the warehouse floor all day.

I still hadn't developed romantic feelings for Cliff, and I didn't know if I ever would. He was a friend, a confidant. He was a safe place for me to land. I was fine if this was to be the extent of our relationship. I only hoped Cliff could be satisfied with it too. I worried sometimes he would give me an ultimatum or grow bored of our friendship and walk away and romantically pursue another. I voiced my qualms to him over the telephone one evening, and he assured me our friendship would never end. He said he cared too much for me to ever abandon me. I believed him but needed to be reminded of it every now and again.

As Perry relentlessly stared at me, I was startled at the echoing ring of the living room telephone. I skipped from the barstool and hurried toward it before a second ring woke Birdie and Della. For the first time all morning, I was wide awake.

"Darby, I tried calling your cell phone first. Did I wake the whole house?" Cliff panted.

"My cell phone is still in my room. I didn't hear it ring. Is everything okay?"

"I couldn't wait until work to tell you."

I spoke quietly into the receiver so as not to wake my grandmother and sister. "Tell me what?"

He started talking a mile a minute. "You know we've been thinking this whole Faulkner and Mitchell thing had blown over since nothing has come of it in over a month? Well, two policemen banged on my door at darn near 4 a.m. this morning. Made Dad awful mad. They were looking for Mitchell. I just talked to Gary, and they went to his house this morning looking for Mitchell too. Scared Tanya's kids something awful. They can't find him anywhere. I'm going to assume Shelly and Dr. Faulkner are next. They may already be in custody. Who knows?"

"Oh me," I worried aloud before noticing Perry had leapt onto the kitchen counter and was devouring my bacon. "Get down!"

"You need to let Della know what's going on. She'll be scared to death if the police barge into her office this morning. They tossed mattresses around and looked under beds and in closets like something right out of a movie. I ain't ever seen nothing like it in all my days."

"I'll wake her right now. Thanks, Cliff. I'll see you at work."

I shooed the cat away from my plate and entered Della's dark room with the violet curtain panels drawn. Perry hopped onto the lavender down comforter, his whiskers dripping with syrup, and snuggled against her. I pulled one of the panels back to cast some light into the room and illuminate the feline hair floating in the air.

Before Mother died, this was the bedroom Della and

I shared. I remembered the iron double bed I rarely slept in was catty-corner to a big olive-green dresser with mismatched mirror. During a thunderstorm I wouldn't stay tucked in next to Della more than fifteen minutes before I ran out of the room and nuzzled next to Mama or Birdie in their beds. Della never followed me. She stayed in this room at the back of the house all alone, determined not to get scared no matter what treacherous weather roared outside the windows. Della was strong-willed from the time she was born. She was strong-willed in pursuing friendships and in pursuing love. Strong-willed in staying here to take care of Birdie, even when it wasn't necessary.

A wooden dollhouse once sat in the corner. It was secondhand, as was everything else we owned, and only came with a miniature plastic couch and a couple of dolls with tangled hair and missing shoes. Our Ken doll didn't have any clothes of his own and wore one of Barbie's T-shirts—lime green with "Rad" written in a lightning-bolt font on the front. The first (and only) spanking I ever got from Birdie was when I put SpongeBob SquarePants stickers on the bedroom wall. Birdie made me get my own switch from a junk tree in the backyard and gave me a long spiel about taking care of things before she swatted my backside. I spent the rest of the afternoon scraping glue and white sticker remnants from the paneling.

That old iron bed and green dresser were both long gone now. When Della moved home five years ago, she splurged on a king-sized poster bed that took up nearly every square inch of the little bedroom. There wasn't space for a dresser or chest of drawers—just a bedside table that seemed miniscule next to the monstrosity of a bed.

"Della? Della?" I stood over her as she slept soundly.

"What is it?" she grumbled from her pillow.

I tapped her shoulder beneath the mounds of blankets. "Come eat breakfast."

She looked to the digital clock on the bedside table. "It's only five thirty. Go away."

"Della, please get up," I said as she hid again. "Why don't you come get a cup of—"

She threw the covers off her head and growled at me, "What do you want, Darby? I don't have to be up for another hour."

"I need to talk to you."

"What in the world do you need to talk to me about at the crack of dawn?"

"This morning the police showed up at Cliff's house looking for Mitchell. They might come to the clinic today."

She became alert and raked her messy dark hair out of her eyes.

"I just thought you should be prepared."

"I'm not worried about it. Brian has nothing to do with any of this. Tell your boyfriend I'm sorry his brother went to jail."

"They didn't catch Mitchell. He'd already taken off."

"Oh, so his brother is a fugitive? You really picked a winner, Darby." She disappeared beneath the purple comforter again while Perry cleaned my breakfast from his paws.

"I'm worried about you." I began to sit on the edge of the bed, but she kicked me away.

"Worry about your in-laws and leave me alone," she moaned before vanishing beneath the blankets again.

● ● ●

Although the sun was welcoming and warm, Cliff and I had lunch in the cafeteria so I could watch the local twelve o'clock news on the small television hanging on the wall. I scarfed down a peanut butter and jelly sandwich and a bag of cheese puffs while expecting to see the SWAT team bust through the door of Faulkner Family Medicine and fly feetfirst into the front windows of the small, brown-brick building hidden behind overgrown crepe myrtles. I was prepared to watch Della emerge from the clinic in a purple ensemble with her arms flailing, but the biggest news story of the day was Farmer Mason's pig being rescued from a well.

"That darn Mason has had at least three pigs fall down that well." Cliff laughed. "You ever heard of such?"

● ● ●

After work, I glanced out the kitchen window and saw Della's car barreling up the driveway with a thick trail of dust behind it. As I rinsed the romaine leaves beneath the running water at the sink, she came through the back door, whistling. She soon entered the kitchen with a spring in her step and a chipper grin.

"You're in a good mood." Birdie smiled at her as she scooped spaghetti with homemade meat sauce from the Dutch oven and into three ceramic bowls.

"I sure am." She took a seat at the bar and her cat hopped into her lap. "Ask me why, sister dear."

"Why?" I asked dryly and patted the wet lettuce with a dish towel.

"Because my boss and dear friend, Brian Faulkner, was not arrested today, nor will he be arrested any other day."

"Arrested?" Birdie screeched and wiped her hands on her stained and tattered plaid apron. "What in Sam Hill are you talking about?"

"Ask Darby. She and Cliff have this crazy idea that Dr. Faulkner is involved in script forgery and who knows what else. Probably trying to pin Jimmy Hoffa's disappearance on him too."

"That isn't true," I mumbled.

Our grandmother leaned against the kitchen counter and looked back and forth between us. "Darby, what in tarnation is she talking about?"

"It's quite the story, Birdie," Della answered. "Go on, sister. Tell her all about it."

"Darby? Please clear this up." Birdie folded her hefty arms and rested them on her large stomach.

"Cliff's youngest brother, Mitchell, has a drug problem. You know that, Birdie. Cliff told you that day out on the porch, remember? Well, Mitchell hangs around with Dr. Faulkner's ex-wife, Shelly. They get pills from Dr. Faulkner."

"What a joke." Della smirked.

"It is true that Shelly and Mitchell pal around together, isn't it? They are both drug addicts?" I asked Della. "And the police were looking for Mitchell this morning. Which means they are likely looking for Shelly too."

"Yes." She paused. "But that doesn't mean Brian has anything to do with this. What kind of sense does it make for the man who wants to see her recover to give her pain pills?"

"It doesn't make sense. I'm just telling you what Mitchell told Cliff." I shredded the lettuce in a large, clear Tupperware bowl.

"So this is what's been going on with you two?" Birdie asked. "I knew there's been an elephant in the room for a while now, and for once it ain't been me."

Della said, "Shelly is just trying to cause trouble for Brian. She's trying to turn their daughter against him. Nobody showed up to arrest Brian today, and no one will. It's simply not true. There's nothing for you to worry about, Birdie."

"Darby?" Birdie looked to me, but I remained quiet. "For crying out loud. You two have been bickering your whole lives long. It's high time you learn how to get along. One day I'll be dead and gone, and all you'll have is each other. You're supposed to be on the same team. You're supposed to root for each other. All this hullabaloo makes my heart sad." Birdie turned back to the counter and began shredding parmesan cheese over the spaghetti.

I locked eyes with Della. "If this is all a lie, I'm sorry for the trouble it's caused you and Dr. Faulkner. I was only trying to protect you."

I pulled salad tongs from the drawer and she answered, "I'm sorry too. For all the things I said on the Fourth of July. I didn't mean it."

I glanced over at her and nodded.

"There, there, girls. That's better."

24

BIRDENA REDD

TUESDAY, AUGUST 22, 2017

I trusted Brian Faulkner's daddy, Patch, as far as I could throw him, and considering he was a man of three hundred-plus pounds, that said it all. I didn't have faith in a doctor with cholesterol higher than my own. If he wasn't smart enough to take care of himself, I didn't see how he could do right by anybody else. Seems he had a lot of misdiagnosed patients. Evelyn Beatty went to Patch complaining of headaches. He pumped her full of ibuprofen until she died from a brain tumor. That was why our family always saw Dr. Millhouse. He ran marathons. I could trust my well-being to a man who ran marathons. He was in his late sixties now, and I saw in the paper he came in first place in some race in Memphis last spring. He was a pillar of health, but I wasn't a bit surprised when Patch Faulkner fell out of a booth at Sit a Spell when he was in his early fifties and died right there of a massive coronary on the checkerboard floor.

The more Darby talked about Brian Faulkner, the more I thought he was as untrustworthy as his daddy.

I hadn't ever talked to Shelly Faulkner a day in my life, but I knew her daddy, Wylie Warren, was a veterinarian in Panola County, and her mama, Jenee, peddled overpriced makeup to anyone within earshot. They lived in a fine cypress house on the north side of town. When you lived in a town as small as the fine point of a needle, you heard things, and I heard Mr. and Mrs. Warren were swingers. Gracie told me they had a fishbowl for partygoers with the same vile interests to put their keys in. Nothing but pure evil, if you asked me, disregarding the sanctity of marriage and instead treating it like a game show where the prize was a romp in the hay with a stranger.

Nothing had come of Darby's claims about Brian Faulkner keeping his wife higher than a hippie in a helicopter, but dirty birds flock together, and I wouldn't doubt any shady dealings coming from a marriage between Patch Faulkner's and Wylie Warren's kids.

Della hadn't told me for sure, but I thought she was smitten with Brian Faulkner. I suspected that when she asked me to make chocolate pudding for the man. You don't take chocolate pudding to just anybody. I didn't want Della to fall for anybody in this town, much less a doctor rumored to be crooked as a dog's hind leg. She didn't need a reason to stay around here when she flourished so well in Tennessee. I knew Della's true love was in some far-off town, and he weren't no rascal like that Kevin fella she fell in love with either. There was a good-hearted man out there eager for her to get out of Clay Station and find him. If she was waiting on me to die before she did it, I wished the good Lord would call me on home.

Darby, though, seemed to have found a good match with this local boy, Cliff Waters. His maw was a maid to all the rich folks around town, and they didn't let just any old riff-raff clean their houses. Must have been a fine, trustworthy woman, and I figured Cliff was all right too. He'd done a good work on Darby. He'd accomplished what I'd tried to do all these years—to coax her out of her shell. When I heard her giggling on the phone behind her closed bedroom door and saw her walking around with her eyes looking upward instead of at the floor, I felt like I was full of sunshine. There was something to say about looking up. When we walk outside, it's our first inclination to glance at the sky. It's a sign of being expectant, hopeful, and Darby did that now. She looked up.

I'd wanted joy and genuine friendship for Darby since she was knee-high to a grasshopper. I'd wanted her to see and to be seen. And I was mighty grateful I'd lived long enough to watch it come to pass.

25

DELLA REDD

The Craigslist inquiry for "escort" produced results that left my face blushed crimson and a lump in my throat. I might as well have typed "prostitute" in the search bar. I immediately deleted the search history on my phone in fear that I would die on the way home from work and the police would discover what I'd been searching. My obituary would probably read: "The depressing debacle known as Della Redd's life ended only hours after she searched online for a male prostitute."

All I needed was a thirtyish-year-old bachelor to accompany me to my birthday party. Surely I could find a respectable man within a hundred-mile radius to agree to drive to Clay Station, show up on my doorstep in a tuxedo, and spend a couple of hours with me at the community center. His only requirements were to sit next to me at the aubergine table decorated with tea candles while we feasted on honey-glazed salmon, walk me to the cake table, and twirl me around the dance floor to a couple of songs. No commitment. No hanky-panky. I solely needed a semi-handsome man to pretend to love me and smile next to me for a few Facebook photos.

Knowing my luck, my escort would take full advantage of the open bar and turn into a drunk gigolo who blabbed our secret to Melanie. Soon laughter would spread throughout the party as he passed out his "escort" business cards to everyone in the room. I suddenly became very nervous at the pathetic and absurd notion. Hadn't I learned my lesson with fake gifts and boyfriends in the past? I tossed my phone on my desk and put the idea out of my mind for good. I would go to the party alone, as I somehow always knew I would. Unless some random man walked into the clinic covered head to toe in poison ivy and there was instant kismet when our eyes met as he clawed his itchy skin, I was destined to go stag. I squeezed my eyes closed and prayed that when I opened them, my knight in shining rash would be standing before me. Instead, it was Rosie Permenter.

"Chest pains since 7 a.m., Della," she groaned.

"Melanie or Camilla will call you back soon, Mrs. Rosie." I reached for her chart on my cluttered desk.

"I couldn't bear to go to the ER. They'd just leave me in the waiting room all day to die. The pain is intense, Della. Please get me back as soon as you can. I only have one aspirin left to chew." She rubbed her left arm.

"Have you been eating Milk Duds again, Mrs. Rosie?"

"No." She shook her head. "Last night I had fajitas with jalapeño sauce. This morning some pepper jelly on a biscuit. But no Milk Duds."

"Have a seat." I nodded to one of the plaid chairs.

Not thirty minutes later, Mrs. Rosie came out of the exam room with Tagamet samples. Not surprisingly, her EKG reading was normal, and she felt much better after a big burp. I bid her good day and filed her chart, knowing I would probably see her again in a couple of days. A cold front was moving in tonight. She'd be back on Monday complaining of pneumonia.

Only Ms. Crosby remained in the waiting room. She attentively watched the soap opera on the television in the corner while chewing on the earpiece of her reading glasses in her hand. I noticed the sun was glaring right on the screen, making it nearly impossible to see the look of misery on the heroine's face after discovering her husband was the father of her sister's baby.

"Ms. Crosby, you want me to shut those blinds for you?" I offered from behind my desk.

"You stay put, dear. I'll get them."

"Just turn that little dial there on the window frame," I said as she stood from the chair and approached the window.

As she grumbled and fiddled with the knob, I looked past her to see a black SUV with tinted windows pull into the parking lot. I wondered who it could be since Ms. Crosby was the last patient scheduled before the lunch break. Before I could put it all together, four men dressed in matching crisp dark suits walked through the front door of the clinic. One of the men, who had the shiniest bald head I'd ever seen, stopped at my desk while the other three walked to the back of the clinic without hesitation or invitation. I was glad Mrs. Rosie had already left. Having those men bust in on her and Dr. Faulkner in an exam room would have given her the heart attack she thought she'd had.

"We're here for Dr. Faulkner, Della," said the bareheaded man standing before me. My heart fluttered.

"You know my name?" I was on the verge of tears. "How do you know my name?"

"We've been watching the clinic for some time," he said in a soothing manner. "There's nothing for you to worry about. We're only here for Faulkner."

"Why?"

"We picked up Shelly Faulkner and Mitchell Waters in Panola County this morning. Dr. Faulkner has been supplying them with narcotics for some time."

I sighed in distress and looked to the back of the eerily quiet clinic. There was no shouting or sounds of Dr. Faulkner being thrown against the wall as he resisted arrest. No crashing of filing cabinets being tipped over or gunfire or Camilla and Melanie shrieking. All was still. Too still.

"Della, what's going on, dear?" Ms. Crosby interrupted the silence from her chair in front of the television.

"I'm not sure, Ms. Crosby. Just sit tight," I said, hoping to pacify her.

The bald man spoke up. "Ma'am, I'm sure sorry, but Dr. Faulkner won't be seeing you today."

"But I need a prescription refill on my blood pressure medicine. I have to see him today. I only have two pills left." Ms. Crosby's eyebrows furrowed with worry.

The agent shook his head. I could sense his anger with Dr. Faulkner for putting poor Ms. Crosby in such a predicament. "If you'll call back in a couple of hours, Della here will explain everything to you and work on getting what you need, okay?"

"Della?" She looked to me for confirmation.

"We'll get this all figured out, Ms. Crosby," I promised as she hesitantly grabbed her purse and walked out the front door, but not before looking back at the soap opera on the television one more time.

I examined the agent standing before me in his expensive suit. The scent of his aftershave was clean and appealing. I glanced to his left hand and noted the absence of a wedding band. He certainly didn't have Dr. Faulkner's thick hair, but he was handsome nonetheless.

Would you like to accompany me to my birthday party in October?

Dr. Faulkner emerged from the back of the clinic with the well-dressed, intimidating men walking closely beside him. Our eyes briefly met, and he looked annoyed. I could see he was sorry he'd been caught, but I feared there was no remorse for the immoral thing he'd done. I was troubled that he didn't look concerned Ms. Crosby was going to be without blood pressure medicine or that Mrs. Rosie would be panicked over chills caused by the imminent cold front and would need his reassurance Monday morning. He didn't care that I felt betrayed. He wasn't the helpful, attentive physician or the man I thought him to be. I had been conned. We all had.

"Cancel the rest of my patients," he ordered before they disappeared out the front door. I didn't know tears were falling until I felt them drip from my chin and onto my keyboard.

"My colleagues are going to take him in now, but Agent Sawyer and I are going to stick around to look through his records. Some other agents will be joining us soon. Please start canceling patients. We don't want anyone else coming in today," the bald man requested.

"What do I tell everyone? Will Dr. Faulkner be back tomorrow?"

"No, he won't. Tell his patients they need to find another doctor."

"What about my job?" I panicked.

He patted my desk. "I sure am sorry about all this. I always hate to see the effects one person's illegal actions have on innocent people."

He moved to the back of the clinic seconds before Melanie and Camilla darted into the waiting room and peered through the window blinds to watch Dr. Faulkner being placed in the back of the SUV.

"What. Just. Happened?" Melanie asked.

"I know what's going on," I said with my head down. I usually delighted in knowing things before my coworkers, but that wasn't the case this time.

Camilla rushed to my desk. "Know what? Tell us, Della."

As I filled them in, they listened intently, mouths agape. Why he would do this made no sense to any of us.

"He must be a drug addict too. He's got to be. That's the only logical explanation. Shelly probably blackmailed him into giving her pills. I bet she said she'd squeal on him if he didn't give them to her anytime she wanted," Melanie theorized with an energy drink in hand.

"If he is taking pills, he's hidden it well. He's never acted strangely at work," I said.

He must've been high when he winked at me and called me beautiful and raved over that chocolate pudding.

"How will I pay my rent next month?" Camilla worried aloud. "I can't go back to my parents' house. They don't even have Netflix. What will we do?"

"What a selfish man," Melanie groaned. "He didn't think about the three of us, did he? How we depend on him. Della, you've probably gotten the worst of it. Don't you live with your grandmother to help her out financially?"

I wasn't quite sure how to respond to a legitimate question from Melanie instead of a sarcastic one.

"I do," I said. "My sister helps, but neither one of us can afford to miss a paycheck."

"We've all been duped. I'd like to gouge his eyes out." Melanie slammed the can onto the counter. "His poor daughter. Both of her parents headed to jail. He sure ruined the Faulkner family name with this stunt."

It was a good thing Remi was already out of Clay Station, because she'd never live this down if she were a young kid walking the halls of Tallahatchie County High. She'd be ostracized, just as Darby and I were for the mistakes of our mother.

"They're rummaging through the files and cabinets in his office. What are they looking for? Is he guilty of other things? Has he been supplying pills to every drug addict in town?" Camilla wondered. "His medical license is as good as gone."

"Della, let us help you cancel appointments. It's going to

be a big job. Show us what we need to do," Melanie offered, and I almost fainted and fell out of my swivel chair.

Camilla and Melanie used phones at the back of the office and assisted me in canceling every appointment in the book, scheduled as far as six months out. When questioned by the patients, I answered with, "Due to unforeseen circumstances, Dr. Faulkner will no longer be practicing medicine. I've spoken with Dr. Wendell's office and they are gladly accepting new patients." With the help of the nurses, we knocked out the task in less than an hour. When the local news station set up in the parking lot and filmed agents carrying boxes, binders, and computers from the office, every line began to ring like church bells. I finally took the phone off the hook and sat at my desk with my head in my hands, overwhelmed by it all.

Before leaving with one last box of files, the handsome bald man, whose name I learned was Agent Mulroney, explained to Camilla, Melanie, and me that Dr. Faulkner was being accused of falsifying patients' medical records and billing insurance companies for services that never occurred. Mulroney said that while Dr. Faulkner hadn't been doing drugs himself, they could prove that he had written unnecessary prescriptions to others besides Shelly. Shelly knew all his shady dealings and probably blackmailed him into keeping her in supply. The Mississippi Bureau of Investigation had been closely watching the Faulkners, local addicts, and pharmacies, so it had been a long time coming. I guess it was a relief he wasn't in an altered state of mind when he told me I was beautiful.

I thought back to the scorching summer day when I'd

visited Brian to inform him of what I thought to be malev-
olent lies. I remembered his hand on top of mine and the
hug we shared. He was manipulating me and knew I would
hang on his every word because of my adoration for him.
Dr. Faulkner used me, and he would have continued to do
so if he hadn't been caught. If I had ever discovered the
insurance fraud, he probably would have taken me to Rare
Company for a steak dinner in exchange for my silence. And
in the frazzled emotional state I was in since moving back
to Clay Station, I probably would have foolishly complied.

● ● ●

When I got home from work that evening, exhausted and
distraught, I immediately walked to Birdie standing in the
kitchen with the potato masher in her hand. Without saying
a word, she reached for me and I fell into her arms like I did
when I was a child. Birdie's hugs were warm, her shoulders
were soft, and resting on her chest felt like the safest place
in the world. It always had.

"It's going to be all right, dear girl," she whispered.

I felt Perry rub against my ankles. "You saw it on the
news, I guess?"

"Prentice called and told me all about it. I tried to call
the office to check on you, but the line was busy. I'm just
so sorry, my love. Who knew Dr. Faulkner would do such
a dumb thing? A rooster one day and a feather duster the
next."

For the first time that day, I laughed.

When I pulled away from her, she ran her fingers through

my hair. The purple pansy I'd tucked behind my ear that morning had long since fallen to the office floor, trampled by the detectives who were hauling things down the hallway.

"I loved him, Birdie. At least I thought I did. I'm such a fool. First Kevin and now this. Why can't I pick a good one?"

"You're no fool." She took my face into her hands. "You're a beautiful, intelligent woman, and you're still young. You're just a baby. There's plenty of time for God to send you the right one. Keep praying. Keep trusting that the best is yet to come."

I didn't know Darby had entered the kitchen until I felt her thin arm drape around the waist of my purple jeans. I turned to her. "I've been so unkind to you. I'm sorry."

She dipped her head, and the lovely bun at the nape of her neck grazed her shoulders.

"I've always thought of you as my fixer-upper. And when you got all fixed up, without my help, I didn't know how our relationship worked anymore. I should have been happy for you instead of envious, Darby. I really am proud of you. I'm proud that you're my sister. Whether you're introverted or extroverted or your knees are covered or—"

"You worry entirely too much about my knees."

I shrugged.

"It's forgotten." She took my hand into hers, and I noticed her short nails were painted light pink.

"Heavens to Betsy! You girls have worn me slap out with your hissy fits and ruffled feathers. If I had my druthers—"

Darby interrupted, "Hold your horses, Birdie. What language are you even speaking?"

26

DARBY REDD

SATURDAY, OCTOBER 14, 2017

The house was chilly and I shuddered beneath my T-shirt as I sat on my bed and watched out the window. The beloved heat of summer and my sun-kissed glow had long faded, and crisp autumn air and pale skin had taken their place. I'd transformed in many ways over the last several months, but my abhorrence of the cold was unchanging. I hurried to grab a sweater before Cliff arrived to take me shopping at Taliaferro's.

While I searched my closet for the beige cable-knit cardigan, I thought about how surreal it was that Della and I were about to turn thirty years old. Despite the long schooldays tolerating ridicule and the dark, lonely hours mourning our mother, worrying for our grandmother, and trying to be unseen (or seen in Della's case), life was fleeting. In my mind, I was still a young girl who enjoyed the solitude of the fields around our house and climbing into the pine tree fork in the front yard to write or listen to Mama's Bob Dylan tape in her Walkman. My aching feet after an eight-hour work shift and the subtle lines forming around my eyes were the only things that reminded me I was no longer fifteen.

It was also hard to believe only six days remained until the party my sister had been planning for nearly a year and Birdie even longer than that. Since Dr. Faulkner was arrested six weeks ago, Della spent her days curled up on the couch with her shedding cat watching television or dashing around the house with the phone glued to her ear, making last-minute arrangements for the party. I didn't hear the excitement her tone once possessed at the mere mention of the celebration. The twinkle in her eye was gone. The elation at the event had been replaced with dread. Now it seemed more like an obligation, a chore. She crunched numbers and fretted over costs since she was now living on unemployment. She hadn't looked for work in Clay Station, as far as I knew, and I was hopeful being without a job would motivate her to leave town and look elsewhere for one.

Faulkner was out on bail, awaiting trial, and his medical license was as useless as Monopoly money. Shelly was out as well, but Mitchell wasn't going anywhere. He had enough priors to keep him in an orange jumpsuit for a while. The scandal was the talk of the town and the subject of an article in the newspaper every week, which only added fuel to the small-town gossip fire. The blinds on the clinic's windows had been drawn tight and brown weeds had overtaken the sidewalk cracks. The crepe myrtles that lined the building were overgrown and in need of a trim. Brian Faulkner's reputation was ruined for good in this town. There were no second chances here.

I was apprehensive about the party on Friday. I was concerned no one would show up, or even worse, they all would.

Not because I was too timid to be among a crowd anymore, but because it was possible the Tallahatchie County High School class of 2005 harassers would attend with a mission to mock Della or pry information out of her about Faulkner. I had recently worried more about the party than Mrs. Dalton's German shepherd while I scrambled eggs in the wee hours of the morning.

●　●　●

"What about this one?" Cliff held up a slinky strapless number that made me shiver just looking at it. It would provide zero warmth.

"I haven't changed *that* much, Cliff," I said as he placed it back on the hook and adjusted his glasses. "I don't know if I'm ready for this." I browsed the rack of dresses. "I'm not as shy as I was a few months ago, but a party? I still get nauseated at the idea."

"You keep shootin' this party down in flames, Darby. Have you thought that you might actually have a good time?"

"No." I slid one hanger after another down the rack.

"This party ain't just for Della. It's for you too."

"It's always been for her."

"You ain't a scared, skittish person anymore. This birthday party is a good chance for you to show who you are now. A new birth, kind of. To announce loud and clear, 'I am Darby Redd! Hear me roar!'" He snorted.

"I may not talk in a whisper anymore, but I don't plan on roaring anytime soon." The faint sound of Muzak played through the department store speakers. "And besides, I've never worried about showing anyone who I am. I didn't care if Melanie Reid and Kelly Ragan and whoever else thought I was shy, and I don't care if they know I'm not anymore."

"I still think you might have a good time. You don't have a thing to worry about. I'll be right there with you. And if it's too much for you, we can always leave and go grab a burger at Sit a Spell."

I smiled at him before holding up a conservative short-sleeved gown in black. "What about this?"

"I like that one. Try it on," he said before pulling a burnt-orange sleeveless from the rack. "And this one too? It's a good one for fall, ain't it? Orange like an autumn leaf."

I reluctantly took the dress from him and stepped into the dressing room while Cliff waited outside the door on a bench.

"I'm still so glad you heard from your mother." My blue jeans fell to the floor and I reached for the orange frock. Much too bold a color for me, but I would appease Cliff by trying it on.

"Yeah. I thought about getting a coat for her while we're here. She left the address of the halfway house where she's staying. No telling what kind of coat she's wearing. Probably ain't no count."

"That's nice of you." I stepped into the maxi dress with a flowy tiered skirt.

Once I zipped the side, I gave myself a long, hard look in the full-length mirror and was astonished to see I had a figure. I tousled my hair on top of my head and posed the way

Della used to when we were kids and she pretended she was a famous supermodel. For the first time ever, I was pleased with my appearance.

"Well? You gonna let me see or not?" Cliff rapped on the dressing room door.

I slowly opened it and stood before him while feeling a bit self-conscious at the evident waistline and bust that had long been hidden beneath bulky sweatshirts.

"Wow, Darby. You look gorgeous." Cliff's eyes were more bulbous than usual beneath the thick lenses.

Gorgeous was an adjective I'd never heard used to describe me. I glanced back to the mirror, my cheeks red from blushing at Cliff's compliment, and I saw my mother's reflection. My mother, who I'd thought was the most gorgeous woman I'd ever seen.

"You mean it?" I asked.

"Of course I do. That's the dress. Don't even try on the other one. I'll get it for you."

"You don't have to do that." I shook my head and glanced at the seventy-five-dollar price tag hanging from the armpit. "I can—"

"Let me do this. It will be my birthday gift to you, okay? I can afford it, Darby," he insisted while continuing to eye me from head to toe. "I've been working overtime. It's really no trouble."

"Thank you." I felt like jumping up and down.

Cliff purchased the dress and a pair of sparkly, strappy nude heels, despite my resistance. I helped him pick out a new suit that fit him like a glove right off the rack and a warm fleece coat for his mother. We joyfully left the department store with the shopping bags swaying in the crook of our interlocked arms.

When I arrived home that night, I found Darby on the couch with two of the TV trays propped in front of her, both covered in receipts and papers and her purple planner scribbled with colored pens and highlighters.

"Where you been?" She glanced over at me as I sat in my familiar spot on the couch.

"I went to Taliaferro's after work and got a dress for the party."

"Darby! You did?" She beamed. "Well, where is it? Let me see it!"

"It's hanging in the hallway. I'll show you later."

"Is it black? You would look beautiful in a bright—" she began.

"It's orange like a traffic cone. Cliff talked me into getting it. Unfortunately, I won't be blending in with the dark tablecloths," I said as she grinned with delight. "What are you doing?"

"Going over the cost of the party again." She chewed on the end of the purple pen. "It's really dipping into my savings. I didn't expect to be unemployed when the time came to pay for everything."

"Why don't you let me help cover some of the cost?" I volunteered.

She looked to me. "I can't ask you to do that, Darby."

"You're not asking. I'm offering. Let me chip in. This party is for me, too, isn't it?"

"Of course, but—"

"I have the money, Della. I want to help," I said as she

smiled with gratitude and patted my knee. "How many are coming?"

She held up one of the papers on the TV tray. "Only seven have RSVP'd 'maybe.' Isn't that embarrassing?"

"Seven more than I thought would *maybe* show." I shrugged and peered over her shoulder at the planner. "Who all did you invite?"

"Don't hate me." She bit her lip.

"I make no promises."

"I posted the invitation on the Class of 2005 Facebook page. There are 114 members in the group. Rachel said she's swamped with work and unable to fly out. I think I burned that bridge. I probably should call her and have a long talk." She exhaled. "I also invited Katie Beth, but she's on bedrest with her pregnancy. Erin responded she may come. Melanie, Jenny James, and Kelly Ragan said maybe." She looked to me. "Of all people, I wish she wasn't coming. She's going to ruin everything like she always did."

"I'll be sure to keep my tissues hidden in my pocket," I said.

Della rubbed her forehead in frustration. "What in Sam Hill am I doing, Darby? I wasted my childhood trying to impress the popular crowd. And then I moved away and was finally secure in who I was and no longer cared about being accepted by people I found unacceptable. And now look at me. Thirty years old, back in Tallahatchie County, Mississippi, and I've invited people I can't stand to our birthday party. And for what? Just so I could walk in with some doctor in an attempt to make them jealous of me? How juvenile is that? What is wrong with me? I'm delusional, aren't I?"

"At times, yes." I poked her playfully. "Della, you've just

been searching for your place. Your tribe. Some security. And you know as well as I do that you have a bright and successful future outside of this old stomping ground. Don't let Birdie, or me, keep you here. We're both fine. You have to live your life. You have to plant yourself in the right place to bloom. Promise me you'll at least think about it?"

"Okay," she agreed.

"Why don't we take a new approach to this party?" I suggested. "Instead of making it some mic-drop moment to gain the acceptance of people who don't amount to a hill of beans, why don't we just celebrate us? Celebrate how far we've come and all the good things we have in store? I mean, that's what a birthday party is for, isn't it?"

"I guess."

"It's their loss, Della." I put my hands on top of hers. "All those girls, they don't deserve *you*. It's not the other way around. You have to believe that. Chattanooga Della believed that. Clay Station Della has to believe it too."

She nodded as Perry jumped into her lap.

"You know Birdie's favorite scripture? Apostle Paul in Philippians? She recited it to you before you hopped in your car and took out of here after graduation. Remember? 'Forgetting what is behind and straining toward what is ahead.' It's time to do that again."

Her eyes quickly watered, but she wiped them with her palm.

"I could post a little something in the Facebook group. Let it be known that we don't want anyone there with ill intentions."

"Then *no one* will come." She rubbed her running nose.

"More room for us to dance, then," I said. "Our own private party. A band and a big old cake just for us. You know I'd prefer that anyway. We'll feel like royalty, being waited on hand and foot."

"Well, purple does represent royalty. And you know how I feel about purple," she said before grabbing her laptop from the cushion next to her.

"Unfortunately," I muttered.

Since it was my first time to post anything on social media, Della found the Facebook group and showed me where to type for all the invitees to see. I tapped the keys while she went to the kitchen to help with the parmesan chicken Birdie was cooking for dinner.

Tallahatchie County High School Class of 2005

For the first thirty years of our lives, many of you found pleasure in our misfortune. Most sneered at our secondhand clothes and frayed backpacks, the off-brand sodas we brought from home to drink with our reduced-price lunches, and the holes in our worn shoes. Some of you tripped us in hallways and stained our clothing with whatever was within arm's reach, whether it was ketchup or playground mud or permanent marker. When our mother died in a tragic accident, you offered us no sympathy or condolences, but instead called her a murderer and even desecrated her grave. Many reading this have been cruel and callous and oftentimes succeeded in tearing us down and making us doubt our self-worth. Maybe you had hurt in your own lives that you didn't know how to deal with, but that was no excuse for being cruel to us.

But the years have come and gone and we've all attained different forms of success.

While many of you have been blessed with beautiful children and spouses, Della and I have not (yet) experienced the joy of being wives and mothers. It's true we still live with our precious grandmother in the shotgun house on Yocona Road. But we are fortunate because we are blessed with the love of family and each other. We are privileged to have our health, a roof over our heads, money in the bank, and hope and a future. We have succeeded because we have forgiven the callous words and actions instead of allowing them to scar us.

We find all of this to be a fantastic reason to celebrate.

If maturity and wisdom have prompted you to outgrow the boorish ways of your youth, we would be pleased to have you join us for a delightful meal of honey-glazed salmon and birthday cake, followed by dancing to the melodies of the well-renowned jazz band Dizzy Davis to celebrate our thirtieth birthday and other achievements. (No gifts, please, as we have everything we could possibly want.) If you have yet to shed your insecurities and worn-out adolescent mentality of unkindness, we would appreciate it if you'd decline our invitation and spend your evening elsewhere.

Join us this Friday evening at six at the Clay Station Community Center.

Or don't.

We'll be fine either way.

Della and Darby Redd

27

DELLA REDD

I went early to the community center Friday afternoon to supervise the placement of the bandstand and tables. I was astounded at the transformation of the large, boring room where the Shriners met for bingo night each week. The cinder-block walls were concealed by purple velvet draperies. The ornate three-tier cake with cascading pansies, courtesy of Cookie's Bakery, sat alone on a simple round table in the corner. Members of the band, resembling the Rat Pack, hauled instruments and amplifiers through the side door and set up around the parquet dance floor. The plastic tables were covered by dark cloths and decorated with the chrysanthemum and tea candle centerpieces I had envisioned while Perry snuggled next to me in my bed. Metal chairs had been wrapped in dark linen slipcovers, and the caterers were fast at work in the small kitchen at the back of the room. It was elegant and nothing short of amazing to see my vision come to life.

I wished I hadn't come by to check on things. It would have been divine to enter the community center at six that evening and be surprised at the stunning change along with everyone else. I hoped it wasn't bad luck for me to see it so soon, the way a bride and groom are meant to remain hidden from one another until the ceremony. But I clung to the hope that the ambience, the band playing, the tea candles flickering on the tables and casting a dim, romantic glow throughout the room would take my breath away when I returned for the party.

My fingerprint was certainly all over the affair, from the numerous yet coordinating shades of purple to the pansies on the cake and the draperies on the walls, but this was going to be Darby's night as well. Since she had posted in the Facebook group, the RSVPs increased by the dozens. Guests commented that her post was well articulated and they looked forward to seeing us both. I was realizing that Darby had always been wise. Even in eighth grade when she consoled me after I was the only one in my homeroom not invited to Melanie's end-of-the-year pool party, she gave me the astute advice not to let Melanie's rejection define who I was.

If I had listened to her then, my high school years would have looked more like my time in Chattanooga. As a kid, she didn't let the words and actions of individuals linger for long. Sticks and stones—that was Darby's adage. The gangly guy in ill-fitting glasses meant the world to me because he'd taught my sister that although it was okay to be quiet and reserved, it was good to open up too. Cliff had chipped away at Darby's cocoon and triggered a metamorphosis. She'd blossomed into a colorful butterfly with outstretched wings.

This night was also for Birdie. I wanted my grandmother to disregard seventy-seven years of burdens and heartaches, if only for a few hours. I hoped the deaths of Mama, Grandaddy, and Aunt Willa wouldn't cross her mind once as she rested in the arms of Prentice Mims on the dance floor.

● ● ●

Mr. Prentice arrived at our house at five fifteen that evening. He was handsome in his tan church suit and sage-green tie. His thick hair was shiny and neatly combed to one side; not a hair was out of place in his impeccably trimmed mustache. He bought a cream-palette wrist corsage for Birdie, who accompanied me to Taliaferro's last week and allowed me to purchase a dress for her. It was a classic cream A-line with lace collar trim and a wide brown belt. She wore her hair in her familiar way, piled in a bun on top of her head, but she allowed me to apply shimmering coffee-colored eyeshadow to her wrinkled lids and maroon lipstick to her thin lips. She looked like a million bucks, and Mr. Prentice couldn't keep his eighty-year-old eyes off her. He said she resembled the same young girl who used to dance in the arms of Joe Edward Redd at the honky-tonk out by Lake Louise. *Spitfire.* That's the term of endearment he used.

I thoroughly examined myself in the full-length mirror on the back of the bathroom door before I left the house that evening. I, too, felt confident in the high-neck, short-sleeved lace dress that was flattering to my figure. I paired it with a small silver clutch and matching heels and twisted a wide braid into a loose bun at the bottom of my neck. I situated the small moth orchid Mr. Prentice purchased for me from the flower shop into the braid and wore the amethyst teardrop pendant Birdie had given me on my birthday the year before.

● ● ●

The sun had already set and a harvest moon was glowing when Mr. Prentice, Birdie, and I pulled into the parking lot in my car. The lampposts that lined the front of the community center glowed softly, warm and inviting. We exited my Cruiser, still damp after driving through the car wash down the street. I couldn't let it be seen covered in dust and dirt from the gravel drive and fields being plowed around our house. Before I'd even shut my door, Cliff's little truck sputtered to a stop in the parking spot adjacent to us. It had not been washed in a month of Sundays.

Darby stepped out in the orange dress and looked absolutely fabulous. It was so refreshing to see her in a bright color. She had allowed me to style her hair in a loose and wispy ponytail with stray hairs framing her slender face. I also did her makeup, but I kept it light. I wasn't jealous of her beauty; instead I was proud of the bold, courageous woman she had become. Even if she had attended the party in gray sweats with her hair hiding her face, I would have been thrilled that she'd attended at all.

I think I was more excited about Cliff's new glasses than he was. He'd picked up the sleek rectangular frames at the optometrist's office only a few hours before the party. Darby had prompted him to get fitted for them last week and explained to him that he didn't have to spend twelve hours of his day pushing spectacles up his nose. Cliff said the thought had never occurred to him. The best part was the glasses remained over his eyes instead of dangling from the edge of his nose. Cliff's hair had grown out a bit and his white scalp was no longer visible through a buzz cut. I knew Darby didn't care about his appearance either way, but I think Cliff felt better about himself since his mini-makeover too. He took Darby's hand below a corsage of fall flowers on her wrist and walked with self-assurance.

I refused to wallow in self-pity because both my grandmother and sister had dates and I didn't. My perspective about the party, about life, had changed. As Darby suggested, this was going to be a celebration of our accomplishments. She was a talented poet with the voice of an angel and a forgiving heart and knew contentment in itself was success. I was victorious in finally taking my sister's sage advice. I refused any longer to base my self-worth on the tragedy surrounding my mother's death or the harsh words spoken to me in school hallways. If forgetting what was behind and straining toward what was ahead was good enough for the apostle Paul, it was good enough for me. And my future was not in Clay Station, Mississippi.

● ● ●

I pushed open the heavy black door of the community center, and my family and I were greeted by the sound of the keyboardist perfectly performing "Autumn Leaves" by Vince Guaraldi. Seeing the room in the glow of candlelight made my heart flutter, and for the first time in a long time, I was proud and confident.

"This is elegant, Della. Absolutely elegant." Birdie covered her mouth with her wrinkled hands topped in costume jewelry she'd dug from her dresser drawer.

Mr. Prentice glanced around the room. "I was just in here playing bingo last week. Don't even look like the same place. You sure this is the Tallahatchie County Community Center? I think we walked into Buckingham Palace." He laughed and nudged Birdie.

"Della." Darby wrapped her chilly hand around my forearm. "You've outdone yourself."

"You like it? Not too much purple for your taste? I'm sorry I didn't include you more in the planning." I searched her glowing face for approval.

"I could do without the purple velvet. A bit too much what I imagine Prince's bedspread to look like." She motioned to the draperies on the walls. "But this is magnificent. Have you ever thought this is what you should be doing? You have a gift for this."

"A gift for what?"

"Party planning, Della. Look around the room. You did all of this. This is your vision come to life. This takes talent, and you're responsible for it. I can't even coordinate my clothing, and you managed to transform a bingo hall into a ballroom."

"You really think so?"

"Yes! Birdie, don't you think Della would make a fabulous party planner?"

"Sure as shootin'." Birdie continued gazing about the room in awe. "There's a lot of money to be made in this, too, dear. Now, you can't always decorate in purple. Purple ain't everybody's cup of tea. But I think you could make the sacrifice, couldn't you?"

"It's just a cake and some drapes on the walls and—"

"Don't sell yourself short. This is fabulous," Darby repeated. "Now, your staff awaits your command."

The waitstaff, hired by Garden of Eatin', stood attentively to the side of the room, dressed in classic black.

"Ms. Redd," the head waiter greeted me, "I hope everything is satisfactory."

"It's wonderful, thank you. Just perfect," I said to the young man in tortoiseshell-framed glasses.

"The staff is at your ready."

"I'm not sure how many guests we'll have," I said nervously.

"Whether it's the five of you or fifty, we will do everything possible to make this evening enjoyable for you all." He smiled and then glanced to the bartender waiting at the back of the room. "The bar is open if you'd like something."

"We don't drink," I said. "The bar is for the other guests. If they show, that is. Otherwise, that's going to be a very bored bartender tonight."

"Understood." He nodded. "But he makes a pretty good mocktail, too, if that interests you. The food is being prepared and will be served promptly at seven. Happy birthday to you and your sister. Enjoy yourself."

"We certainly will, young man," Birdie called as he walked away.

We chose a table beside the dance floor and sat down as spotless glasses filled with water were placed before us. I guzzled the frigid ice water, and as it numbed my throat I became a bit anxious at the thought no one else would arrive. I quickly and purposefully changed my mindset. Even if it was just the five of us all evening, we'd enjoy our meal and dance. We'd allow all ten servers to wait on us hand and foot. We'd rest easy in our beds tonight with full stomachs and full hearts and enough leftovers to last us until Christmas.

Darby leaned into me and asked, "When you and Faulkner's stepsister discussed the catering, did she mention anything about him?"

"Not a word," I said. "She's sweet as pie and still honored the discount, but no conversation about his arrest. I'm sure she's embarrassed."

I looked to Mr. Prentice and Birdie sitting across from me, talking quietly, sharing secrets the way lovers do. He muttered something amusing and she cackled loudly, like a hyena, before playfully swatting at his arm. The sight of them flirting like teenagers made my heart leap in my chest. Grinning, I then looked at Darby and Cliff. He tapped his long, slender fingers on the table to the jazz ballad while Darby subtly swayed to the beat. Before I could lean into Darby and pose my request for her to do what would have been unthinkable just a few months before, I saw Melanie and her husband walk into the room, with Camilla on Melanie's heels.

I sighed and announced to our table in a deflated tone, "The nurses are here."

"Well, that's good, isn't it?" Birdie turned her heavy body in the slipcovered chair.

"We'll see," I said as I stood from the table and approached them.

Melanie and Camilla were both wearing black cocktail dresses that hit above their knees. I typically only saw them in scrubs and had to admit they did clean up well. Camilla's long, dark hair was in beachy waves and Melanie's dishwater-blonde locks were held in a loose bun with invisible bobby pins. Melanie's husband was dressed in a khaki sports coat and crisp blue jeans with a crease down the leg.

"Della, this is my husband, Daniel," Melanie said as her husband with the large cranium extended his hand and gave me a warm smile. Melanie met him when she went off to Mississippi State, so I hadn't a clue about his history or if he was a bully in his younger days like his wife.

"Nice to finally meet you, Della," he greeted me kindly. I immediately felt remorse for ever thinking his head resembled a watermelon.

Melanie nudged Camilla in her bony ribs and she finally spoke up. "Hey, Della."

"This really looks lovely," Melanie said as she glanced about the room.

"Very purple," Camilla added.

"But we wouldn't expect it to be any other way, would we, Camilla?" Melanie cut her eyes at the youngster by her side.

"No one is here yet," I said, somewhat embarrassed at the empty room.

"I talked to Erin and some of the others. They will be here."

"I see a bar." Camilla tapped at Melanie's pale bare arm. "I'm in the mood for something fruity. With an umbrella."

"Mel, I'll get us a table." Daniel removed his arm from his wife's waist. "Della, again, thank you for the invitation. It's wonderful to finally meet you."

He turned on his heels and followed Camilla, but not before stopping to greet my family on his way to the empty table beside them. Cliff stood to shake his hand and they conversed for a moment.

"Your husband seems like a nice guy. How did he end up with you?" I teased.

She playfully shrugged. "Listen, Della. I really appreciated what your sister wrote in the Facebook group. It made me stop and think of the awful way I've treated you all these years. As kids and then when you moved back and started working for Dr. Faulkner. You haven't deserved any of that."

"Melanie—"

"Let me finish, Della. I don't know why I picked right back up with my despicable behavior when you came back to Clay Station. Maybe because Camilla thought picking on you was funny. But one line Darby wrote in that post stuck with me."

"Which one?"

She squeezed her eyes closed, as if trying to remember. "'If you have yet to shed your insecurities and worn-out adolescent mentality of unkindness,'" she quoted. "That struck a nerve. I am insecure. Always have been. Probably stems from having a daddy who told me I wouldn't count for anything. Said I should have been a boy. Angry there was no boy to carry on the Reid family name." She avoided my eyes. Probably because if hers caught mine, she'd cry. "But that doesn't matter. I have been unkind and adolescent. I'm too old to play the mean girl. I apologize."

Birdie was right. Hurt people do hurt people. It wasn't an excuse, but at least there was something to pin Melanie's malice on—an unsupportive father who made her feel less than. I wondered what reasons the others might have had for hurting me and Darby so. Did Kelly Ragan grow up in a household where her mother lived vicariously through her? Pushed her to be the head cheerleader, the straight-A student, the popular one at all costs because she wasn't? Did Devon Drake live with parents who threw dishes and blows at one another? I'd never know. But I found relief, I guessed, in knowing there was a reason of some kind for the things Melanie had done.

"Thanks for that, Melanie. Apology accepted," I answered. "You know, I've been adolescent and unkind as well. I've thought terrible things about you."

"Apology accepted," she repeated and paused for a moment. "Camilla will never apologize, though. As my grandmother would say, that dog won't hunt."

"Your grandmother says that too?" We laughed. Together. Instead of at each other. I continued, "I know I was a weird kid. I was extra. Always tried too hard to fit in. Lied to do so. And I'm still weird. I wear flowers in my hair and light-up sweaters and give everyone a hard time about mayonnaise. I've given you plenty of ammunition."

"You are weird. I won't deny it," she said. "But you're a good person, Della. You should be treated kindly. And one of us, someone, should have shown you compassion when your mother died." Her eyes were downcast, ashamed.

"Well, enough of that." I cleared my throat before I did something really weird like sobbing and pulling her into my arms. "Have a drink and enjoy yourself while we wait on some others to get here."

"I'd like to say hello to your sister and grandmother first, if that's okay?" she asked as I pinched my own hand to ensure I was not hallucinating.

"They'd appreciate that."

● ● ●

People began trickling through the door to the dancing flames from the tea candles and soft jazz welcoming them. I was in such a tizzy at actual bodies moving around the shadowy room that I could barely process whose faces I was seeing. There was no mistaking Erin, though. She arrived solo, in a classy cornflower-blue romper with ruffled sleeves.

She approached me, grinning, and said, "Everything looks fantastic. Goodness, Della, you really outdid yourself."

"Thank you." I felt my cheeks blush as she stood before me, her long gold earrings shining against her honey-colored hair.

For years I'd wanted to thank Erin for her quiet support—for the sympathetic glances and the consoling nods. I'd always been too intimidated to talk to her about it, but I knew now was the time.

"You were always nice to me." She stopped scanning the room and looked at me. "You didn't treat me like the others did. It's long overdue that I thank you for that."

"I could have done more." She shrugged. "I could have said something to them. I could have reached out to you. I could have—"

"You could have joined in their bullying, but you never did."

"I was proud to see you finally take up for yourself, and for your sister, when you smacked Kelly. She could be pretty terrible back then. Well, I guess she still can be." Erin rolled her eyes. "I try not to associate with that crowd anymore. Devon is friends with their husbands, which is the only reason I even invite them to our Christmas party. Honestly, I could live the rest of my life without listening to Jenny talk about her obsession with Louis Vuitton bags. I've found some great friends in a small group of ladies from my church. In fact, we get together for Bible study on Tuesday nights. Maybe you and Darby would like to join us?"

"Darby and I would both like that." I smiled as the band played the unmistakable percussion intro of "Mambo Inn" by Count Basie. "Speaking of Devon—"

"Migraine." She cut me off and casually chewed her bottom lip.

I suspected Devon didn't have a migraine, but instead was one of those Darby mentioned as still possessing the juvenile mentality of spitefulness. The last time I saw him at Piggly Wiggly, Devon had a receding hairline, and his once-athletic physique had changed due no doubt to buckets of hot wings and pitchers of beer. He sneered at me like I was a leper when we passed each other at the deli. I was relieved he hadn't shown up and put a damper on the evening.

Erin walked away while the room buzzed with chatter and the soundtrack of Count Basie, and I watched the wait-staff line rectangular tables with chafing dishes. I counted the guests loitering around the bar and conversing at tables and was pleasantly surprised to reach the number twenty-five. Twenty-five people had taken the time out of their busy schedules to celebrate my twin and me. Not a one uttered a nasty remark or even questioned me about Dr. Faulkner. It appeared they were all genuinely enjoying themselves. Some of the faces I recognized and others approached me to rein-troduce themselves. "We had geometry together." "I moved to Clay Station our sophomore year." "You may remember me. I was in ROTC." These classmates had never been on my radar because I was too busy wasting my time pining for the approval of the popular group to notice others who had also been exiles of the clique. Cheyenne Cooper, Cicely Buford, Tatum Winfred. We could have encouraged one an-other if I hadn't been so self-absorbed and tossed them aside because they were "nobodies." I was no better than Melanie or Kelly Ragan. I hadn't verbally ridiculed anyone, but I was judgmental just the same.

As I took in the scene of the bustling room, a heavyset man wearing a lilac tie over a crisp white button-down ap-proached me.

"Della? You don't remember me, I'm sure, but we had American history together. Mrs. Firestone? Third period our junior year?"

"Hi." I stretched out my hand and he wrapped it in his—warm and soft like a fleece glove on a winter's day.

"Matthew Borden," he introduced himself. "Fatty Matty? I played the trumpet in the band. Had a face full of zits and a wispy mustache that wouldn't grow no matter how much I prayed over it. I gave up on the mustache, but my face is smooth as a baby's butt now." He let go of my hand and grazed his flawless cheek.

I laughed and was struck by his dazzling brown eyes with flecks of green. "Matthew. Yes, I remember."

I did remember. I remembered Matthew walking down the school hallway lined with burgundy lockers in khaki pants with his trumpet case, his large thighs rubbing together and causing his feet to bow outward. Like Darby and me, he, too, endured high school hell, but I never befriended him. I never showed him the compassion I had coveted.

"Still Fatty Matty though." He winked at me and patted his round stomach. "I love what your sister wrote in the Facebook group. A lot of these folks tormented me, too, but I got out of Tallahatchie County and did all right for myself. Moved to Fort Payne, Georgia, and started a little car lot. Clunkers and the like. But now I own the largest dealership in DeKalb County. I don't tell you that to toot my own horn, but I happened to be in town visiting my dad this weekend and decided to stop by to celebrate my accomplishments right along with you. And, of course, to wish you and your sister a happy birthday. I always remember you as real nice girls. Never once called me Fatty Matty."

I never called him anything. I wished I could go back in time and strike up a conversation with him before

Mrs. Firestone started a lesson on the industrial revolution. Ask him to meet me at the arcade after school. Call him by his full name of Matthew.

"My wife died in a car accident two years ago. Very similar situation to your mother. My Ginger was a drinker. Hit a telephone pole and that was that." He shrugged his hefty shoulders.

"Oh, Matthew, I'm so very sorry."

"I believe God's ways are higher than mine. Have to trust His plan is best. That keeps me going."

"Saint Paul called us to forget the past and strive toward what lies ahead."

"Indeed he did." He grinned. "Philippians."

"What about your kids? How are they?" I fished.

He chuckled. "No children for Ginger and me. The drinking took such a toll on her body. Wasn't easy for her to conceive. Again, I have to trust in a higher plan. A better one than my own."

"Your faith is inspiring. I sure am glad you decided to stop by this evening." I motioned to Mr. Prentice and Birdie seated in their chairs. Birdie was tapping her feet, which were about to bust out of her black flats, to the upbeat song. "Would you like to join my family at our table?"

He smiled to reveal perfectly aligned teeth that must have been the product of braces. "That's awful nice of you, Della. I'd like that."

"Come along, then. I'll introduce you," I said. "And I love that lilac tie."

● ● ●

Darby remembered Matthew and the trumpet solo he performed for a band recital at school. "So What" by Miles Davis. I had no recollection of it, so I must have skipped out on the assembly. Being the jazz aficionado I was, my ears would have perked at the distinctive, smooth intro. I would have sought out Matthew Borden after his solo and talked jazz with undoubtedly the only other kid at Tallahatchie County High School who knew who Miles Davis was. Matthew and I conversed about our favorite genre of music as we slowly marched down the buffet line and the long-awaited salmon was served on our white plates. I had also requested one small dish of prime rib for Camilla in case she came. Not that I was very concerned if she blew up like a balloon from the fish, but I didn't want her medical emergency to hinder the party.

"We're having a fabulous time, Della and Darby. The food looks amazing," Jamie Gibson cheered as she passed me with her plate and pink cocktail in hand.

I thanked her and said to Darby in line behind me, "I think we're a hit."

When Matthew and I reached our table and settled in our chairs, Darby held up her fork with a bacon-wrapped vegetable and said, "I've never tasted finer asparagus in my life. Have you, Birdie?"

"I declare. It's real fancy. Boy, I tell you what, Prentice, have you ever had asparagus cooked like that?"

"I don't think I ever had asparagus." Mr. Prentice chortled. "Not too keen on any vegetable that hasn't been dredged in bread crumbs and then tossed in Crisco."

"I can't believe I'm saying this, but the hollandaise sauce isn't half bad either."

Birdie laughed heartily and her hefty shoulders bounced like she was on a trampoline. "Della just ate a condiment! I never thought that dog would hunt."

● ● ●

When the chafing dishes in the buffet line were nearly empty, guests piled onto the parquet dance floor. As I scanned the crowd, I noticed Kelly Ragan was not among them, which was okay by me. She probably took offense at Darby's intelligent words, which proved some mean girls were destined to remain mean.

"Well, I'm full as a tick on a hound dog." Birdie covered her mouth to suppress a burp.

"I don't know about y'all, but I need to burn off a few calories," Matthew said with a cackle and tossed his linen napkin to the table. "Della, would you care to dance?"

"That would be nice." I nodded and felt warmth in my cheeks.

Cliff, Darby, Mr. Prentice, and Birdie all pushed away from the table cluttered with empty dishes and soiled napkins and followed us onto the floor. Matthew took me into his strong arms, and I sank into him the way I took to my comfortable place in the crook of the couch after a long day. He felt warm and safe in a way I thought only Birdie could feel. We slowly moved about the floor as the band began Glenn Miller's "Moonlight Serenade," and I rested my head on his broad shoulder and looked to Darby wrapped in Cliff's arms beside us. She casually gave me a thumbs-up before Cliff whisked her into a turn and her back was to me.

Before the song was over, Mr. Prentice put his hand on Matthew's shoulder and asked to cut in. Matthew cheerfully complied, placing my hand into Mr. Prentice's, his palm rough like leather and his knuckles speckled with gray hairs. Then Matthew turned to Birdie and twirled her around by one hand. She giggled like a schoolgirl and said, "Hold your horses, young man! I'm not as agile as I once was."

Mr. Prentice nimbly slid his worn brown loafers across the parquet and pulled me along with him.

"You've still got moves, Mr. Prentice. I bet you were a real ladies' man back in the day."

"I put on my muscle rub before I left the house."

"Well, don't get too crazy," I said. "I did not put mine on today."

"I'm glad we have a few minutes alone, Della," he said close to my dangling silver earring. "I don't think I've had the chance to tell you what your Birdie means to me."

"I know you love her, Mr. Prentice." My mouth was closer to the top of his gray head than to his ear, as I was nearly three inches taller than he was.

"When you spend two long years watching the person you love more than anybody else die, you wonder if you'll ever find love again. And after that, if you can even think of being with somebody else, it's for one reason only. Love. I love your grandmother, Della. I intend to take care of her as long as the good Lord allows me."

I felt light as air in the old man's embrace because his promises lifted a twenty-five-year-old weight. Since the night my mother died, I'd felt responsible for Birdie. Even as a little girl in pigtails, I worried she'd be the next one to be ripped away from me and Darby. Every morning I asked if she'd taken her pills. I popped a quarter into the pay phone in the cafeteria at school on my lunch break to call Piggly Wiggly and confirm she was okay. There was always the foreboding thought that she would die and leave Darby and me alone. I feared we'd end up in foster care or we'd be split up. I thought that mindset would fade when we reached adulthood, but it didn't. I called home multiple times a day when I lived in Chattanooga. Even while I was out with friends at trivia night, an ominous vision of Birdie falling on the floor and gasping for air would cross my mind and I'd quickly excuse myself from the pub table to give her a call.

When Darby phoned to tell me Birdie had a stroke, it was my worst fear realized. I couldn't bear to think about life without her, but now it was time for me to humbly loosen my grip on my grandmother. Just as she'd given me roots and then wings, it was my time to do the same for her. It was time to release her into Mr. Prentice's care.

"You're never too old for love, dear girl. And you? Well, Della, thirty ain't nothing. You've got plenty of time to find love and get married and have young'uns of your own. Maybe you're well suited for that fella over there swirling my Birdie around." He cut his eyes toward Matthew. "He'd better keep those hands above her waist."

"Thank you, Mr. Prentice." I pulled him into a tight hug and inhaled the scent of the menthol muscle rub on his shoulders.

"Della, Della!" Melanie interrupted our embrace. "Look at the door. Look!" She took my head into her hands and swiveled it to the left.

I squinted my eyes across the dim room to see the figure standing near the entryway. I wasn't sure, but it appeared to be Brian Faulkner, right there in the flesh, standing in the threshold. I knew for sure it was him when other guests began to notice him. I saw their mouths moving, but their snickers and whispers were drowned out by the jazz melody. I suspected if the band knew who he was and the local infamy surrounding him, they would abruptly cease to play and shine a spotlight on him standing there, looking sheepish, with his hands deep in the pockets of his dress slacks. The lead singer of Dizzy Davis would likely pull the microphone close to his mouth and announce, "Ladies and gentlemen, Dr. Brian Faulkner, prescription forger and insurance scammer, has just entered the building."

Camilla rushed to Melanie, me, and a thoroughly confused Mr. Prentice and gasped, "Is he even allowed to be here? Shouldn't he be under house arrest or something?"

"I don't think so." I glanced down at his shining leather shoes. "I don't see an ankle monitor."

"The nerve of that man! How dare he show up here?" Melanie balled her fists and tightened her hot-pink lips into a straight line.

"I'll go see what he wants. Excuse me, Mr. Prentice," I said as I walked away.

"Della?" Darby reached out for me when I passed her and Cliff on the dance floor. "Why in the world is he here?"

"You need me to throw him out, Della? I may be nothing but bones, but I can toss a man out by his collar if need be," Cliff offered. "Years of wrestling with my no-good brothers taught me that."

"No, no, Cliff. Everything is fine." I patted his shoulder as if he were a dog about to let loose on the mailman.

As I got closer to Dr. Faulkner and his chiseled, handsome face and fresh haircut came into plain view, I felt every eye in the room on the back of my neck. My face and chest flushed warm with hives.

I was greeted by his familiar scent and asked, "Dr. Faulkner?"

"Hi, Della." He awkwardly shifted from one foot to the other. "You look beautiful."

"Thank you."

"You think anyone has noticed I'm here?" He slyly grinned and nodded to the crowd behind me.

"Why are you here?"

"I was invited, remember? My stepsister *did* cater this event. And by the way, the leftovers on that plate right there look delicious." He pulled his hand from his pocket and pointed to a half-empty plate on the table nearest to us.

"Yes, you were invited. Before you were arrested and stripped of your medical license and I lost my job."

"Oh, that. That must be why everyone is staring. I thought it was because I look so handsome this evening."

For the first time, his flattering wit was lost on me.

"I think you should go."

"I don't intend to stay," he said. "I had the party saved on my phone calendar, and when I saw the reminder today, I wanted to stop by for just a minute. To apologize."

I tilted my head. "Apologize?"

"Yes, I owe you, Melanie, and Camilla apologies. Because of my imprudent actions, you are all unemployed. I bear that burden. Despite what you may think, I am remorseful. I truly am repentant for what I've done to my employees and patients who have trusted me all these years."

"I'll call Melanie and Camilla over so you can—" I turned to summon them, but he reached for my arm.

"No, Della." He shook his head. "You know how they are. They'll relish the opportunity to cuss me up and down in front of a crowd. They thrive on applause, you know? I don't want that to overshadow this lovely evening. I trust you'll apologize to them for me."

"I will."

"The day you came to the house to tell me what you knew, I took advantage of the fact that you had feelings for me. Instead of coming clean to you that day, I worked you. I took you by the hand. I gave you a hug. I would have done anything in that moment to save my own hide. I'm not proud of that. That's not who I really am."

"Thank you for that." I looked to the purple polish on my toenails extending from the sparkling heels. "Why did you do it, Dr. Faulkner? Why did you supply pills to Shelly and her friends? You knew the consequences. I can't understand."

"Greed," he responded, looking ashamed. "I falsified medical records. I received money from insurance that I shouldn't have. And for what? For Remi. She's going to medical school. It seemed like an easy way to provide for her. And to provide for Shelly too. She spent money quicker than I could make it. Shelly knew what I was doing, and she was in on it with me when we were married. And then, when she became dependent on pills, she used everything she knew as blackmail. She lorded my crimes over me. I just got in too deep, Della. And now I've lost everything."

I almost wanted to reach out to him, to console him. But good sense prevailed, and I refrained.

"You were a faithful, competent employee. And if I had any sense about me, I would have jumped at the invitation to be your date this evening. I should have been flattered that someone as lovely and kind as you found something about despicable me attractive."

"You're not trying to manipulate me now, are you?" I brazenly locked my eyes with his.

"I have nothing to gain by it anymore," he answered. "Well, I've caused enough uproar. This night isn't about me or how I've fallen from grace. It's an evening for you and your sister to celebrate. I'll go now."

I nodded.

"Happy birthday, Della." He took both of my hands into his, and I was relieved that I felt nothing. It was as if I were holding the lifeless plastic hands of the mannequin at Taliaferro's Department Store. I wouldn't be his pen pal in prison or smuggle a file in a cake to him. Every sentimental feeling I'd ever possessed for Brian Faulkner was gone. "I wish you all the good things."

And just like that, he turned and disappeared through the heavy wooden door.

Melanie and Camilla rushed to me as soon as he was gone, and I told them about the apology he offered to the three of us. I kept the rest of our conversation secret. It was no one's business but ours.

• • •

When it was time to cut the cake, the lead singer of the band called for Darby and me to convene at the table where the cake was so beautifully displayed. The crowd of guests surrounded us and sang while I suppressed tears of joy. After we blew out two white candles on the top of the three-tiered cake, Darby and I exchanged a quick hug and posed for a photo for Birdie before the servers sliced into the intricately decorated tower of white icing.

Matthew and I continued to talk about our love of jazz while we devoured the deliciously rich dessert. We shared stories of arriving home from school with degrading signs on our backs or stains on our clothes from the spiteful hands of others. He remembered a time Devon dumped the cafeteria garbage can over his head—on class picture day, no less. And when he was done reliving the painful memory, Matthew laughed. He didn't bellyache or act like a victim. He laughed at the past, and I laughed with him. What a relief it was to no longer be flooded with anger and resentment at twenty-year-old wrongdoings. To put them, once and for all, in the rearview mirror. Amid the sound of our harmonizing laughter, wounds were unexpectedly healed.

"Did you get out of here and go to college, Della? From what I remember you were a pretty smart kid." Matthew dabbed icing from the corner of his mouth with a napkin.

"Yes." I pushed the empty cake plate away. "I moved to Chattanooga after graduation. Went to community college and got my associate's degree. I came back to Clay Station a few years ago when Birdie had a stroke. I think it's time for me to get out of here again, though. Birdie and Darby say I did a pretty good job planning this party tonight. And to be honest, I enjoyed it. I'm thinking of maybe learning more about party planning and going back to Tennessee. I sure loved it there. I loved the air, the views, the people."

"Well, I'll be." He bounced with an enthusiastic laugh. "You've never been to Fort Payne, have you? I'm only an hour south of Chattanooga. I can see Lookout Mountain from my office."

"Well, I declare." We exchanged warm smiles. "The Lord sure works in mysterious ways, doesn't He?"

"I can attest to that." He winked at me, and I recognized without a doubt that it was a sincere act of endearment, absent of any manipulation.

● ● ●

While Matthew and Cliff both talked with a small group on the other side of the room, I saw an opportunity to approach Darby while she sat at the table alone and sipped her ice water. I pulled out the chair next to her and said, "I know we don't give each other gifts, but—"

"What do you want now, Della? I showed up, didn't I? I've eaten. I've chatted. I've danced," she teased me.

"And you've had a great time, haven't you? Admit it. Social situations aren't half bad, are they?"

"Surprisingly, I've enjoyed myself very much." She brushed some crumbs from the linen cloth into her manicured hand and tossed them on the empty cake plate.

"Well, then, I'm going to take credit for this party. I'm going to say this party is my gift to you. This lovely evening is what both Birdie and I have given you. It was her idea, after all. And her Visa is what rented this space. Which I will pay off since disability is her only income."

"And you want what?" She crossed her arms and rolled her eyes in good humor.

"You don't seem the least bit nervous to me. That hair of yours hasn't been tugged on once this evening. You're among friends. Not to mention that handsome man in sleek frames over there adores you." We both glanced at Cliff, who was looking very animated and flailing his hands around as he told a story to Matthew.

She tapped her wrist where a watch should be. "Get to the point, sister."

"Aside from writing poems, you have another God-given gift. And I want you to share it."

"I can't sing, Della." She adamantly shook her head.

"Can't never could." I smirked.

"Fine, then. I won't sing." She reached for the sweating glass of water. "Won't never will. How about that?"

"Your voice is what Mama passed on to you. I think of her every time I hear you sing. Birdie does too. I think Mama would be really proud of us, Darby. And if she were here right now, you know what she'd want more than anything? To hear you sing. You don't put a lamp under a basket. You put it on a stand for all to see. It's time to get out from under the basket."

She hesitated. "I wouldn't even know what to—"

"'Ode to Billie Joe.'"

"Oh, Della!" She chuckled. "I haven't sung that since we were kids."

"It was Mama's favorite, Darby. You know that. When she hung clothes on the line. When she swung us around the living room and we felt like we were flying. When she held you while the thunder boomed outside the window. That song represents so many moments of our childhood."

"Della, I . . ." She fidgeted, uneasy in her chair. "It's not even a happy song. Actually tragic when you think about it, yeah?"

"Every person in this room grew up with that song. They'll sing right along with you."

"Still." She sat silent for a few minutes and surveyed the dark room with squinted eyes. Finally, when she realized I wasn't going to leave, she huffed, "You owe me, Della Marie Redd."

She stood and passed Cliff, Mr. Prentice, and Birdie, who were walking back to the table.

"Where's your sister off to?" Birdie gently lowered herself onto her chair after Mr. Prentice pulled it out for her like a true gentleman.

"She's off to shine, Birdie."

Darby silently stood to the side of the bandstand and waited for the current song to conclude. Then she leaned into the guitar player wearing a fedora and skinny black tie. While she spoke into his ear, he appeared to cheerfully agree to what she said and then approached the lead singer, who bore an uncanny resemblance to Sammy Davis Jr.

"All right, all you cool cats," he said into the microphone. "We've got a real special treat for you tonight. The birthday girl herself, Ms. Darby Redd, is going to sing one for us."

The room erupted in cheers and applause, and Birdie looked to me with tears forming in her pale eyes. "She's really gonna sing, Della? What did you say to get her to do this?"

"Not much." I shrugged. "There's never been anything we could say to her, Birdie. She had to find the courage to do it herself. And thanks to Cliff here, she did."

Cliff sat at attention in the chair next to me. "She's really gonna sing?"

I patted his lanky hand resting on the table. "Thank you for giving her the confidence to share this gift with others."

"Oh geez, Della." His words and mannerisms resembled Goofy the cartoon dog. "I didn't do nothing."

"Don't sell yourself short, Clifton. You're good for Darby. You saw in her what Birdie and I have both overlooked all these years. You accepted her for who she is. You never forced her to bloom. And that's why she did."

"She's taught me a thing or two. I've learned I ain't got to gab all the time. I can give those hamsters on a wheel up there a little break." He tapped his temple. "There's a lot to be said for just being still. You can listen a lot better when you ain't talking."

The guitar player grabbed an acoustic from the stand behind him and pulled a wooden stool beside Darby and sat on it. I could see the apprehension on my sister's beautiful face as he strummed the first chords, and for a moment, I was nervous for her. But when she belted out the first lyrics perfectly, the partygoers cheered. And just like that, the uneasiness vanished. Darby looked like a natural, as if she'd been onstage her whole life. As if she were singing to a sold-out crowd in Madison Square Garden. She relaxed and raised the rigid arms at her sides to lift the microphone from its stand. She'd always been content being in the shadows, at the teacher's side reading a book, in the privacy of her bedroom penning what I imagined to be picturesque words dripping with emotion and wisdom. But now she appeared to be content being seen and heard, front and center. Her light had finally been placed where it belonged—on the lampstand.

When she reached the locally famous line, the crowd shouted the lyrics from the parquet floor surrounding her.

I clapped my hands in delight and looked to Birdie. She was staring at me from across the chrysanthemum center-piece while tears left clean streaks through her bright rouge, and she mouthed the words, *Can't never could.*

EPILOGUE

DARBY REDD

A thrush singing songs to daybreak woke me from beneath the mounds of fleece blankets that had shielded me from the cool autumn night air. The air mattress beside mine was empty, and the smell of dark coffee alerted my senses and prompted me to stretch. I peeked through the opening of the flimsy tent flap and saw Cliff squatting beneath the bald cypress and poking at a crackling fire. The silver coffee kettle was wedged between two of the tree's conical knees as a flame roared around it.

Because of the popping fire, I couldn't hear the Tippo Bayou flowing slowly at the bottom of the bank where we'd pitched our tent. It was such a peaceful noise and had helped muffle the sounds of Cliff snoring on the air mattress beside me the night before.

I leaned onto my elbow and pulled back the tent flap. Cliff looked over to me and grinned before tugging on his flannel jacket.

"Happy birthday."

"Thank you." I smiled.

"How'd you sleep? Get too cold?"

"No, I slept quite well, actually." I yawned. "How long have you been awake?"

"A while." He poked at the fire. "That dadgum thrush started whooping and hollering before it was even light out. Glad he woke me up, though. I wanted to make sure coffee was ready when you woke up."

Cliff reached for the tin cup beside him on the cold ground scattered with leaves and filled it to the brim. Then he rummaged through his backpack and pulled out two extra-large honey buns wrapped in cellophane.

"Breakfast of champions." He stood, his long, thin legs covered in sweatpants, and carefully walked the few steps to me so the hot coffee wouldn't spill.

"Thank you." I sat up on the thick air mattress covered in blankets and gently took it from him.

Cliff sat on the bright-blue tarp that had served as the porch for our tent. Last night we'd reclined on it for hours, watching a small, quiet fire flicker and listening to the trickling of the cold stream. We talked about everything from Cliff's grapefruit allergy to my latest poem.

I read it for him by the dim light of the lantern hanging above our heads as moths flocked around it. It was about Mama, as so many of my sonnets were, but it was different from the others. It wasn't about the black ice or her being a victim of circumstance. It wasn't about the social anxiety that caused her to drink. Instead of making excuses for my mother's irresponsibility, my poem held her accountable.

Aside from acknowledging her liability, I also forgave her in ways I didn't realize I needed to. Cliff engaged in conversation with me that made me confront feelings I hadn't dealt with regarding her death. Cliff had served as a therapist of sorts by letting me vent to him. His listening ear aided me in digging deep and realizing emotions and thoughts even my pen and paper hadn't discovered.

We both chewed on our sweet rolls and Cliff popped the top on a Coca-Cola can. The sound echoed throughout the trees with scant orange and red leaves hanging from their branches. The sun hadn't even been up an hour, but our glucose was soaring. And it was quite all right by us both.

My phone chimed beneath the mountain of blankets. I dug around until I found it and read the text aloud.

"'Happy birthday, sweet sister! Can't believe I'm awake this early, but Matthew and I are going to have breakfast at our favorite restaurant on Lookout Mountain before we go on a hike. Since it's our birthday, I think I'll splurge on the chocolate-chip pancakes. Glad to have the weekend off. The wedding last Saturday about did me in and I need the break. Bridezillas are the worst! I'll give you a call later today, and don't forget Matthew and I will be in town next weekend. Let's plan on dinner with Birdie and Mr. Prentice. I'll bring Perry. I know you've missed eating meals with cat hair in them. Love you.'"

"I'd wager you do miss that cat a little bit," Cliff said between bites of the glazed honey bun.

"Not true." I held the steaming cup of coffee to my lips. "There's nothing better than coming home after a long day to a dander-free couch and a clean toothbrush."

I thought about my spotless home. As part of Tallahatchie's historical renovation project, the derelict First Southern Bank on the court square was converted into apartments. Mine was a one-bedroom that once served as an office on the top floor. The window in the small living room overlooked the Tallahatchie County Courthouse, with its stately slate columns and manicured grounds dotted with magnolia trees. My only complaint about the location was the roaring of eighteen-wheelers that had to veer off the interstate across town and travel Main Street to reach the sawmill in Panola County. As they rumbled down the sleepy street, they shook the glass panes and rattled the gray picture frame that held a photo of me, Della, Birdie, and Mama sitting together at a picnic table at Sand Hill Methodist's homecoming when Della and I were toddlers.

Since Mr. Prentice and Birdie said "I do" last spring in an office at the courthouse that loomed over my apartment, they lived together in my lifelong home on Yocona Road. Mr. Prentice's farmhouse was deemed too large and the land too much of a burden to tend to. His nephew took on the place and got it operational again. Cows grazed the long-empty pastures and chickens pecked at grain right outside the back door.

I stayed on with them for a month or so until I saw an ad for the renovated apartments in the newspaper. Birdie and Mr. Prentice both insisted I live with them forever and play Rook every night after supper and listen to them hee-haw about Mr. Prentice's latest attempt at a cross-stitch. But I knew it was time to go. Della went back to Chattanooga only a few weeks after our last birthday, with Matthew's encouragement. She'd spread her wings and flown, and it was past time for me to do the same.

In thirty-one years, I'd never gone to sleep in an empty house. Because I'd always relished silence and favored re-treating to my bedroom to write, I didn't think I would have to adjust to being alone. However, for the first few weeks, it was foreign to me. The stillness was deafening at times and allowed more decibel space for the echoing of the forklifts in my mind. It was unfamiliar knowing there wasn't someone on the other side of my closed bedroom door, just a few steps away when thunder roared or the wind howled. But having Cliff visit nearly every evening to watch television with me on the used couch I purchased or to help me make supper in the quaint kitchen with limited counter space helped me to adjust. As the days wound down on the assembly line, I coveted the silence and comfort of my own place. I was a big girl now. I went to the grocery store alone. I paid my own bills. I finally felt like a grown-up.

I was content as the quiet, reserved schoolgirl who ate lunch alone. I was content as the bashful woman who lived with her grandmother and twin. I was content being a loner, without a friend in the world. And now I was content liv-ing alone and navigating my friendship with Cliff. I was pleased knowing that Birdie and Mr. Prentice were grow-ing older together rocking in the metal chairs on the front porch of the old clapboard house, and that Della had finally found love and companionship in Matthew and friends in Chattanooga. She was thriving there and shadowing a pres-tigious party planner, with hopes to one day branch out on her own. Della finally made peace with Clay Station and she, too, rested easy knowing Birdie was being cared for and I was doing all right on my own. She'd made peace with our mother's reputation and the classmates who harassed her. She'd made peace enough to finally leave for good.

"We got time to do a little fishing this morning before we head out?" Cliff asked.

"Yeah," I agreed. "Birdie wants us to stop by for lunch and Mississippi Mud birthday cake. Then all I need to do today is paint these chipped fingernails and get some laundry done. Don't have a thing to wear to church in the morning."

"What you gonna sing?"

"Tanya and I have been working on 'I'll Fly Away.' She really can sing like a bird." I picked at the flaking copper polish on my short nails.

Gary and Tanya had been regularly coming to Sand Hill Methodist for a few months, and I'd found a friend in Tanya. She and Cliff's brother were planning to marry in the little chapel after Thanksgiving. They'd turned their lives around, living in harmony and even helping take care of Cliff's dad.

A preacher from Enterprise, Alabama, was assigned to Sand Hill last summer, sending old Reverend Guidry and his nugget ring back to Louisiana. Pastor Parks brought with him seven little ones and his wife, who had a heart for missions. We'd done several outreaches in the community, and it was fulfilling to join God where He was at work. Pastor Parks's wife also had a gift for worship and music. She played the piano and violin, but she couldn't carry a tune in a bucket. I stepped way out of my comfort zone when I offered to lead Sunday worship for her, and I recruited Birdie and Mr. Prentice and some of the other blue-haired members to start up a choir. I wasn't on a stage for the world to see, like Birdie had always desired, but it was a place where I felt at ease. I guess I could thank Della for that. After I sang at our thirtieth birthday party, a void I didn't even know I had was filled. Each Sunday it did my heart good to look out on that congregation of mostly octogenarians and hear their soft, scraggly voices join mine. My lamp was finally on a stand.

Dr. Faulkner's stepsister, who owned Garden of Eatin', showed up one Sunday a few weeks back with her husband and two little ones in tow. The big, uppity church in town had snubbed them since the controversy with the once-prestigious Dr. Faulkner. That was what our town usually did when the mighty, or even the unmighty, fell. But we took them in with open arms at Sand Hill. And if Mitchell or Shelly or even Dr. Faulkner himself decided to visit after they'd served their time, we'd welcome them too. Pastor Parks regularly preached that Jesus died for the sinner, not the saint, and the parishioners at our small country church were determined to live by that.

Sometimes when I was standing beside Mrs. Parks playing the satin oak upright piano in the corner of the church, I'd think about walking down that red-carpeted aisle in a white gown to greet Cliff. When he cocked his head just right or winked at me from behind his sleek, rectangular frames, it was not uncommon to feel a flutter in my chest. Once I was done spilling out words that I didn't know lived within my head and my soul and he took my hand into his long, thin fingers, I was overwhelmed with a feeling I couldn't quite describe. The only thing I could compare it to was when I stepped out from behind the microphone at the community center last October and I felt full. Like everything was as it should be.

Something about Cliff made me feel something. Made me know something. Was that love?

It just might be.

A NOTE FROM THE AUTHOR

When I was in middle school, I was teased by a group of pretty girls with hair that didn't frizz in the humidity. They had slender waistlines and dates to the homecoming dance. For whatever reason, I was the bane of their existence.

However, I don't just relate to Della and Darby in this story. I see myself in Melanie and Camilla too. I was oftentimes cruel and callous to classmates. If anyone I teased and taunted back then happens to be reading this, I apologize. I was a hurt little girl who hurt others in a futile effort to feel better about myself.

God has a beautiful way of healing our insecurities and changing our hearts and actions. What people said about me all those years ago—and what I said about them—doesn't mean squat in the grand scheme of things. Our worth is found in Him alone.

And in Him, we are flawless.

ACKNOWLEDGMENTS

Dave, thank you for being the best agent and cheerleader ever. Kimberly and Julie, I appreciate your constructive criticism/suggestions on the first draft of *Della and Darby*. You are responsible for putting a far superior book into the hands of readers.

To my family, friends, and social media/blog followers—your daily doses of love and encouragement are never lost on me.

Jesus, I can do nothing apart from You.

DISCUSSION QUESTIONS

1. In what ways do you relate to Della and Darby?
2. Do you relate to Melanie and Camilla in any way?
3. Do you really think Darby was content being timid and reserved?
4. Did you for root for Della and Dr. Faulkner's relationship?
5. Have you ever felt responsible for someone else's happiness the way Della felt responsible for Birdie's?
6. Do you think Darby and Cliff will ever be more than good friends?
7. Who was your favorite character in the book?
8. Who do you think changed the most in the book?
9. Did Birdie speak any wisdom into your own life?
10. Have you carried any resentment from your youth into adulthood?

ABOUT THE AUTHOR

Susannah B. Lewis is a humorist, blogger for *Whoa! Susannah*, and freelance writer whose work has appeared in numerous publications. The author of *Can't Make This Stuff Up!* and *Bless Your Heart, Rae Sutton*, Lewis studied creative writing at Jackson State Community College and earned her bachelor's degree in business management from Bethel College. She lives in Tennessee with her husband, Jason, their three children, and seven dogs.

● ● ●

Visit her online at whoasusannah.com
Facebook: @whoasusannah
Instagram: @whoasusannahblog
TikTok: @whoasusannah